WATER TRAP

"Look!" said Sullivan.

Two Canada geese, mated for life, swam like lovers in the dark water. But Morris did not see them. He was squinting at the odd form at the near edge of the pond. Could pass for the feet and legs of a man. Morris walked nearer. By God, it was a man, facedown, studying the edge of the pond. What was he looking for? The hell he was looking for anything. His head was *in* the pond! The angle of his head in the water said it was not a man at all, but a body.

"I think you're standing over our host," Sullivan said.

"By God, you're right. It's Melvin Newton. How did you know?"

"The thousand-dollar suit, and his shoes are down at the heels. You can always tell a cheap rich man by his shoes, Morris."

"Never been a cheaper man," he admitted. "Or a deader one."

MURDER
ON THE
LINKS

John Logue

A Dell Book

Published by
Dell Publishing
a division of
Bantam Doubleday Dell Publishing Group, Inc.
1540 Broadway
New York, New York 10036

ISBN: 0-440-22062-9

Printed in the United States of America

Published simultaneously in Canada

April 1996

10 9 8 7 6 5 4 3 2 1

OPM

To Joshua, Rebecca, and Akiva

"April is the cruellest month . . . "
T. S. Eliot

CHAPTER ONE

Morris stepped onto the unending green of clipped Tifton grass, scattering dew over the tops of his old, favorite walking shoes. The 10th fairway spilled emptily down into the far shadows and might have been a steep sea rolling between the hundred-year-old Georgia pines. First rays of the sun leaked between the great trees, giving life to azaleas and dogwoods and rosebuds, making a garden of the Augusta National Golf Course. The only sound across the vast acres of blooms and shadows and ponds tamed and vegetable-dyed to an unearthly blue, was a mower cutting the fairway grass in just one direction, toward the 10th green—cutting the grass to the exact fraction of an inch as posted in the locker room for the attention of the players yet asleep in their beds. Already the mower had cut the grass on the practice range to the exact same fraction of an inch and in just one direction, away from the tees. Players could judge by their practice shots the *precise* distance they would roll on the course itself.

Detail. Obsession with every nuance of the course and of The Masters tournament had been its tradition since Bob Jones and Cliff Roberts built Augusta National and opened it to tournament play in 1934.

Morris's walking stick eased into the soft ground as he circled the practice putting green, mowed by hand to a speed to shake the most hardened nerves in the game. The old, original Manor Clubhouse stood like a block fortress under its tin roof. Expansions had been carefully designed to keep faithful to the simplicity of the original building.

Morris had known Bob Jones only at the end of his life, and only after a spinal disorder had lashed him to a wheelchair but left his great intellect and wit intact. Morris knew him well enough never to call him Bobby. It was the diminutive the world would always love him by, and Jones, the last gentleman, could only grit his teeth and bear it.

Restless . . . having conquered the world of competitive golf and retiring from it at age twenty-eight . . . Jones bought the Augusta property, with Cliff Roberts, to build the ultimate golf course from his own imagination. Morris looked down across the 18th green into the long valley of the property in the first daylight and could feel Jones's esthetic sensibility rise up with the mist off Rae's Creek hidden in the trees. The land had been planted as the South's first nursery, started in 1857 by Baron Prosper Jules Alphonse Berckmans, a Belgian. It was a name to predict the "business royalty" of the Augusta National membership. The members had sometimes been described less charitably as a gathering of "modern-day robber barons." But Jones, though a seeker after perfection, somehow remained the democratic man, the best loved hero in the history of American sports.

Jones had especially loved Julia Sullivan's husband, the late Monty Sullivan, as gay as Jones was serious. Jones even drank more than his share the day Monty won The Masters, exactly twenty years ago, a popular victory that had been the occasion last night of a modest celebration by certain Augusta National members in Julia's honor. In truth, the old guard had drunk, and even sung into the late hours, remembering Monty. Morris looked toward Newton Cottage, where he and Sullivan were staying, but it was too early on a Sunday morning for Julia Sullivan to make her appearance.

Morris turned on his cane. Writhing out of the ground at the corner of the clubhouse was a great wisteria vine, the first ever introduced to America. Morris squeezed his cane at the evil quality of the vine twisting against itself, though under it was a scattering of gay umbrellas and lawn chairs empty at this hour of the country's most powerful families.

Morris felt the first morning breeze lifting itself over the property. He took a deep breath of pines and newly mown grass and early April: the air had a quality about it—Morris gathered another deep breath—true enough, it smelled of *money*. He laughed to himself. A friend of his once incurred the wrath of the permanent sitting chairman, by writing that "no one dared breathe in the atmosphere at Augusta National until Cliff Roberts had breathed it out." Roberts was only angry that it was written. He did not deny it. In the beginning, you had to be on a first-name basis with him or Jones to hope to be invited to join Augusta National. Roberts had been a powerful man in investments and securities and ran the club from New York City for forty years with an iron will. All club rules and regulations were decided by one vote: his own. When Roberts was deep into his eighties and could no longer manage the steep fairways or hit the golf ball out from under his own thin shadow, he passed an early night with old friends and members at the Manor Clubhouse, in which he had a room as narrow and severe as might belong to a junior officer in a harsh army outpost, and when the others had gone happily to bed, Roberts eased down to Eisenhower Pond, which the former president had suggested be built on that exact site, shot himself in the head, and fell dead in the pond, denying even God the right to conclude his absolutely orchestrated life.

Morris poled his way around the clubhouse and along the driveway until he looked down the allée of giant magnolias that stretched for two-fifths of a mile to the commonplace traffic of Washington Road, which led past the Scottish Rite Temple, a chiropractor with a home practice, Julian Smith Park, the Free Will Baptist Church, SLICK TAYLOR SEAT COVERS—with Slick's aging sign reaching back into the decades—and on past the Dixie Vim filling station, none of which predicted an entrance of magnolias to freeze the hearts of three generations of the greatest players in the modern history of golf.

Morris made his way back along the practice range, which ran to the front of the property. He could imagine Monty Sullivan lashing balls to his caddy, stopping after every swing to wave to some crony of the merry night before, or to salute a fan he'd never met in his life, or to rag even Hogan himself, who tolerated Monty's happy enthusiasm for life for the pureness of his swing, which that year won The Masters itself. Morris had to laugh out loud again at the celebration that followed.

"What are you laughing at, old man?"

Two graceful hands and arms reached around his own great bulk from behind him. It was a voice the angels envied but the devil copied.

"I'm sorry, but womenfolk are not allowed out on Augusta National grass until a proper hour," said Morris.

"Even in their bare feet?"

"Never in their bare feet."

A slim, bare foot appeared from behind him.

"Shocking!" said Morris.

The other foot stepped around and the person above them both, Julia Sullivan, was in a brief skirt and blouse as bright as spring itself.

"You know what they threatened to do to Sam Snead?" said Morris.

"No. What did they threaten to do to old Sam?

Buy him a hairpiece? Make him pick up a check for the first time in his life?"

Morris said, "He once made a bet he could play a practice round here in par or better . . . barefoot."

"Good for Sam."

"He did it too. Easily. Up in West Virginia, he didn't know they had shoes until he was in his double-digit years. Cliff Roberts threatened to bar him from the course forever if he tried it again."

"He should have worn his shoes the next year and played naked," said Sullivan, giggling at the idea of Sam in his shoes and famous hat, naked as a jaybird.

"You . . . are . . . incorrigible." Morris lifted her entirely off the grass with no effort.

"If this is the new threat, I'll take two of them," said Sullivan, kissing him straight on the mouth.

Morris set her down, shaking his formidable head. "I can't believe it. And in the broad daylight. It's almost as wicked as what happened here years ago to the British Ryder Cup captain."

"What happened to Sir Whoever-he-was?" Sullivan straightened Morris's vast belt and buckle.

"Poor chap, very serious fellow, was rooming with something of a scoundrel over behind Jones Cottage; nothing could be done about it, you see, the American scoundrel was the defending champion." Morris's voice took on the clipped agony of the old Englishman. "The good British captain came down the next morning to complain to Mr. Roberts. 'Outraged,' he was. Seems his American roommate had come to bed late, terribly late, 'with a woman of the night, don't you see. Bad form,' said the·Englishman. 'Inexcusable,' and all that. 'The rounder never turned out the light.' "

Sullivan laughed until he had to hold her up off the wet grass.

"Oh, the story raged through the press tent all that day," said Morris, "with the great British writer and commentator, Henry Longhurst, offering six-to-one odds that his country's esteemed Ryder Cup captain 'never closed his eyes till daylight.' "

"Enough," begged Sullivan, collapsing against him. She punched him in his substantial ribs. "Why didn't you ever introduce me to such a scoundrel?"

"Oh, you know him well."

"Not well enough." She punched him again.

"You're all talk, Sullivan."

"Think so?" She loved her bare feet on the damp grass.

"Maybe not," said Morris, shaking his head. "It's awfully early in the morning. Let's take a walk."

"Sure." She raked the grass gently with her bare toes. "Out on the course?"

"No," he said. "I don't want to bother it, lying out there by itself. Not even its pins fixed in its greens. Let's walk back to Eisenhower Pond. We won't see it during the tournament."

"Is it rough walking?" She loved the feel of her bare feet in the damp grass.

"Oh, hell no. Not at Augusta National. There is no *rough* anything. Not even off the fairway. Jones didn't believe in it. He built all the terror into the greens."

Sullivan took Morris's wide arm like a true fol-

lower. He was careful to stay on a winding path behind the members' cottages, just off the 10th tee.

Soon they were lost among the giant pine trees.
"Look." He pointed to the top of one of them, ris-
ing like a mast on a Spanish galleon. Fixed so high
in the tree as to make you dizzy was a lightning rod.
"Not even God is allowed to strike a tree at Augusta
National," marveled Morris.

"I've been coming here twenty years, woman and
girl, and I never knew they did that," said Sullivan,
bending her head back against him to get a better
view. "Tell me, back there . . . what were you laughing at?" She turned her blue eyes and slim nose and
pleasantly long face up to his, her thick brown hair
swirling to her shoulders like a young girl's.

"You . . . partly. The part that was married to
Monty. The year we were celebrating last night, the
year he won The Masters."

"Oh, God." She laughed at the memory.

"Every time he emptied his glass, Monty called
somebody else in Denver to replay the last round.
All night he called them," said Morris. "Kept the
whole damn city awake. Every putt he sank got ten
feet longer with the telling. By daylight he was putting them in from across the state."

"And Demaret and Burke," said Sullivan, "took
the laces out of all of his shoes—golf shoes, dress
shoes, even the two shoes he was wearing. He wore
all of them that way for a month, all the way down
to the tournament in Miami. Even in his tuxedo he
went without laces in his shoes, even on the golf
course. Started a new trend that year among teen-

agers. All I can remember of that month is one long drink and the laughter."

"Until the wreck in Texas," said Morris.

"There's that," she said, touching his face.

"I still can't believe Monty died, and we lived through it," said Morris, reaching down to rub his stiff left knee.

"Yeah," she said. "And you loved him better than I did, John Morris, and I was crazy about him."

"What was Monty, twenty-two years older than you were?"

"Yeah. That's what I loved best about him. And he had the quiet, deliberate, cautious outlook on life of a nineteen-year-old fraternity boy."

"He did think seriously enough about his investments to own downtown Denver," said Morris.

"There's that." Sullivan grinned. "And aren't I glad." She flicked the key to her beloved Cessna jet, which she wore on a chain around her neck.

"Oh, we could live on my Associated Press retirement . . . and my freelance writing," said Morris, ". . . for at least fifteen minutes. Did you have a famous time last night?"

"Better than that. I love it that so many members and players and writers still remember Monty. Best thing, it wasn't sad. It was just the way he would have had it. Even Hogan raising a toast. I think I did cry at that sight, Morris."

"Hell, Monty would have wept at Hogan making a toast to any mortal. I'm glad we never practiced any fake guilt, Sullivan."

She laughed. "Maybe it'll come on us in old age."

"It better hurry," said Morris.

She picked up a large pinecone and threw it, just missing him by an inch, and then stepped faster through the dew and the shadows. "Come on, Morris. Where is General Eisenhower's famous pond?"

"Right there." He pointed through the trees.

The first sun was glancing off the pond, which was dug in a somber rectangle, as a formal pond might be imagined by a five-star general.

"Look!" said Sullivan.

Two Canada geese, mated for life, swam like lovers in the dark water. But Morris did not see them. He was squinting at the odd form at the near edge of the pond. Could pass for the feet and legs of a man. Morris walked nearer. By God, it was a man, facedown, studying the edge of the pond. What was he looking for? The hell he was looking for anything. His head was *in* the pond! Morris was poling himself forward as fast as he could swing his stiff left knee until he stopped over the prostrate man. The angle of his head in the water, away from life, said it was not a man at all, but a body.

Morris resisted the temptation to lift him out of the water. He bent and felt the man's left wrist, lying on the damp grass. It was stone-cold stiff. The man had been dead for a long time.

Morris was careful to disturb as little of the site as possible.

Sullivan hadn't seen the man, as she was watching the geese, and couldn't imagine why Morris had begun running and stumbling forward. Now she was standing behind him, her eyes open but not yet understanding what they saw.

Morris followed with his own eyes the sprawled right arm and hand, still visible in the shallow water. The sunlight bounced off the shiny metal of . . . he could see . . . under the hand . . . a gun . . . barely submerged.

He pushed himself erect with his cane, which sank into the soft ground.

"Look carefully, Morris." Sullivan's voice might have been cautioning a small child. "I think you're standing over our host."

Morris, startled, bent back over the the body, which was dressed in a suit—a dark-gray pin-striped suit. He bent until he could just see the left cheek of the face shimmering under the water.

"By God, you're right. It's Melvin Newton. How did you know?" He turned as if accusing her of a felony.

"The thousand-dollar suit," said Sullivan, "and his shoes are down at the heels. I noticed them last night. You can always tell a cheap rich man by his shoes, Morris."

"You're all charity, Sullivan." Morris shook his head at the sight, suddenly a more intimate one. "Never been a cheaper man," he admitted. "Or a deader one."

Melvin Newton had been a bastard, all right. Never any doubt about that. And now he was as dead as he had been unattractive.

"He was the last man alive I ever thought would kill himself," said Sullivan, bending over, her hands on her knees to get a surer look.

"You see the gun," said Morris.

"Oh, yes."

"Aren't you supposed to faint, or call for help?" said Morris, unable to take his own eyes off the death scene. A school of tiny minnows swam past Newton's head, fluttering the long, sparse strands of black hair that he would comb over his thin skull, fluttering them on the surface of the water as if they were alive.

"I'm not the fainting type," said Sullivan. "And I've grown used to your friends turning up dead in games and tournaments."

"Listen, he was no friend of mine," said Morris.

"We're staying in his cottage."

"*We* are staying in his cottage," Morris said, "because *he* invited *you*."

"Don't get technical, Morris. We're standing over a dead man. What do we do now?"

"Do you want to stay here while I send for the police?"

Sullivan folded her arms under her stylish bosom. "How would it look for them to come and find two dead men?"

"Tell you what, we'll both go after the police," said Morris. "Our boy here isn't going anywhere. We can send a Pinkerton man to watch over him. Did Newton seem despondent to you last night?"

"No. The word for how he seemed was *arrogant*. That's how he seemed last night, and how he seemed any night in the last twenty years I had the bad luck to be sitting at his table."

"Funny, his old man was such a championship guy," said Morris. "And one of Bob Jones's charter members here."

"Yes, and the old man would get drunk and sing Irish drinking songs with Monty."

"Just what Monty always needed," said Morris, "a drinking, singing companion. Well, the apple fell a long way from the tree when Melvin Newton, Jr., hit the ground."

Sullivan put her long fingers on Morris's thick wrist and twisted her lips as if something had just provoked her memory. "Isn't this the pond where . . ."

"Yes," said Morris. "Where Cliff Roberts shot himself and fell dead in the water."

"This is a terrible coincidence, Morris."

"It's plenty terrible. You know I've never been addicted to coincidence. It always seems to be the bedfellow of bad intentions."

"You don't think somebody killed Melvin Newton? The gun is still in the water, under his own hand."

"He was a nasty guy. The kind people kill. Maybe, somewhere, he had one friend. I never met him. Not that we all wouldn't trade on his daddy's memory and his own grudging hospitality."

"Oh, he made you pay. You had to put up with the sour sight of him," said Sullivan. "They'll have to hire six pallbearers to carry him to his grave."

"Sullivan, you are terrible. And terribly correct."

Morris looked over the manicured grass, which grew exactly to the waterline. There was no sign of a struggle. Morris regretted his own big footprints in the dew, but he had been as careful as possible.

He looked again at the body, in its oddly formal sprawl. This arrogant man, who lusted after the job of chairman of Augusta National the way he lusted after rival publishing companies . . . killing himself in the same way as the first chairman, Roberts, in the same Eisenhower Pond. How could it be?

"I'm trying to remember when he left the party last night," said Morris.

"I know he left early," said Sullivan. "His wife was looking for him. She even asked if I had seen him. In fact, she left without him. I'm sure of it. I saw her leave."

"I wonder where he went, or who he met, if anybody?"

"He met his Maker," said Sullivan, stepping back from the sight of him.

"We'll have to tell his wife," said Morris.

"We'll have to tell her immediately."

Morris opened his mouth.

"I know . . . *I'll* have to tell her immediately." Sullivan paused. "Somehow . . . I don't think Phyllis Newton will faint."

Morris found it hard to believe—five hours ago they were still toasting Monty Sullivan, and the sounds in the bar had been like old times. The only sound missing had been Monty's wonderful Irish tenor. But he would have loved the party in his name

and in Julia's honor. Morris remembered Monty all
those years ago in his newly won green jacket, The
Masters champion at play among his peers, his dark,
shaggy hair in his eyes. And then Morris remembered that Julia had buried him in the jacket. Morris
ignored the dead-still pond under his feet and was
back among the glad sounds coming out of the clubhouse bar the night before.

"Morris, are these people friends of yours?"

The firm hand on his large arm belonged to Edgar Benefield III. He looked as tall and tanned and
erudite and appropriately graying at the temples as
a Benefield-the-third ought to look.

"I never met any of them in my life," said Morris.
"When did you get in? Is Jerusha with you?"

Benefield nodded that she was.

"Julia will be happy to see you both."

"We're staying just down the hall from you in
Newton Cottage," said Benefield, wincing at the
thought of their host.

"Any port at a Masters tournament," said Morris.
"Hell, Newton's not a bad guy . . . when he's in a
coma. I understand you are now partners with him."

The noise Benefield made was two shades darker
than a laugh. "He bought us out. Simple as that. A
small literary press can't compete in the marketplace
anymore, Morris. My father is lucky to be in his
grave. He never could have imagined Benefield
House as part of the Newton romance publishing
empire. Truth is . . . I took the money and ran." Edgar finished his drink with a scowl, as if it were the
worst medicine imaginable.

"I doubt I helped the financial cause, with my *History of the Ryder Cup Competition*."

"A very fine book, Morris. My father was proud to publish it."

"My mother, God bless her, lived to buy a copy," said Morris. "So I know you sold one. Julia Sullivan claims to have read it. But you can't trust Sullivan. How is it working out . . . the new ownership?"

"Don't even ask." Benefield stood in the old Manor Clubhouse as comfortably as if he'd come with the furniture. Morris was always surprised to realize that Edgar was not a member of Augusta National. He came from an old Boston family, founders of one of the most distinguished literary presses in the country. And Edgar in his youth had been a truly fine amateur golfer. Qualified for the U.S. Open twice and for the National Amateur eleven times, and came within a stroke of winning it in a tournament that Morris had covered at Shinnecock Hills, on Long Island, twenty years ago. Edgar had even made the cut that year after the first two rounds of The Masters. The Augusta National course with its wide, open fairways and slick, precipitous greens suited his long, somewhat erratic tee shots and his deft putting stroke. So long as Edgar was not actually a threat to win The Masters, he could dominate his nerves and play well in it. Bob Jones, the greatest amateur golfer of all time, loved it when a fellow nonprofessional played well at Augusta. Odd that he never invited Edgar Benefield to join his club. Morris thought again that he would have been the quintessential member. Morris knew him to be a bright man, and an engaging one, but somewhat weak—a condition lethal to any championship hopes in golf and sometimes even dangerous in a man under stress. Hence the family publishing house, under Edgar's leadership, being sold to Philistines. Well, hell, nobody was perfect, thought Morris. And Edgar had a lovely putting stroke. Not to mention a perfectly beautiful wife.

Coming toward them, as if she'd heard his thoughts, was Jerusha Benefield: tall, still blond—by secular intervention—and stylish in every way, her nose tilted by the gods and her chin up, as she always carried it, not in arrogance but just to meet the world on her own terms. She was the one woman who could turn his head with Sullivan in the room.

"Hello, Morris," she said into the back of his neck, in the depths of a big hug.

"I don't think I'll be able to speak for three or four days," said Morris.

"You best hug her again. You may not have another chance in a long while." Edgar Benefield was entirely serious.

"Where are you going?" Morris backed away to study her answer. She was the only person he ever knew who had absolutely green eyes.

"To Paris."

"Now, there's a town," said Morris. "I'd even vote for the river running through it."

"Yes." She smiled her agreement.

"Don't you need a traveling companion?"

"Yes."

Morris took her near arm. "Do pop over to see

us, Edgar. We'll be hanging out on the Left Bank. In some unpronounceable brasserie."

"I don't think I'm invited."

"Of course you are invited," said Jerusha, reaching for Edgar's arm, which he withdrew.

"I can't live the rest of my life in another country," said Benefield, obviously resuming an old argument. "You remember I had a hard enough time visiting Mother when she moved back West. I can't help it. I'm just an Eastern American person."

"Jerusha, you're going for the rest of your life?" asked Morris, truly surprised.

Jerusha Benefield only nodded her head.

"You love Paris that much?"

"I'm going back to my painting. And I'm never giving it up again." She said it matter-of-factly, in no way posturing.

"I remember you painted," said Morris, who had been in their Manhattan apartment more than once. "I'm a total barbarian, Jerusha, when it comes to art . . . Sullivan says I'm a barbarian when it comes to anything . . . but I loved that big painting of the sea, at night, that you did that hangs in your living room. Goddamn, can't you paint on both shores of the Atlantic? This country can't afford to give up its most beautiful specimen of woman."

She laughed. She had a free, deep laugh. Better than a stylish laugh. Then she said, looking with care at Edgar, "I have to build a life to paint in."

"Without me," Benefield said, more desperately than angrily.

"Always a place for you in my life, Edgar."

Morris shifted his weight from bad leg to good leg, feeling caught in the most awkward moment of two friends' lives.

"And a place for the children?"

"Of course. But they aren't children. They are married and gone to their own lives," said Jerusha. "Time I went back to my own."

"Tell her not to talk rubbish, Morris." Benefield looked at him for help.

Morris tightened his grip on Jerusha's arm. "I'm an optimist, for everybody's life . . . except my own," he said. "I know this world is big enough and small enough for two people who love each other to find their separate lives and be together. The famous Julia Sullivan and a certain oversized, undergifted writer have been doing it for years."

Jerusha Benefield kissed him on the lips.

Morris was equally startled by the soft touch of her lips on his and the simultaneous deep slap against his backside.

"Don't kiss that man, Jerusha Benefield! Until you've had your tetanus shot. He hangs out with golfers and other unseemly jocks. No telling what you might catch," said Sullivan, pushing Morris aside and hugging Jerusha like a sister.

"Excuse us. We've got to find a conversation," said Sullivan. "We have our lives to catch up on." She lifted herself up on her toes and also kissed Morris on the same lips. "But I won't go too far, old man."

Morris watched them disappear out onto the

lighted terrace. They were two smashing women of a certain age. The young would kill to have what they were both born with. Morris looked back, but Edgar Benefield had disappeared into the crowd in the bar.

"Damned shame, the woman's leaving him."

Morris turned back around, having to control his mouth to keep from wincing at the sight of his host, Melvin Newton, Jr.

Newton's flat voice made it clear he didn't think it was a shame at all.

Morris forced himself to shake the man's hand, thin and dry, as if it were dying from the absence of human warmth. His expensive pin-striped suit served only to make Melvin Newton less attractive. With his dark, thinly hooded eyes and narrow mouth, and with long, sparse black hairs painted over his narrow skull, he stood in an expensive slouch, contemptuous of everything he saw.

"How are your quarters?" Newton asked, knowing damn well how they were, since he owned them.

"Fine. Truly fine," said Morris, honestly. "Understand you and Benefield are now partners." He enjoyed saying the word *partners*.

"Hardly." Contempt lifted the hoods of Newton's dark eyes. "Benefield couldn't make a go of it. Not half the man his father was. Not much wonder his wife is leaving him."

"I understand he got a damn good price for Benefield House." Morris had no idea what price he got and bit his lip to keep from smiling.

"My price," said Newton. "And my House. I call all the shots. His office of president is just an empty suit."

So much for Edgar's old title. Morris was sure Newton had the most unattractive smirk he had ever seen.

"I knew you were a big noise in publishing," said Morris, now entirely careless of Newton's response, "but I didn't know you were into South American poets." A Benefield House poet from Argentina, whose lifetime work hadn't sold five thousand American copies, had recently won the Nobel prize in literature.

Newton laughed, a nasty sound. "And no longer will Benefield House be 'into' poets from Argentina. Believe me."

"I believe you," said Morris.

Newton began, "How's your paramour . . . ?"

Morris looked down, directly into Newton's dark eyes, until the man was plenty aware of how he'd best not refer to Julia Sullivan, if he was going to refer to her at all through his own teeth.

". . . How's Julia?" asked Newton, looking around the crowded room, not giving a damn how Morris answered or how Julia was.

"Yeah, she's fine," said Morris. "I'll see you later, Melvin." He walked off toward the singing in the bar, knowing Newton despised to be the man left standing in a lapsed conversation.

"Sweet guy, that." The voice could belong only to Jackie Burke, the greatest Ryder Cup competitor America had ever had and one-time champion of

The Masters, and longtime best friend of the late Jimmy Demaret.

"Do you think there is a country that needs a Newton? We could pay the air freight," said Morris.

"The cold war's over. We wouldn't want to start another one."

"How's Houston?"

"Hot. Already. Just the way I like it."

"It agrees with you," said Morris. "You look like you could tee it up here and win again."

"Sure I could. From the ladies' tees." Burke thought about it. "I bet I couldn't, at that. I'd still have to putt the icy-fast greens."

"Who do you like in the tournament?" asked Morris.

"Raymond Floyd."

"One of the kids, huh?" Morris smiled.

"I swear he's playing the best golf of his life. Funny how we pull for the guys nearest our own generation."

"They're getting thin on the ground," said Morris.

Burke nodded that it was true, but he did so without any self-pity. "I also like Couples. And Davis Love. The way they hit the ball, Morris, it's a sin. Of course, there are all these great Europeans."

"You never lost to a European in your life." Burke, in his youth, had achieved a priceless record in Ryder Cup competition.

"I didn't have to play these guys, Ballesteros, Faldo, Woosnam."

"You played against some great ones."

"How's Julia? I've only seen her from across the room," said Burke.

"She's unsinkable. She loves you fellows for remembering Monty."

"I can never think of Monty without thinking of Jimmy," said Burke.

"They were a pair," agreed Morris. "You couldn't beat 'em, and you damn sure couldn't out-sing 'em."

Burke laughed.

Morris would have paid a lot to see a multicolored sweater and a pair of Irish eyes and two of the surest hands that ever picked up a golf club come walking into the room, harmonizing with Monty Sullivan.

A couple of members of the club from Houston pulled Jackie Burke away in a swirl of handshakes.

"Young man."

Morris was always ready to smile at a greeting like that. He got a warm handshake from Michael Compton, chairman of Augusta National and the man responsible for the party in Monty's memory. Compton smoothed his silver hair with one hand as if it were a portion of the family legacy. With him was his thin, thin aristocratic, but accommodating wife, Aeriel. She was far too formal to hug Morris, but offered a genteel hand in an old-fashioned glove. The Comptons were old New York money. As carefully as they stood in the crowded room, they might have been alone in their Upper East Side town house, gracefully holding martinis like passports to a grander life. Morris knew that Compton wanted to be United States senator from New York, a position his father, the former governor, never attained while alive. There had been a scandal of some sort in his gubernatorial administration. Morris couldn't remember just what. . . . He smiled and chatted with the Comptons as if his mind was entirely occupied with their small talk.

"Julia is out-of-her-mind-happy with the party," said Morris.

"She is such an adventurous woman," said Aeriel, with true admiration. "Flying her own jet plane. Astonishing."

"That's Sullivan," said Morris. "You just missed her. She's out on the terrace with Jerusha Benefield."

"The most beautiful woman in New York, I think," said Aeriel, with not a hint of envy.

"But not for long," said her husband.

"Did you hear she is moving to Paris?" said Aeriel.

Morris nodded that he had. "To take up her painting again. . . . She was just telling me."

"But never to come back?" Aeriel Compton could not imagine being a permanent exile from her beloved Manhattan.

"I don't know. . . . Never is a long time," said Morris. "If I were Edgar, I'd practice my French. I don't think even golf can take the place of Jerusha."

Not meaning to embarrass Michael Compton, Morris said, "Too bad Edgar is not a member of Augusta National. You fellows might help take his mind off his troubles. I always believed Edgar would have been the perfect member here—fine player, gentleman, distinguished publisher, all that. Did he never care to join the club?"

Compton was shocked at such an open question. A breach of every etiquette. His martini shook in his glass. He was too much the gentleman to say what he thought.

Morris liked the man, but felt more curious than diplomatic.

"Of course he would be a fine member," said Compton, almost in a whisper. "We are in several clubs together in the city."

Morris interpreted his answer as an apology.

"We'd best attend to our guests, Michael," said Aeriel, again offering Morris her white-on-white glove. He imagined himself accepting it like the Count of Monte Cristo.

"Goddamn, Morris, you suckin' up to the big cheese?"

It could only be the ungallant Eddie Hayward, pudgy, with a new double chin but none of the joyful appetite for life that ought to go with it, the most unpopular defending champion Augusta ever had. *And one of the least talented*, thought Morris. Eddie, at age forty, caught lightning in a Scotch and soda last year for four improbable days, and he was prepared to live off The Masters title for the rest of his career. In Hayward's company was an obviously uncomfortable Tom Spears, still darkly handsome and slender in a dinner jacket from another decade.

Morris ignored Hayward's comment. He did shake his hand and the hand of Spears, an old friend.

"Don't pay any attention to Hayward," said Spears.

"No," agreed Morris. "How have you been, Tom? Haven't seen you since this time last year." He spoke as if Eddie Hayward had disappeared into the dark outside the clubhouse.

"I'm the old, familiar unemployed," said Spears, twisting a white golf tee between his thumb and finger, with regret.

"Not again."

"Oh, yeah. That makes seven club jobs I've pissed away in nine years . . . if you're counting. I don't think I was cut out to help some stockbroker take two strokes off his 36-stroke handicap."

Morris shook his head in sympathy. Spears had won The Masters, not once but twice—putting him safely among the great players of his time. But his time had passed him by. Arthritis in both hands had ruined any chance Spears had of a second career on the Senior Tour. He was left among the "silent" great players whose names never became household words, who still had to make a living with their hands, arthritic or not.

"No reason to settle down," said Morris, "as long as you're still among the last of the bachelor champions."

"Some champion," said Spears. "And who the hell would have me? I did get a hug earlier from the beautiful Julia Sullivan."

"I hope you didn't flatter her. She's too cocky already."

"Morris, you are as close as anybody to Melvin

Newton," said Spears. "I want to ask a favor of you." He touched Morris's arm. "It could mean a lot to me."

"Listen," said Morris, "I'll do anything I can, legal or illegal, to help the cause. But I doubt I have any more influence with Melvin than you do."

"I'll take my chances. I'm staying down the hall from you and Julia," said Spears. "Maybe I can catch you at breakfast."

"Done," said Morris.

"Nobody can help a man who's got shit for hands, especially that turd Newton," said Hayward, angry with them both for ignoring the defending Masters champion.

"Better than shit for brains," said Morris, before his mind edited his tongue.

Hayward gave him his idea of a hard, tough look, but was careful not to step nearer to Morris's formidable bulk.

"Come on, Eddie," said Morris. "This is your big week. Relax and enjoy it." Morris did not have to add, *You'll never know another week like it.*

"Goddamn right," said Hayward, smoothing his thin, blond hair, tucking in one of his chins, and shooting the cuffs of his shirt a half-inch beyond the sleeves of his green Masters jacket, which could not hide the soft fat his body was quickly dissolving into. He walked off without looking back at the two of them.

"Swell fellow, Eddie," said Morris.

"Ain't he a joy," said Spears. "But I have to give him credit. The bastard has already milked more money out of his one Masters title than I ever did out of two."

"It's the gathering phenomenon . . . television," said Morris. "Today it can make a celebrity out of a billy goat."

"I guess I missed out by a decade," said Spears, able to muster a bright smile against his dark good looks.

Morris knew Spears had been married twice, but each marriage faded along with his game, and his financial independence faded as well.

"See you tomorrow, Morris," he said. "I'm going where the singing is. Maybe some of the good times will rub off on me."

Morris winced to see a champion and a good man reduced to such a state.

A large, ungainly man with a round face that needed shaving five minutes after it had been shaved took Morris by the arm. "Did Tom Spears touch you for a loan?" asked Gerald Acton.

"No," said Morris.

"He will," said Acton, tournament chairman of the Tees and Pin Placement Committee, and husband of the fifth-richest woman in America. He was the same height as Morris, though his own large body had long gone to flab. Morris looked around, but Acton's wife, Louise, was not in sight. Then she came out of the bar, bearing a drink in each of her firm hands. To Morris, she looked quite handsome but somewhat out of place in a pale blue gown. She was always most comfortable in a pair of jeans and a roughout jacket. She'd inherited an enormous electronics fortune. Her husband of twenty-six years never actually held a job, so far as Morris could judge; he was content to sit on the board of directors, and climb the social ladder of New York, while spending all his energy and Louise's money on other women. Louise seemed glad not to be bothered, giving over her own life to her charities. She did love golf. Her father had been an amateur champion, and she'd won a few local tournaments in her youth. Morris had seen her from time to time at tournaments around the world. He liked her and her friendly smile. She even wore a short, friendly haircut, guaranteed to give her no trouble in wind or rain.

Morris kissed her on the cheek.

"Careful, I'll douse you in martinis." Louise had a low, husky way of speaking that was more friendly than sexy. Her billion dollars might not even have existed.

"I've been doused that way before," said Morris.

"I'm shocked," said Louise. "Where's Julia?"

"Last I saw, she was huddling with Jerusha Benefield."

"Who's moving to Paris, I hear," said Louise.

"I don't think it's a secret," said Morris.

"Do you think she'll invite us over?" asked Louise, lifting her glass to Morris's and, maybe reluctantly, to her husband's.

"Cheers," said Morris. "I've already invited myself."

"You always had a crush on those green eyes of hers," said Louise.

"I don't deny it," said Morris, "unless Sullivan is in the room with a five-iron in her hand."

"Guess you heard the club is letting Sid go," said Gerald Acton, pronouncing words carefully, ready to assume whatever opinion Morris might have about Sid Norton. The only thing Morris trusted about Acton was his wife, Louise.

"Hell, no, I haven't heard that," said Morris. "What happened?"

"According to Melvin Newton, defender against moral turpitude, bit too much of the grape," said Acton, lifting his glass as if it had been the specific culprit.

"I've known Sid Norton for twenty-five years, and I never saw him drunk . . . when I wasn't drunk," said Morris.

"Well, he's out. Had a nasty scene just now in the bar with Melvin. You know Melvin when he's riding the horse of self-righteousness."

"I hate it," said Morris, as if to himself. Sid had been a good, solid, professional player in the years after Hogan and Snead. Won a few good tournaments. Bob Jones hired him as the teaching pro at Augusta National. Jones believed only a good player could be trusted as a good teacher.

"I think I'll look Sid up," said Morris. "He might need somebody to get him to bed."

"Good for you, Morris," said Louise. "Always looking after your boys." She meant it, patting him on his wide back. "I've got to have my annual down-and-dirty talk with Sullivan." She brushed her short hair off her forehead as if it threatened her hazel eyes.

"Oh, Lord, nobody will be safe," said Morris.

"Tomorrow," she said. "Tell Sullivan I'll look her up."

Morris kissed her again, this time on her firm lips.

Morris searched the bar, but Sid Norton was nowhere to be found. Maybe he'd already left for home. Morris hoped he wasn't too deep in his cups to drive. Morris also looked for Newton, but he was nowhere to be found.

Jack Nicklaus and Arnold Palmer—now there was a pair—each grabbed Morris by an arm. They wanted him to settle an argument about a tournament in Scotland a hundred years ago, when they were young. Morris remembered the incident perfectly. They were both wrong.

"Morris, damn you, we're gonna get another historian," said Palmer.

Morris drifted around the room and onto the terrace and back to the bar, soaking up memories of the good times, and wincing at the crude laughter of Eddie Hayward, Melvin Newton, and Gerald Acton, three lost souls who belonged together in the next life sharing some obscene moment.

Happier sounds came from deep inside the bar. The Squire, Gene Sarazen, nearing ninety and crafty as ever with his gentlemanly opinions, was telling sportswriter Furman Bisher how the overlooked, perilous little No. 7 was the greatest golf hole at Augusta National. And who could argue with the Squire, who must have given strokes to Old Tom Morris. The ever courtly Byron Nelson, who had once ruled this course and this tournament in the same royal manner as Palmer and Nicklaus, had his gnarled, magical hands on an actual club to the attention of his famous protégé, Tom Watson. Dr. Cary Middlecoff himself, a one-time Masters champion, was telling the eternal runner-up, Tom Weiskopf, about the time, after his back gave out, that he shot in the 80s here at Augusta, and tossed his car keys to his caddy and told him to leave them in the trunk with his clubs ... and he did, by God, *locked* safely in the trunk, leaving Middlecott stranded outside with his odious eighty. And then he was telling about the time on the *Wide World of Golf,* in the early days of television, when he stroked a ninety-foot putt that rolled and broke ten feet over two huge mounds and dived straight into the cup, and a woman among the small clutch of live spectators around the green said to her husband, "I always knew these television matches were fixed." And Weiskopf laughed with the grace of a man who might have won four Masters titles but had long accommodated himself to finishing second to immortality all four times. Gary Player, Masters champion and golf's first physical fitness addict, insisted to *New York Times* columnist Walter Edwards that he was "hitting the ball better than I've ever hit it in my bloody life." Edwards winked at Morris; both had known Player for over twenty-five years and on four continents and had never heard him admit to hitting it any other way. But God help the man chasing a leading Gary Player over the last nine holes of any tournament; he had many qualities, but mercy was not among them. The two new "golden boys" of the game, Fred Couples and Davis Love, were laughing together about something, but they were too far away for Morris to know what it was; just as they had distanced themselves this year from the games of all of golf's other pretenders to the throne. Eddie Hayward insinuated himself into a conversation between Johnny Miller and Ken Venturi, two ex-Californians, golden boys from separate eras who had won the U.S. Open and were now too polite to turn their backs on Eddie and his vicious criticism of the condition of the immaculate Augusta National course. There was something about golf, thought Morris, that brought out the best and the most murderous in the human species.

CHAPTER TWO

The Pinkerton guard was an old hand. Barton was his name. James Barton. He was a heavyset man whose large head sat right down into his shoulders. He asked again about the body facedown in Eisenhower Pond, unable to reconcile the idea of it with the perfect symmetry of the grass under his feet.

"You say it's Mr. Newton? No doubt about it?"

"When you get there," said Morris, "you can identify him for yourself. We'll tell Newton's wife, and call the police."

"The club ain't gonna like it," said Barton, shaking his large head.

"No," said Morris. Then he thought of the average age of the members; death was no stranger among them, not even suicide.

Barton called on his walkie-talkie for another

Pinkerton man to replace him outside the club-house. Then he began a rolling, bowlegged walk toward Eisenhower Pond, looking back now and then as if to be sure he was not being sent on a fool's errand.

Morris watched Sullivan climb the stairs inside Newton Cottage to knock on Phyllis Newton's door. From the top of the stairs she raised one fist to let him know he owed her one . . . a big one.

Morris picked up the phone in the living room and dialed the Augusta police station. A Sergeant Reese put him through to a Detective Fannin.

Morris gave his name and told the detective in precise terms who he had found dead and where.

"You are the John Morris who used to be with the Associated Press?" asked Detective Fannin, catching Morris a bit off guard.

"Yes," he said, "but I've been freelancing for a couple of years now."

"I knew you once," the detective said, but he didn't explain when. "You could see enough of the dead man's face to be certain he was Mr. Newton?"

"Yes," said Morris.

"Oh, shit," said the detective.

"Absolutely," said Morris.

"If you'll wait for me at the clubhouse, I'll be right there," said Fannin.

Morris couldn't imagine when he had *known* Detective Fannin. He couldn't remember a Detective Fannin in Atlanta during the murders at the U.S. Open. Or in Sparta when the football coach Harry Carr was killed. Morris shook his head, then dialed the clubhouse. The club chairman, Michael Compton, was having breakfast.

"Don't bother him," said Morris. "I'll walk over and visit with him."

Compton was sitting at a long table with his committee members when Morris interrupted him. Compton stepped reluctantly away from the table.

Morris told him what he had found at the pond.

"Good Lord," said Compton. "I was angry with Melvin for missing the committee breakfast. I was about to send for him." Compton smoothed his silver hair as if it could sustain him in the crisis. "Do you think I should tell the other committee members?"

"Yes," said Morris. "The Pinkerton men know. I sent a guard down to watch over the body. Everybody on the grounds will know about it soon enough."

"We'll have to call the police," said Compton. His hands shook in spite of himself.

"I've spoken with a Detective Fannin," said Morris. "He's on his way."

Compton bit his lip at the vulgar necessity of a detective on Augusta National's holy ground of golf. "The press will be onto it soon enough."

"Yes," said Morris. "But they won't be here for a while. Not after a long Saturday night. Better to see what the detective has to say first. And he and his team will want to examine the site without interference."

"His team?"

"Oh, yes. A photographer, a medical examiner,

probably a couple of others. They'll have to docu-
ment what happened, even if it turns out to be suicide."

"You don't think it could be . . . anything else?"
said Compton. He couldn't bring himself to say the
ultimate word, *murder*.

"I'm not the detective," said Morris. "Of course,
there's the gun in the water, just under his hand.
But tell me, did Melvin strike you as the kind of guy
who would kill himself?"

Compton smoothed his silver hair as if getting in
physical touch with his own insight. "No," he had
to admit, biting his upper lip. "But I don't know
what kind of person does kill himself."

"A desperate person," said Morris. "But then . . .
who can ever say he knows any other man?"

Compton frowned at the complexity of that question.

"I thought Melvin wanted to own the world,"
said Morris. "Never occurred to me he wanted to
leave it."

Compton had to smile at the truth of that. Then
his face was grimly back in place. "It's going to be
a mess."

Morris nodded. And thought: It tells you
something . . . that neither one of us is broken up
about Melvin Newton lying dead . . . or running over
with sympathy for his wife.

Compton might have read his mind. "I'd better
get over and break the terrible news to Phyllis."

"Do visit with her," said Morris. "But as we
speak, Sullivan is telling her what happened. They

could both use a little friendly support. It's not going to get easier." Morris did not say that Phyllis was stronger than Octagon soap. He didn't have to. Michael Compton knew her well enough.

Phyllis Newton was holding a cup of coffee in one hand when she opened the door to her suite. Her blue robe did nothing to hide her considerable girth. She did not conceal her surprise at seeing Julia Sullivan.

"I'm sorry to bother you, Phyllis. But I have some awful news. May I come in?"

Phyllis Newton's hard face congealed into granite, as if sending notice that she was equal to any news whatsoever.

The sitting room was immaculate, with a copy of *Southern Accents* opened on the coffee table to an even more immaculate room.

Sullivan knew better than to soft-pedal the news. "Morris and I took an early morning walk. Phyllis . . . I'm sorry . . . but we found Melvin dead. At Eisenhower Pond." She reached over and touched Phyllis's hand, which clenched into a fist. Phyllis shook her graying dark hair in iron disbelief.

"I'm sorry," Sullivan said again, not surprised by Phyllis Newton's formidable composure.

The new widow sat with her own thoughts, without speaking. Then she said, "What happened to him?"

"It seemed," said Sullivan, "as if he had shot himself."

"Ridiculous!" Phyllis made a terrible laugh. "He

wouldn't kill himself if he was the last man on earth." She folded her thick arms under her solid bust, as if she were prepared to debate the matter.

"It seems terribly illogical," agreed Sullivan.

"Then why do you say he killed himself?" Phyllis accused her.

"I said 'it seemed' he killed himself. He was lying in Eisenhower Pond, with a handgun in the shallow water just under his own hand." Sullivan flinched, stating the harsh details. But they seemed to punch through Phyllis Newton's iron-plated composure.

"Well . . ." Phyllis breathed her exasperation through her open mouth.

"Of course, the police will have to determine what really happened," said Sullivan.

"The police?"

"They are on their way," said Sullivan.

"Will . . . I have to talk with them?" The idea of it violated Phyllis's composure even further.

"Yes, you will," said Sullivan. She took that moment to ask Phyllis, "Then Melvin hadn't been depressed?"

That terrible laugh again. "Melvin? Never! If some big deal blew up . . . he was angry. Depression was for the weak. He loved to say that. Melvin was not a weak man."

"No," said Sullivan. Then she said, "The party seems to have happened a thousand years ago. You must have fallen asleep afterward and not missed him." She said it offhandedly, as though it was a natural thing to have happened after a party.

"Of course I missed him," said Phyllis, as if she

had been accused of some negligence. "I was furious at him." The fury reappeared in her face, as though Melvin were still somehow responsible for disappointing her. "Of course . . ." She might have been talking to herself. . . . "I'll have to speak with the police. . . ." She said it as though preparing herself for the ordeal. Surprisingly, she looked to Sullivan for help.

"Just tell them what happened," Sullivan said. "Don't edit what you say. Be straightforward. It's the best thing. The police hate to find out something that's been deliberately omitted." Sullivan said it with genuine concern for the woman, whom she'd never admired.

"Yes . . ." Phyllis seemed to make up her mind in the direction of candor. "I was furious with him. Not that he hadn't failed to come home before. He could be a fool for some young thing. Show me a powerful man who can't be." She said it as a challenge to the male species. "But never *here*. At his precious Augusta National." She said that as if she despised the chair she was sitting in. "He would never admit it, but he wanted the chairmanship, you know." She all but smiled, as if that was one lust Melvin Newton had been denied. "Of course, I didn't call the clubhouse. I waited!" Her face was again full of insult. "At least he had the decency not to . . ." The sentence trailed off.

Sullivan had no trouble finishing the sentence in her mind: . . . *be found lying dead in someone else's bed*.

"I know he looked forward to Masters week," said Sullivan. "All the members do. The whole world of golf looks forward to the tournament. It just doesn't make sense, his killing himself . . . and especially this week."

"No!" said Phyllis Newton. "Of course he didn't kill himself! The police must realize—powerful men have powerful enemies. Find the man he left the party with, and you have his killer. That's all I have to say on the matter." She looked at Sullivan as if she had been subjected to violent cross-examination.

Sullivan felt embarrassed to ask one last question. "Did Melvin travel with a handgun?"

Phyllis looked up, as if the thought had not occurred to her. "Yes," she said, then closed her mouth and her expression and made no offer to describe the gun or to look for it.

Sullivan could sense that Phyllis was already beginning to regret her rare candor and would surely hold it against her later.

Now Phyllis began to weep carefully into a handkerchief that appeared from out of the pocket of her robe. Sullivan touched her arm. Phyllis was flesh and blood, for all her steely resolution.

Stepping out of the passenger's side of the police car was a young man, nervous, very nervous, with red hair, a slim build, freckles, still more like a boy than a senior detective. He stepped immediately toward Morris.

"Mr. Morris. Detective Fannin. Henry Fannin." He stuck out a slim but firm hand.

His face seemed so young, and suddenly familiar,

to Morris, but he couldn't remember where he had known him.

Fannin might have been listening to his thoughts.

"I used to see you here," said Fannin. "Several years in a row. When I was a kid. I grew up in Augusta. I worked as a flunky in the press tent. Even took a week off my first year at college to keep it up."

"Hell, yes!" said Morris. "Henry." The name and the face—an even younger face—and all the freckles, came to mind. He'd been an energetic kid. A dependable runner, for all things. Never sticking his nose where it shouldn't be. But knowing everything that was happening. And how to round up any absent writer whose office needed him "right goddamn now." Morris shook his hand again, as if he were now truly greeting him and as a longtime equal.

"I still remember the year I wanted a tournament ticket for my girlfriend," said Fannin. "That was before tickets were impossible. But I didn't have a dime. You snagged me one somewhere."

Morris remembered the year exactly, when Nicklaus had won his third title. "The ticket came from Sullivan, *my* girlfriend," said Morris, enjoying the description. "Sullivan could get a ringside ticket to the Second Coming."

"I remember her," said Fannin. "Is she still that beautiful?"

"Yes, but for God's sake don't bring it up. She's too vain already. And what happened to your own girlfriend?"

Fannin laughed. "She's my wife. We have two children."

"I guess the ticket must have worked," Morris said, remembering the way the young Henry Fannin was respectful but never afraid, not even of the most temperamental players, or "big shot" writers, or even of Cliff Roberts himself.

"I used to read a lot of the stuff written in that tent," said Fannin. "Yours was always the fastest and the truest."

"I'll settle for fastest," said Morris, more flattered than he would admit.

"It's ironic . . . but I came out here . . . as a police officer—just a junior member of the team—when Mr. Cliff Roberts killed himself," said Fannin.

"That must have been rough," said Morris.

"Yes. He was an autocratic old man. But a very shrewd one, even a fair one, as I remember. I can see him picking up any discarded cup and carrying it to a trash bag. God help you if he saw you throw one down."

"Melvin Newton was no Cliff Roberts," said Morris.

"No." Fannin shook his head. "To be truthful . . . between you and me"—it was obvious the detective trusted Morris implicitly—"I couldn't stand him."

"I don't know anybody who could," said Morris, indicating with his hand and arm the way to Eisenhower Pond, which Fannin knew as well as he did.

"Let me tell my driver again how to find us. He can bring the others when they get here." Fannin stuck his head back in the passenger door to speak to a heavyset young policeman behind the wheel.

The Pinkerton man was glad to leave the body to them, and promised to keep what he had seen to himself. Detective Fannin knelt, careful not to disturb the site, much as Morris had done less than an hour before. He shielded his eyes from the early slant of the sun with the palm of his hand.

"No doubt. That's Mr. Newton," said Fannin, rising awkwardly from one knee.

"If there was a struggle here, I can't tell it," said Morris.

Fannin bent forward and seemed to count the separate blades of grass around the legs and torso. He shook his freckled face. "The lab may turn up things we can't see. But I doubt it. Suicide becomes more convincing when you stand over the body like this. You'd be amazed how much it resembles the death of Mr. Roberts. We'll know a great deal more if he left a suicide note."

"If he had, you would have heard from his wife."

"It's possible he left it in the clubhouse."

"It's possible," Morris said, but without conviction.

"Do you know if he traveled with a handgun?" the detective asked.

"No," said Morris.

"But you are staying in his cottage?"

"We are. But the word *cottage* is something of a misnomer. It's a large house with numerous suites and bedrooms. The members gave a party last night in memory of Monty Sullivan's win here at the Masters twenty years ago. Julia was married to him then. The party was really in her honor. Melvin and his wife invited us to stay with them. I wouldn't say we were close to either of them."

"I've seen his temper. He could be a nasty man," said Fannin.

"He could be even nastier if you were doing business with him . . . or so I hear," said Morris. "He didn't have a shortage of people who weren't crazy about him."

"Even looking at him here . . . I get the feeling you still don't believe in his suicide," said the detective.

"I'm not much for coincidence. Two club members dead by their own hands . . . in the same pond. Give me a break."

"Imitation is a form suicide often takes."

"Cliff Roberts was as tough as they come. But he was an old man who didn't want to die by the inch," said Morris. "I said to Michael Compton that Newton still wanted to own the world . . . he didn't want to leave it." Morris was embarrassed at rehearsing the phrase he had coined. He knew damn good and well it was headed for print in his *Atlantic* piece, which had taken a violent turn of narrative.

"Who else is staying in his cottage?" asked Fannin.

"Let's see," said Morris. "There's Edgar Benefield and his wife, Jerusha. Remember them?"

Fannin nodded that he did. "Speaking of beautiful women," he said.

"Indeed," said Morris.

"Are the two families close?"

"Hell, no," said Morris. "Benefield recently sold the family publishing house to Newton. He told me he did it for the money. He hated the idea of selling out an honest literary press to a romance publisher. Said his father was better off in his grave than knowing about it."

"Wouldn't he very sporting to take a man's money and then kill him for giving it to you."

"No," said Morris. "And Edgar Benefield is a fine amateur golfer and a true sportsman." Morris did not add *but maybe a weak man*. He went on: "Then there's the club chairman, Michael Compton, and his wife, Aeriel. Their own suite of rooms in another cottage is being remodeled."

Fannin raised his sandy eyebrows for any further insight into the Comptons, whom he knew by sight.

"Old money, the Comptons," said Morris. "Old, old money. A decent enough guy, really. His wife is thin and formidable. But not unlikable. But the old rich keep to their own kind. Compton's father and Newton's father had been great friends."

"I do remember old Mr. Newton," said Fannin. "I remember the year he died, during the tournament. All the members were sick about it."

"He was a great friend of Bob Jones's, and a charter Augusta member," said Morris. "The man lying here was a pale imitation of his daddy."

Fannin nodded his agreement. "Anybody else in the cottage?"

"Yes. Spears. Tom Spears. The two-time Masters champion. Remember him?"

"Oh, yes. A nice man. He was already finished as a player when I was a kid. I once had to get him from the locker room to be interviewed, after he'd shot an embarrassingly bad round, in the eighties, in fact. He was absolutely a gentleman about it. Made no excuses to the press. He even gave me a souvenir. I still have it."

"I remember the interview," said Morris, who had written a sidebar about the arthritis that was destroying Spears's game, though Tom had made no reference to it, or given any other alibi in the interview. "What kind of souvenir did he give you?" Morris was curious, but not surprised by Spears's generosity.

"Well"—Fannin was embarrassed—"it was a sketch. A charcoal sketch he had done—of me—working in the press tent . . . I was just a kid," said Fannin, almost as an apology for being the subject of a sketch.

"I didn't know Tom was an artist," said Morris. "I'd like to see it."

"Can't say much for the subject, but he's good . . . it seems to me. God knows I'm ignorant about art."

"Tom told me he's just lost his seventh club job in nine years. He just doesn't have the temperament of a teaching pro. He's a damn fine man, and a true champion," said Morris.

"How did he come to be staying with the Newtons?" the detective asked.

"Michael Compton suggested Newton invite him. He must have known Tom was out of a job. Newton could hardly say no to the club chairman. And Spears is a two-time champion and an honorary member of the club."

Morris suddenly remembered he was supposed to meet Tom Spears for breakfast. He looked at his watch. It was still early. He also remembered— maybe it was the idea of a club pro that triggered his memory—Sid Norton was being let go as Augusta National's pro. Melvin Newton had accused him of excess drinking, according to the unlovely Gerald Acton, who was also staying in the Newton Cottage with his wife, Louise. Morris explained it all to Detective Fannin, whom Morris could now only think of as the freckle-faced Henry.

"Jesus. If Newton did travel with a handgun, everybody in the goddamn club had access to it."

"Including his wife, as well as myself and Julia Sullivan," said Morris. He shook his head at the number of times he had been a logical suspect in the death of an athlete.

Fannin smiled. "What time did you leave the party?"

"Late," said Morris. "With the Lady Sullivan. Neither of us saw Melvin Newton leave. In fact, Phyllis asked Julia if she had seen him. Julia said she hadn't. And we were among the last to go. Of course, when the party was going full blast, the Cuban army could have left and we wouldn't have missed them."

"Would you say the Newtons were happily married?"

"More like an armed truce," said Morris.

Through the trees came Fannin's heavyset driver, a thin photographer with a video camera, two middle-aged police officers, and a rather delicate young woman with the face of an archangel.

Morris caught the name of the young woman only: Dr. Karen Moseley. She had short, blond, very fine hair that seemed to float above her high, classical forehead. She might have been a model for a Botticelli painting rather than a medical examiner carrying a heavy metal case.

She left her small hand in Morris's large one, saying, "I know who you are. You were a friend of my grandfather's." She had a wispy voice that floated above her with her hair.

"Your grandfather was . . ." Morris churned the name Moseley through his memory. Christ, he'd better behave himself; everybody in Richmond County was keeping up with his ass.

"Dr. . . ."

"William Moseley . . . Oh, hell, yes," said Morris.

She nodded her halo of fine hair, pleased that he remembered her grandfather.

"A very wise man. And a very funny one. He also saved the lives of more than one golfer by helping catch a killer in Atlanta."

"He told me it was you who did that." She set her case down by the dead man as if she were an hourly employee reporting to work on a construction site.

"Is your grandfather still living?"

"No. He died two years ago."

"I'm sorry. But then, he damn near lived forever."

"He was ninety-one."

"An amazing man. Is he why you became a medical examiner?"

"Very much why. My father was recalled to military service and killed in Vietnam. My grandfather became a second daddy to me. Gave me my first bicycle. Paid my tuition to medical school. I loved him." She was not embarrassed to say it in front of her peers. "Not that I will ever be as bright as he was."

"Oh, I bet he was proud of you."

She didn't deny it, leaning over the dead man.

The photographer, a tall, thin, morose man with a hooked nose, began panning the scene with his video camera, first taking in the entire pond and continually tightening the focus until the dead man's hand under water must have filled the entire frame. When he had finished with his video, he began shooting with a 35-mm Nikon. The whole time he said nothing, as if he and the body were brothers in silence.

The young Dr. Moseley waited until the photographer was satisfied and then began to touch and probe the corpse as if there were some possibility of life yet hidden inside of it.

Detective Fannin took a pencil from his coat pocket and carefully stuck it down the barrel of the handgun and lifted it out of the water into the sunlight. He held it until all of the pond water had dripped from inside the revolver.

"A thirty-eight Smith & Wesson," said Fannin, turning the revolver this way and that on the end of the pencil. "It's his, all right." He pointed with his other hand at a set of initials traced into the side of the barrel: MLN. "Wonder what the *L* stands for?" said Fannin.

"Lamar. Melvin Lamar Newton," said Morris. "I always thought it was a very literate name for a very barbarous man."

Dr. Moseley looked up at him with a smile that was more amused than angelic. Fannin didn't edit his own chuckle.

"A little help, please," Dr. Moseley said to the two middle-aged policemen who had been on their hands and knees collecting any loose debris from around the body and dropping it into plastic bags. With one of them on each side, they lifted the very stiff and very dead Mr. Newton until his head was clear of Eisenhower Pond. His right hand, frozen in an awkward salute, dripped pond water on the grass. Both of his eyes were locked open, one of them running with muddy water as if he were weeping for his late existence. A neat hole penetrated just above his right ear and exited with a shattering of his left temple, both wounds cleansed by the pond water and maybe by the tiny fishes.

"What do you think?" Fannin asked after young Dr. Moseley had made another tour of the dead body with her gloved but elegant hands.

"He's been dead all night. It will be a bit difficult

to pin down the exact hour he died . . . his head being in the water so long. But I'd guess he's been here at least since midnight. Maybe longer."

She pointed to his right temple. "Even the lake didn't wash away all the powder burns. He was shot at close range. I think the barrel of the gun might have actually touched his temple."

"Anything inconsistent with a suicide?" Fannin asked, dropping again to one knee to examine the wounds.

"Not really. We'll have to check the angle of the bullet, but it probably won't show us much. The gun seems to have been held remarkably level. If he shot himself, he wasn't trembling."

"Not likely he was shot from that close by a stranger," said Fannin.

"Just the one bullet missing from the cylinder?" asked Morris.

"I didn't break it open," said Fannin, "but that's the way it looks."

"Did he fall directly into the water?" Morris asked. "No chance he was dragged into it?" He still found it difficult to believe in the great coincidences between the deaths of Mr. Roberts and Mr. Newton.

"Hard to tell. Maybe impossible. The grass doesn't appear much disturbed. We'll examine his flesh and his clothes microscopically. Still, we may not know that."

"Wouldn't there be a grass stain on the right side of his face . . . if he fell on it in the grass?" said Morris.

Dr. Moseley looked back at him with one of her

unearthly smiles. "It's possible. But he's been in the water, perhaps all night. We'll have to see."

"Would a submerged hand show positive in a paraffin test, if he fired the gun?" Morris asked. "And I know I'm making a nuisance of myself."

"I see why my grandfather liked you so much," Dr. Moseley said, without looking up from the mud-filled mouth of the corpse.

"Damn problem is," said Fannin, "here at Augusta National, they fertilize the grass within an inch of its life . . . on the golf course and off. The paraffin test is just a test for traces of nitrate. He'll probably test positive for nitrate from one end to the other, even the hand that's under water. Hell, we'd all probably test positive for nitrate just from touching the grass ourselves."

"True," said Dr. Moseley, "though I hadn't thought of it."

"You finish up here," said Fannin. "There's an access lane we can send the ambulance down when you're ready. It should be at the clubhouse by now."

"Right." Dr. Moseley was bent over the corpse again.

Morris leaned on his cane and looked at the early sun slanting through the huge pines. It was so quiet, they might have been in a national forest. The great migration of golf fans in their multicolored plumage wouldn't come winding down the fairways until the practice rounds began tomorrow. Not even one Augusta National member had ventured down to check on the corpse. It would be indiscreet to intrude on a suicide, even of a longtime member. They were leaving it entirely to the police.

The two Canada geese sailed across Eisenhower Pond, as if it were going to be a perfect Sunday.

Morris and Detective Fannin made their way through the trees back to Newton Cottage. Sullivan was sitting alone on the front steps, her chin in her hands, like a small girl who has lost her pet frog.

Morris introduced her to "Henry."

Of course, Sullivan remembered him immediately. "You've still got your freckles, Detective," she teased.

"And two children." Morris did not mean to say it as plaintively as it sounded, causing Sullivan to raise one eyebrow at the children they would never have.

"How did his wife take the news?" asked the detective.

Sullivan turned it over in her mind . . . remembering the questions she had asked and Phyllis Newton's iron-plated answers. "She never flinched . . . until she finally wept," said Sullivan, oddly protective of this woman she'd never been fond of.

"When did she miss him?" asked Fannin.

"She missed him, all right," said Sullivan. "She was angry with him for not coming to the suite from the party. She didn't call the clubhouse." Sullivan hesitated, then said, "A matter of pride." The detective nodded. "Melvin had a wandering eye. But, apparently, he was always on good behavior at Augusta National. I can tell you his wife thinks it is

'ridiculous' to believe he killed himself. If I can remember . . . she said, 'powerful men have powerful
enemies.' She believes if you find the person he left
the party with, you'll find his killer."

"If there was a killer," said Detective Fannin,
doubtfully.

"Oh, yes," said Sullivan. "Melvin travels with a
handgun. But I didn't ask if it was still in the suite."

"I've got an opening on my staff," said the detective.

"Sorry, she's already employed . . . looking after a
failed, middle-aged writer," said Morris.

"Who owes her a very large favor," said Sullivan,
putting her small fist under his nose.

"I'm sure the revolver was his," said the detective.
"It has his initials engraved on it." He held up the
plastic bag with the handgun in it. "Who's inside
with his wife now?"

"The Comptons—Michael and Aerial.
Henry . . ." She felt comfortable with his first name.
"I'm sure Phyllis regrets every word she said to me
. . . before the shock of Melvin's death wore off. I
think it would be best if you didn't quote me. I warn
you, she is one formidable woman."

"And now a rich one," said Morris.

"He controlled the fortune in the family?" said
Fannin.

"Oh, hell, yes," said Morris. "He inherited a publishing company. And turned it into a press to print
money. I think Phyllis was once his secretary. It's
not something that comes up in her conversation.
She's now one of the richest women in America.

Unless Melvin left his millions to the Baptist church. Somehow I don't think it's likely."

"She could have taken a moonlight walk with him down to the pond and pulled out the old revolver," said Sullivan, almost to herself.

"I'd rather take a moonlight walk with a live cobra," said Morris.

"Maybe he did," said Sullivan.

"I have to go up and interview her," said Fannin. He did not look as if he expected to enjoy the experience. "If you two would keep the details of what happened to yourself, until I've talked with those who were close to Newton, I'd appreciate it. And thank you . . . Julia." He settled on her first name, to her obvious pleasure. "You don't know how much you've helped me."

"Oh, yes, she does," said Morris. "You'll be getting a bill. Don't doubt it."

They watched the detective disappear into the cottage.

"You think there's any chance Phyllis killed him?" asked Morris.

"A tiny chance. I don't think she cared that much about him. She just enjoyed the power of being Mrs. Newton."

"It shouldn't be too hard to find out who left the party with Melvin," said Morris.

"It may be harder than you think. People were coming and going. Even Phyllis doesn't know when he left, and she was looking for him. Did you miss him?"

"Hell, no. I would have been looking to avoid

him," said Morris. "I guess the next question is, Who stands to gain from his death?"

"If I said 'the world,' God would get me," said Sullivan. "Phyllis now has the money and the power. And she doesn't have to put up with his playing around. Better than that, with his *being* around."

"It's too late for Benefield to get his publishing house back," said Morris. "It now belongs to Phyllis."

"Still, revenge can taste terribly sweet; nobody loves it better than the literary types," said Sullivan.

"If you are talking about the possibility of revenge, you'd better include most of the members of Augusta National and a substantial quantity of the human race . . . all of whom had some bone to pick with Mr. Melvin Newton. Sid Norton, for one. Melvin was helping throw him out as club pro . . . said he was a drunk."

Morris looked at his watch. "I'm supposed to meet Tom Spears for breakfast. He wanted me to use my influence, such as it was, with Melvin about something. . . . I don't know what. I'd better go find out."

"You do that," said Sullivan. "But remember . . . you owe me one . . . a big one." She measured the size of his obligation at about seven feet up from the cottage steps, where Morris left her standing.

Tom Spears set down his coffee cup. With his dark good looks and his halfback shoulders in the white golf shirt, he might have been headed for the first tee and a run at his third Masters title.

"I'm late," said Morris.

"I'm surprised you made it at all," said Spears. "I heard you found Melvin's body. Everybody in the club wants the inside scoop"—he indicated the roomful of breakfast eaters, who were suddenly very silent—"but they are all too polite to ask. I'm just an 'honorary member,' too poor to be polite. What the hell happened, Morris?"

"That's what the police are here to find out. I'm not supposed to talk about the details until the detective has finished his interviews."

"Is it true he shot himself at Eisenhower Pond, the same as the Old Man, Cliff Roberts?"

"So much for the Pinkerton man keeping what he saw to himself," said Morris. "But I don't know what happened. Neither does the detective . . . yet. I expect he will be talking with you before the day is over."

"With *me*. Why me?" asked Spears, fear opening his brown eyes, as if he had been accused of capital murder.

"You knew Melvin. And you were staying in his cottage. I'm sure Detective Fannin will question everybody staying in the cottage. Tell me, did you see Melvin leave the party last night?"

"Yes," said Tom, stroking his strong jaw between his thumb and forefinger.

"Who was he with?" Morris kept any emotion out of his voice.

"I hate to say it. I'm sure it doesn't mean anything." Spears looked at Morris, as if for agreement. "Sid Norton left with him. You know I like Sid. I always have. Sid was angry. And more than a little drunk. And you know a man had better hold his whiskey at Augusta National. They've bounced more than one member who couldn't. Melvin looked around the room as if for somebody to get Sid away from him. Melvin had trouble with the door. He wasn't too steady himself. I expect he'd knocked back a drink or two like the rest of us."

"What time was that?"

Spears thought. "I didn't look at my watch. I stuck around another hour . . . maybe hour and a half. I got back to my room at one-thirty. I did look at my watch then. Must have been around midnight when they left. Maybe a little before. I'm not sure. Is it important?"

"Maybe," said Morris.

"Depends on if it was suicide or . . ."

"Yes. No reason, at the moment, to think it wasn't. Except . . ." Morris paused.

"He wasn't a guy you would figure to kill himself," said Spears.

Morris nodded in agreement.

"Every man alive has thought about it," said Spears. "It occurred to me when these began to go. . . . " He held up his two hands, which were twisted slightly with arthritis. "But hell, no. That's too big a leap in the dark, Morris. You can take a lot of pain and failure before you try that."

"Newton was feeling no pain . . . and sitting on top of the publishing world. Tell me," said Morris, "what did you want me to use my influence to get him to agree to?"

Spears drank the last of his coffee. "A Japanese automobile company wants me to make a commercial. For next fall's model. It's the biggest chance I've ever had, Morris, to pick up some serious endorsement money. But the damn thing . . . the ad . . . would be built around my two Masters titles. They want to shoot me in the car coming up the Augusta National entrance . . . between the magnolias . . . here to the clubhouse."

"Hogan did it years ago, for Cadillac," said Morris. "You know Hogan. He said he would drive the car, but he wouldn't speak. He didn't either."

"I ain't Hogan," said Spears. "The club wouldn't agree to it. Compton, as chairman, didn't have a real objection. But Newton was on the executive committee. He said, 'Hell, no. Fuck the Japanese.' Something like that. I wanted you to talk to him."

"Now your problem is solved," said Morris, with no inflection in his voice.

"Look, I didn't kill the bastard. I'm broke, Morris, but I'm not crazy."

"No." Morris looked into his unblinking eyes and remembered what a relentless competitor Tom Spears had been, never flinching no matter the pressure. He was a player who extracted the last measure of his own ability. Who gave no mercy, and asked for none. But he was asking now with his eyes, for understanding.

"Do I have to tell all that to the detective . . . what's his name?" said Spears.

"Detective Henry Fannin. Yes, tell him exactly what you told me, Tom. It will be awkward for you

and Sid. But you didn't kill the man. And I'm sure
Sid has an explanation for leaving with Newton. Better that it come out right now. For God's sake don't
try to hide anything. Fannin's okay. In fact, you
know him."

"The hell I do." Spears had his chin between his
thumb and forefinger again, as if it could strengthen
his memory.

"He worked in the press tent when he was a kid.
All red hair and freckles . . ."

"By God, I do remember him. I even remember
his name . . . Henry," said Spears.

"He said you did a charcoal sketch of him. That
he still has it."

"Why were you and the detective talking about
me?" Spears's shoulders seemed to widen in his golf
shirt.

"Fannin asked me who else was staying in the
Newton Cottage. I told him."

"And you told him I was out of a job." Spears cut
his words into separate accusations.

"I did. I gave him a quick sketch of each of us
. . . myself and Sullivan included. I also told him you
were 'a damn fine man and a true champion.' Fannin
remembered you very well, and agreed with that description."

Spears's anger subsided, but not entirely. "How
is my private business *your* business, Morris?"

"When a man is lying dead on the ground, Tom,
a detective can ask any question he pleases, and you
damn well better answer as honestly as you are able.

You will have a chance to do that this morning."

Spears lifted his empty cup and set it back down, his anger with it. "I'm sure you're right, Morris. No hard feelings. I guess I'm just sick of my own failure." He looked at his two hands as if they had betrayed him.

"Do you still sketch?" asked Morris.

"In fact, it's one thing I can still do with my hands," said Spears. "But I hope Henry is a better detective than he is an art critic. It's pretty ordinary stuff. I've been doing it since high school. Just to amuse myself. My mother taught art at a junior college in California, years ago, before she got married. She piddled at it when I was a kid, enough to interest me."

"Have you tried to sell it?"

"Oh, hell, no. I don't even give it away. Usually. It's just . . . literal stuff."

"I'd like to see it," said Morris.

Spears, with his first enthusiasm of the morning, said, "I did a series of sketches of Sullivan—over the years, actually—here at Augusta."

"Jesus . . . I would kill to see them," said Morris.

"Between jobs, Augusta is the only place I'm sure to show up every year," said Spears. "I have a cheap space rented in an old warehouse. If it hasn't burned down."

"Promise to show me the sketches," said Morris. "And I promise I will speak with Michael about the commercial. Hell, I'll talk with him about it anyhow. I'll kick his ass if I have to. Or find somebody a lot more powerful than myself to kick it. I can't imagine he won't allow it. He's not that bad a guy." Morris thought to himself, Newton would have been an argument of a different sort; he'd not been a man to back down from a nasty decision.

"It's a deal," said Spears, holding out his right hand. "Careful how you shake it."

Morris wondered what the club members in the room, staring at them, thought . . . or imagined they had agreed on.

Morris walked through the dining room toward the pro shop. An unfriendly hand caught the bottom of his jacket. Morris stopped, and stood without speaking until the hand released his jacket.

"Is it true that big-shot Newton shot hisself?" Eddie Hayward did not disguise the smile on his puffy face.

Morris resisted the urge to dump his plate of eggs in his lap.

"What were you and he and Gerald Acton laughing about last night?" asked Morris. "I believe Detective Fannin will want to speak to you about that. A man is laughing one minute and dead the next. Funny thing." Morris left him sitting with his mouth open and egg on his fork.

Sid Norton was nursing a hangover with a cup of black coffee. His hair, which had been fading for years, had now gone entirely white. He smiled, but he looked as if his face might break.

"Hello, Morris. You still speaking to us has-beens?"

"Bullshit, Sid. You're still in your prime."

"Yeah. Tell it to the executive committee. You heard I got the ax?"

"You're sure it's final?" said Morris.

"When the tournament's through, I'm through." The coffee cup shook in his hand. "They say it's the booze, Morris. I can tell you, last night it was true."

"How the hell did you get home? I looked for you," Morris said, with no hint of what Spears had seen.

"I didn't. I slept on the couch in the living room of Newton Cottage."

"Be damned. I didn't see you."

"I was drinking that 'invisible whiskey.' Gets many a husband in trouble. But you know me, still the widower. Tell me, Morris, what happened to fuckin' Newton? And my head hurts too bad to pretend I'm sorry."

"He's dead, Sid. That's all I can say. You can ask Detective Fannin. He'll be talking to the clubhouse staff and to everybody who spent the night in Newton Cottage . . . though I doubt he knows you did."

"Jesus. Did somebody kill the bastard?"

"Looks like suicide. That's all I can say. It's up to the detective to find out. You might remember him . . . Henry Fannin, used to work in the press tent when he was a freckle-faced kid."

"Yeah. Nice kid. And now he's a detective? God, Morris, where has time gone?" He drank the last of his coffee, holding the cup in both hands.

"Has the booze really been that bad?" Morris asked, touching Sid on his forearm.

"Not really. I can't drink like I used to. Who the

hell can? I had a couple too many one night and got into an argument with Melvin. Over nothing. He didn't like my new line of men's shirts in the shop, for God's sake. Not a reason to run me off after twenty years. The members damn sure liked 'em. They bought every one of 'em. The truth is, Morris, he got the idea his bloody-awful wife had the hots for me. And maybe she did. She took some lessons. Terrible athlete. She had no intention of taking up the game. That bitch. I'd cut it off first. I don't know what she told Melvin, but it wasn't in my favor. Damn her."

"Did you tell this to Michael Compton?" asked Morris.

"I tried to. He wouldn't let me finish a sentence. He just said the executive committee agreed—I'd done a good job, but it was time for me to retire." Sid set his empty cup down so hard, he cracked it on the counter.

"I'm sorry," said Morris. "Do you think Melvin's death might change their attitude?"

Sid looked at him for a hint of accusation, but didn't see any.

"No. I'm history, Morris. But by God, I'll ask them again."

"Does it surprise you that Newton may have killed himself?"

"Oh, shit, yes. That bastard. If you told me he killed somebody, I could believe it. Is it true he shot himself?"

"Look. You talk to the detective about it. One piece of advice, Sid. Don't conceal anything. The police are touchy about that. I'd better tell you. Somebody saw you leave the clubhouse last night . . . with Melvin. What happened?"

"Goddamn, Morris. Are you after me too?" Norton's hands shook more violently.

Morris didn't answer him.

"He told me I was a washed-up drunk. I followed him all the way to his cottage, telling him what an asshole he was. He wouldn't answer me. He just disappeared up the stairs. I lay down on the couch and the next thing I knew, it was morning. And my head is still killing me. But I didn't kill the son of a bitch, Morris. I wouldn't waste gunpowder on him. Do you think this detective will believe me?" His voice was as shaky as his hands.

"Look, Sid. Tests will probably show he killed himself. Just be straight with Fannin. Tell him exactly what happened. What time did the two of you leave the clubhouse?"

"Hell, I don't know," said Sid. "After midnight. I think. Not that late. But it's all too late for me, old friend."

"Listen, are you gonna be okay? I mean, does the club have a retirement program?" Morris had known Sid for thirty years and didn't hesitate to ask him.

"Yeah," said Norton. "I'm fine. I've got a nest egg put away. And I have to say, they made me a fair deal. I only wanted to work another couple of years, Morris. I didn't want to be kicked out like an old dog."

"Sid, you'll be surprised how much you enjoy

having time of your own. I've been retired a couple of years from the AP. I miss some of the excitement, my old buddies. But I like getting up in the morning with nobody to tell me what to do or where to go."

"Yeah, but I'm just an old hack, Morris. I don't know anything but golf."

"Clubs will be begging for you, Sid. You'll have to beat 'em off with a one-iron."

"Yeah," Sid said, unconvinced.

Morris stepped outside the clubhouse and walked directly into the flabby person of Gerald Acton.

"What's this, Morris? About Melvin?" Acton's dark jowls swung with his jaw when he spoke.

"He's dead, all right," said Morris.

"What happened?"

"Detective Fannin is the man to ask."

"Did he kill himself?"

"Maybe."

"That I'll never believe," said Acton. "I heard him on the phone to his tailor, ordering a dozen new suits. Man doesn't need to be buried in but one new suit."

"You better tell that to the detective."

"I don't like it," said Acton. "I don't like anything about it. Somebody killed him. This detective better be finding out why. And who. Not a damn one of us is safe. Suicide, my ass." Acton's jowls swung in agreement.

"Why do you say nobody's safe? Suicide or murder . . . it was very likely a personal matter."

"Bullets don't care whose heads they splatter. I

don't like it." Acton shifted his vast, loose weight toward the clubhouse door, a man very much in need of a Bloody Mary. He disappeared inside without so much as a nod.

Morris wondered for the hundredth time how Louise Acton could ever have married such a man . . . and wondered again why on earth she stayed with him. "It is a puzzlement. . . ." he quoted to himself.

Jerusha Benefield saw Morris coming up the cottage steps and opened the door. She had obviously been waiting for him. She was frightened and glad to have a consoling hug. Sullivan was across the room and making a small fist at Morris, who was looking over Jerusha's shoulder.

"What on earth happened to Melvin?" asked Jerusha.

"The last thing that happens to any man," said Morris. "Question is . . . *how* did he die?"

"What do you think?" she asked.

Morris could only shake his head; he didn't know.

"Edgar is upstairs talking to the detective. Fannin is his name. He knows you, Morris." It was a mild accusation. "I already spoke with him," she said. "But I couldn't help. I don't know anything. I went to sleep early. I sleep so soundly, I won't hear the end of the world."

"Did you like Melvin?" asked Morris.

Jerusha flinched as if he had meant to offend her. Then she thought about it, her green eyes concentrating. "I despised him. I'm embarrassed to say it, standing in the man's own cottage."

"I didn't like him either," said Morris.

"He could be a nasty man." She twisted her hands as if she were washing them of his memory. "He always spoke down to Edgar, who is a far better, brighter, kinder man. It killed him to sell Melvin his company. I begged him not to do it. I have money, Morris. Enough for us to live on. But not enough to have saved Benefield House. Melvin meant to keep the publishing house name alive, but to destroy what it stood for. I hated it for Edgar. But I couldn't do anything about it. I can't even do anything about us. I can't live with his silences anymore, Morris. It's that simple. He began to disappear inside himself years ago. I need a life. I'm going to find it." She did not say it as an apology.

"What time did you go to bed?" asked Morris.

"Not long after ten o'clock. I was exhausted. But I had a grand time talking to Sullivan. You are a lucky man, John Morris."

"You are right about that. But don't be telling Sullivan. She's over there now, shaking her fist at me."

Jerusha turned to see a big, fake smile pasted on Sullivan's face.

"What time did Edgar go to bed?" asked Morris.

"I knew you were going to ask me that," said Jerusha. "The detective did. I don't know. We have separate bedrooms. I never woke up until the sun came in the window. Edgar said he came in about one A.M. and read. He reads late at night. It's an old habit. Edgar is not a man to hurt anybody, except himself."

"What do you mean?"

"He's hard on himself. I liked his shyness as a young man. It's become bitterness, Morris."

"I'm sorry," said Morris. "Still, he's a sportsman of the old school. I've always liked him for that. No hope you two will stay together?"

"It will have to be in Paris. Do talk to him, Morris. I'm afraid this detective—as polite as he is—is going to frighten him."

"I'll do that. Let me go speak to the Lady Sullivan."

Morris crossed the room and put his arm firmly around Julia Sullivan's shoulders.

"Don't think you can flirt with a beautiful woman and come over here and hug up on me," she said.

"There is room in the world for two beautiful, smashing women. But just barely," said Morris.

She couldn't help but smile. "I admit," she said, "I'm crazy about Jerusha."

"On the other hand, there is only room for one devastating man at a time." Morris posed with his hand on his cane.

Sullivan rolled her eyes and giggled in spite of herself. "Yes, one huge American 'hunk' at a time. How can the world stand it?"

Morris took on a great look of modesty.

Sullivan punched him in the arm. "What have you learned?"

Morris told her everything he'd found out since breakfast.

"What do you make of it?"

"Madness. His or somebody else's."

"How about greed, or ambition, or revenge, or lust—one of the great 'verities' you have such faith in?"

"By all means a possibility," said Morris, looking up the stairs at the slow descent of Edgar Benefield.

He stopped between the two of them.

"Did you survive our Detective Fannin?" asked Morris.

"Barely. He's a persistent young man."

"Did you remember him?"

"Only after he told me about working the press tent as a kid. Then I remembered him very well. A dependable young man."

"What did you tell him?" asked Morris.

"I left the party . . . it was after midnight . . . it was close to one A.M. Went up to the room and read. Jerusha had turned in hours before. If I could sleep like her, I think I might want to keep on living."

"Edgar Benefield . . . behave yourself," said Sullivan.

"I'm losing my publishing house, and my wife. What the hell else is there?"

"There's always Paris," said Morris, "and golf."

"Thank God for golf," said Edgar. "Although I'm not sure I ever want to pick up another club."

"Baloney," said Morris. "You ought to get out on the Senior Tour when you hit fifty. Take your mind off your troubles."

"Do you think I could?" asked Benefield, who seemed never to have considered such a thing. "I've always been an amateur."

"And a damn good one," said Morris. "What did

you tell Detective Fannin about Melvin? How did he seem to you last night?"

"His old, overbearing self," said Benefield. "All I heard from him all night was his opinion . . . about everything. I'll be honest. I look forward to never seeing the man again, Morris. And here I stand in his own cottage." Edgar might have been his wife, saying the same thing minutes before.

"Did you see Sid Norton sleeping here on the couch, when you came in . . . or anytime later?" asked Morris.

Benefield shook his head. "I don't know if I even looked at the couch. I might have missed him. Did he sleep here?" Benefield shifted his weight as if the idea of it concerned him.

"Yes," said Morris. "He said he left the club, fighting with Newton—trying to fight with him. Newton wouldn't talk to him . . . went upstairs, left Sid in the living room, and he fell asleep on the couch. Maybe a bit before midnight."

"Damned if I saw him," said Edgar. "But it was pretty dark in here, only a lamp or two burning, and I was tired and headed for my room."

"Did you know Melvin traveled with a gun?" asked Morris.

"Yes. He showed it to me more than once. Made me nervous the way he swung it around."

"Is the detective upstairs, going through his things?"

"Yes."

"How is Phyllis?"

"She's taken to her bed."

"The devastated widow," said Morris.

"At least." Benefield's voice revealed nothing. "I'm not hungry. But I'd better eat anyway." His eyes flickered, ever so slightly, to see his wife approaching.

Morris climbed the stairs to their rooms and made notes on a pad. He'd actually dozed off when the phone rang. It was the detective, who had finished his search of the cottage and had spoken with everyone who spent the night there.

"Where can we talk?" asked Fannin.

"Out back of the cottage," said Morris, "there's a porch."

Now the sun was shattering through the pines and glancing off the grass in all its April fury. Fannin sank in a deep rocking chair as if submerging himself in his doubts.

Morris waited for him to speak.

Fannin began by shaking his head, making a semaphore of his freckles. "Not a hint of a suicide note. Nothing. Man just left the party and walked out and killed himself. Makes no sense at all, Morris."

Morris only shook his own head, leaving the detective to fill up the silence.

"Somebody *killing* him makes a lot more sense," said Fannin. "But who? Why? If you set out to kill every asshole in Georgia, the population would suffer grievously."

Morris had to smile.

Fannin said, "You're right. His wife laughs at the idea he killed himself. A nasty laugh."

"I know it," said Morris, speaking for the first time.

"It's not the 'poor-widow-who-can't-believe-her-husband-capable-of-a-foul-deed' sort of thing. I believe she could see him killing anybody but himself. Still, there's the bloody thirty-eight in the pond with him. And no witnesses."

Morris leaned back in his own rocking chair and poked his cane at the porch railing, keeping his silence.

"Gerald Acton said he heard Melvin order a dozen new suits over the phone. Not the thing a stingy man who's about to kill himself would do," the detective said.

Morris nodded his agreement.

"Now I'll have to ask his damn wife if she knew about the suits." Fannin shook his head at the life of a detective. "I did ask her if her husband was in good health."

"An illness? I hadn't thought of that," said Morris.

"Well, he didn't have one. He'd just gotten his annual physical."

"Why would a man who was about to kill himself get a physical? While you are asking Phyllis if she knew Melvin had ordered twelve new suits, you might ask her if she had the hots for the club pro, Sid Norton."

"What? Norton didn't mention anything like that to me," said Fannin.

"He told me Melvin thought she was trying to come on to him . . . and that she might have been.

Phyllis took some lessons that Sid says she really had no interest in. Sid certainly had no interest in her. Conan the Barbarian would have no interest in her. It was after the lessons that Melvin accused Sid of being a drunk. Helped get him fired."

"Sid told you this?"

"I doubt Sid was trying to hide anything from you. He was probably just hoping it wouldn't come up. It's embarrassing to him. But you can ask him about it yourself."

"I will," said Fannin.

"Did Tom Spears tell you he saw Newton leave the party last night?"

"Yes. He said he left with Sid Norton chewing him out . . . maybe a bit before midnight."

"That's what he told me," said Morris.

Fannin was now sitting on the edge of the deep rocking chair. "Tell me what Sid told you, and what you saw yourself."

Morris recounted Norton's story, saying Sid might have been asleep on the couch when he and Sullivan got to the cottage last night, but it was dark and they didn't see him.

"The Actons didn't see him either," said Fannin. "I would trust Acton's wife, Louise."

"Gerald himself is not one of your favorite members?" said Morris, smiling.

"Not among my favorite human beings," said Fannin.

"He's a beauty. I will never understand why Louise married him. Or kept him after she did marry him." Morris hesitated. "But you must realize—no man can imagine any appealing woman happy with anybody... but himself." Morris laughed into the Sunday morning silence. "Don't you dare tell Sullivan I said that."

"Oh, no. One death is all I'm prepared to investigate at Augusta National. What's more and more appealing to me, Morris, is the obvious: the poor son of a bitch, Melvin Newton, killed himself. Period."

"Funny thing," said Morris, seriously. "Gerald Acton surprised me... with his reaction. He's afraid."

"Of what?"

"Of whatever killed Melvin Newton."

"He didn't say that to me," said Fannin.

"Maybe a couple of Bloody Marys lifted his courage, such as it is."

"Maybe. Nobody I've talked to admits to so much as hearing a gunshot last night."

"At the party you couldn't have heard a cannon shot," said Morris.

"What do you truly think happened?" asked the detective.

Morris propped himself to his feet with his cane. There was something tugging in the back of his mind that he ought to tell Fannin, but he couldn't remember what it was.

Morris said, "Oh, I think somebody we know very well stuck a gun to Newton's head and shot him to death... probably for good reason."

"Who?"

"I don't know. And I don't want to know," said Morris.

"Maybe the autopsy, or the lab, will tell us something we can't see for ourselves," said Detective Fannin. "But when we're all done, I'd settle for the one simple decision—suicide."

"Call me," said Morris.

"I will, indeed." Fannin stepped back inside the cottage with his jacket over his shoulder, like a young country doctor making a house call.

CHAPTER THREE

Practice rounds at Augusta National had long been lost in a sea of spectators. There was a lifetime waiting list for tickets to the tournament proper. So fans drowned the course from Monday until Wednesday just to see the practice rounds. Morris lamented the old days when he could walk along the fairway with the pros, swapping stories between shots, even with those foursomes playing among themselves for higher stakes than they were going to win on Sunday.

Morris pegged a folding seat into the soft ground and sat down just to the right of the enormous, totem-beast pine tree on the right side of the No. 7 fairway. None of the crowd sprawling through the trees and hills, and gathering at the 12th tee like hungry voyeurs awaiting a traffic accident, lingered in this deceptively tranquil site. The Squire, Gene Sarazen, always insisted this anonymous, 365-yard No. 7 was the best golf hole at Augusta National. Its narrow fairway required an immaculate three-wood or longiron; its near-vertical green, rising from front to back, demanded an approach shot that stayed below the hole. Not even the breath of God could stop an errant putt struck from the top half of the green. Sarazen loved the 7th hole, for it might have been lifted right out of Scottish lore. Morris remembered Greg Norman, the Shark, detonating a wedge shot that scraped the low-lying clouds before falling to the No. 7 green and being sucked all the way down to the fairway grass by the enormous backspin on the ball inflicted by the angle of the wedge. For all his power, and his appealing talent, Norman had never learned the "dead" iron that floats onto a green without benefit of backspin. Bob Jones himself had been a master of such shots. It was the near-forgotten art of soft hands and informed touch that Sarazen so admired in the correct playing of the hole. The sight of Tom Watson, under his Hogan cap, brought Morris back to the present. Watson reached the sky with his own wedge, but with so soft a touch that it struck the tilted green two feet below the hole and came to rest dead even with it. Watson lifted his hat at the quiet applause from the gathering of fans around the green. Of course, he missed the putt. The red-haired, freckle-faced young man from Kansas City had dominated golf for six years in the 1970s and '80s but now in his early forties he had seen time itself unnerve what had been the best putting stroke in golf. He left the green with his head up, chin out, not conceding a stroke to the quiet dignity of the game he loved.

The aging Gary Player, in his chosen black, left his approach in the front right bunker, but holed the sand shot for a three, and lifted it out as casually as if he had expected it to fall, which, indeed, he had, as the greatest sand player in the history of the game.

Fred Couples, with his easy, double-jointed take-away, seemed hardly to touch the ball with his wedge and yet it flew the green as if self-propelled. His chip back onto the green seemed to turn over one dimple at a time, then it was just rolling, then it was spinning past the hole and six yards into the fairway. Couples simply ran his hand through his abundant hair and grinned his matinee-idol grin at the vagaries of gravity; he was a man subverted by a hole he could drive the distance of.

Paul Azinger bent his rake-handle-lean self over his approach shot. His hands gripped the club in an unnaturally strong position, but his swing was dead-blocked against a hook, resulting in a low, crashing fade of a tee shot, directly opposite the rolling, right-to-left layout of Augusta National. Azinger, like that great fade-shot artist Lee Trevino, would be an improbable winner of any Masters. But when he stroked his five-foot putt for a par, Azinger was string music; it was too bad he was playing in the wrong arena. Morris focused his binoculars on the No. 7 tee. Filling the lenses was John Daly. He

stood in his odd-lot clothes like a sackful of door-
knobs. His rough blond hair seemed to have been
cut with a pair of hedge clippers. A cigarette hung
out of his mouth like a barroom challenge. He took
the club . . . My God, thought Morris, *it is a driver*.
. . . He took the club back around his neck and sent
the ball in the air until it was smaller than a hail-
stone. Morris, with his glasses, followed its passing
like a meteor until it came down dead and buried
beyond sight in the front left bunker, 360 yards from
the tee. The crowd around the No. 7 green never
saw it, never heard it land, but the news of the flight
of the ball ran along the fairway like a surf-line of
rich gossip breaking over the green grass. There was
a certain old, faded doom in young Daly's eyes as
he walked rapidly to the fate of his ball.

Now Raymond Floyd came up the seventh fairway, trailing the extralong shafted iron he had used
off the tee. He played a low punch shot from deep
in his stance that would have brought tears to the
eyes of the Squire himself. It ran up the green and
stopped dead at the hole for a gimme three. Raymond smiled a smile from his early days as the most
ready gambler on the tour, often playing practice
rounds for more money than the tournament's
grand prize. In his middle years he settled down into
a happy family life and won the U.S. Open and the
Masters and the PGA and became one of the great
touch players in the modern history of the game.

Nicklaus. Even in the twilight of his playing
days . . . just to see him over the ball in his yellow
sweater . . . just to see the concentration in his eyes

as he lifted his head, and then again, and then again, and then again, each time dipping his club-head to the ball as if in unspoken collaboration, and then turning his head to fix the ball with his left eye only, and spanking it smartly into flight and watching it, commanding it to stop, spinless, in the middle of the green. He bent over the four-foot putt, having made more critical putts from that distance than any man since Jones himself; he relaxed over the putt for maybe thirty seconds while the tension grew in the eyes of the spectators and in Morris's own eyes, until some impulse ran from Jack's eyes to his hands and the putter drew itself back and then forward sending the ball directly to the hole, but just to the right of it so that the ball spun 300 degrees around the cup and spilled out of the lip. Nicklaus stared at it as if seeing the passing of a golfing age that would not come again.

"What had Bob Jones said? 'He plays a game of which I am not familiar.' "

Morris turned at the familiar voice of Walter Edwards, golf writer for the good, gray *New York Times*. "Do you suppose we will ever see his like again?"

"No. Not us. We're too far down the road, Morris. And a golfer like him comes along once in a century. And this century is nearly done."

"I'm gonna steal those lines," said Morris.

"Of course you are. You were trained by the Associated Press, weren't you?" Walter, lean as a whippet, laughed with his hand on his old friend's wide shoulder. "I say, you had a call in the press tent. From that detective chap . . . Fannin . . . our old copy boy."

"You remember Henry?" said Morris.

"Of course I do. Saved my anatomy more than once when they were looking for me in New York and I was still sleeping it off."

"Not the *Times*; sleeping it off." Morris said in mock astonishment. "Do you know what he wants?"

"Of course I know what he wants. Haven't you seen my press pass? He wants to tell you something about the postmortem."

"But you don't know what?"

"I would have found out if we had been talking over the bar and not the telephone. He would speak further only to you."

"Do you think Newton killed himself?" asked Morris.

"Shit, no. Newton was the most self-centered son of a bitch in New York City."

"Maybe he got drunk out of his mind and did it—in some horrible stupor. Hell, maybe someday we'll all do it. How can any of us ever know another human being?"

"Sure. And maybe he did it in his sleep. I can tell you, many a business victim of Melvin Newton's in New York would have been pleased to pull the trigger. As for you, Morris, you'll never shoot yourself. Sullivan would kill you on the spot."

"You're right about that. How about you, Walter? What are you doing with your life? In fact, where were you last night?" Morris raised one hardly skeptical eyebrow.

"Drinking at Sullivan's party. And I left with a wife. My own, in fact. Morris, in truth, I hope they pass it off as suicide . . . let it go at that. Something tells me we will hate the reality of what happened."

"You say everything better than I do, Walter. And you couldn't be more right. I'd best go see what our boy Henry has learned. Tell me—" Morris lifted himself off his portable seat—"who do you like in this bloody golf tournament?"

"Couples."

"You think he's ready to win a major?" Morris asked.

"No. But he has such length . . . 'When length was fatigue and breadth was but bitterness sore . . .'"

"Jesus . . . now you're stealing from that well-known Georgia sportswriter, Sidney Lanier."

"Go talk to your detective. Tell me what he says."

Morris saluted with his binoculars.

Morris eased among the long, anonymous rows of word processors in the press tent, where he was still favored with a seat and even a telephone. He was rung straight through to Detective Fannin.

"So what did Dr. Moseley learn?" Morris asked.

"Not much that we couldn't see for ourselves. Newton was probably dead by one or two A.M. Food still undigested in his stomach. He had been drinking . . . but was just barely drunk. He should have been in control of his faculties. Couldn't tell anything from the paraffin test. Just as I thought, he was covered in nitrate from the fertilizer on the grass. But the bullet was fired from his own gun, the one in the pond. No doubt about that."

"Did he actually fall into the water?"

"Yes. He wasn't dragged in. No trailing marks in the soft ground, no smudged grass stains. His eyes were open, and the mud in the pond was driven into the sockets when he fell."

"That's cheerful."

"Dr. Moseley thought you might find it so. She said to give you her special regards."

"Thank her for me. And let's all have a drink when this sorry business is over. As far as mud in the sockets, I doubt Dr. Moseley is any more squeamish than her legendary grandfather, who would have laughed at the clap of doom, and frequently did," said Morris.

"You've got that right."

"Was Newton ill in any way?" asked Morris.

"No. The bastard would have lived forever. His arteries were clear as a young man's."

"Comes from evil living," said Morris. "What about the wound itself?"

"The barrel of the thirty-eight was placed directly against his temple. The burns were tremendous, and the trauma of the entry was devastating. If Newton didn't shoot himself, he wasn't shot by a stranger. Unless he was invisible."

"Whoever shot him, his intent was invisible," said Morris.

"No shortage of people who despised him . . . with good reason. But it's a large step from there to killing him. If it's any comfort to his widow, I don't believe Melvin Newton ever realized he had been shot."

"What about the angle of the entry?"

"Dead level. Almost oddly so. No upward angle. Almost as if he were shot by a giant reaching directly across at arm level."

"A man of any height could level a gun at his head," said Morris.

"Or a woman. But it would take a steady hand," said the detective.

"Did you find anything in his pockets? Or in his papers?"

"We found a lot of corporate shit. Most of it we are checking with his lawyer and his chief operating officer . . . a man named Milligan. A nasty sort of guy."

"It would take a nasty sort of guy to wheel and deal for Melvin Newton. He would also need the capacity to eat a lot of the shit you speak of," said Morris.

Detective Fannin's young voice rose with his own curiosity. "There was one very strange entry in Melvin's business calendar . . . which he kept in his breast pocket." Fannin pulled it from his own pocket. It was a slender, black, expensive business calendar . . . or organizer, as it was actually called. Luckily, the calendar hadn't gotten wet. Fannin turned to the last entry—apparently made yesterday—in Newton's own hand. Morris could see all the other entries were quite precise. "This last phone number was scrawled down in a hurry," said Fannin.

The area code and the seven numerals ran above and below the printed line . . . *as if it were maybe written in the dark*, Morris thought but did not say.

"If you can believe the calendar," said the detective, "this last number was entered sometime yesterday."

"Of course, you've called the number," said Morris.

"Oh, yes," said the detective, his voice again rising as if he held the receiver to his ear at that moment. "It's a very private number . . . for the *president of the United States*."

Morris was appropriately amazed.

"The son of a bitch answered this number himself," said Fannin. "I can tell you . . . I didn't do a very good job of explaining myself. Disturbing the president, on a Sunday afternoon. I could hear his wife complaining in the background."

"I can imagine," said Morris. "I would have been expecting a mistress . . . or maybe a bloody stockbroker to answer. What did the president say?"

"First he said he never heard of Melvin Newton. Then he asked his wife. She'd never heard of him either. The president had no idea how Melvin got his private number. Then when I stammered around about who Melvin Newton was—and what happened to him—and why I came to be calling his private number . . . the president backed up a little bit. Said he had met several members of Augusta

National over the years. He might have met this Newton. But he hadn't recently given him his private number. He was sure of that. Not that one of his aides might not have. He said he would check on it and let one of his aides get back to me."

"It's a bloody mystery," said Morris. "Now I wouldn't be surprised if Melvin was a big campaign contributor—with his company's money, of course—and if he had his hand out for some big favor. Don't suppose you asked him that?"

"I'm just a country detective, Morris. I'm not into accusing the president of the United States of lying over the death of a man he never heard of."

"You'll go a long way in Richmond County," said Morris. "I wouldn't have asked him either. But I know people I can ask."

"Would you do that?"

"Yes. Did you ask Newton's wife about the number?"

"I did. She insisted she never opened Melvin's business diary. She had no idea why he had the president's private number. I don't think much could shock this woman, Morris. But that number did surprise her. She wasn't faking her own curiosity. I also asked this Milligan, his operating officer. He had no idea what the telephone number was about."

"You must remember, President Eisenhower was a dues-paying member of Augusta National all during his administration, and afterward. I expect, as the president indicated, any one of Augusta's two hundred and seventy-five members has likely met him. . . . In fact, rich and powerful as they are, any one of them has likely met every president who has sat in the White House in the last thirty years. Not to say the presidents would remember them individually. Probably the telephone number has nothing to do with Newton's death. But it makes you want to know why it was written down."

"Yes," said Fannin. "Be my guest and find out."

"Anything else?"

"A number of business notes in his diary. This Milligan could explain most of them. They had a long phone conversation yesterday."

"But not about the president?"

"He swears not," said the detective.

"You could subpoena the president."

"I forgot how funny you can be, Morris."

"Yeah. I'm funny as cholera. So how will the Augusta police department list the death of Melvin Newton?"

"A very politic question," said the detective. "But I think 'probable cause of death . . . self-inflicted wound with a thirty-eight revolver.' "

"Let's hope the buck stops right there," said Morris.

"But while we hope . . . we'll keep plugging away," said Fannin. "We're keeping the body here until all the tests have been run. We're asking his widow to stay at her cottage until we know the results. She had no objection."

"I wouldn't be surprised if Phyllis has forgotten who he was."

"Not very gentlemanly of you, Morris, cutting down a lady in her grief."

"What did Red Smith write about the great geld-ing Kelso ... 'the unkindest cut of all.' " Morris laughed, and missed Red in the same breath.

"Let me know anything you find out on that end," said Detective Fannin. "By the way ... New-ton's wife did know about the twelve new suits he'd ordered. In fact, she suggested them. His tailor was about to go out of the country for a long European vacation."

"Must be nice," said Morris.

"You should know—you were on a worldwide, all-expenses-paid vacation for twenty-five years," said Fannin.

"Kiss my ass, Henry," Morris said, laughing in spite of himself.

Lounging in a chair under the great oak tree was Julia Sullivan, like an advertisement in *Town & Country*.

Morris lifted the glass out of her hand and drank it to the ice.

"Tell me ... *everything*," Sullivan said, pushing an empty chair toward him with her sandaled foot.

Morris, careful to keep his words between them, quietly told her everything he had learned from De-tective Fannin.

"Do you think the police will stick with suicide as the cause of death?" Sullivan asked.

"Unless something else turns up. Nobody in the mayor's office is going to be pushing to charge a member of Augusta National with first-degree mur-der. How is the widow holding up?"

"Phyllis put on her best show of being upset—after her visit with the detective," said Sullivan. "She said she got the feeling she 'was under suspicion.' "

"I don't imagine it will keep her up nights."

"No, but she enjoyed being distraught. I got the feeling she wants to leave Augusta National for good—and can't wait to put Melvin Newton safely in the ground."

"I don't doubt it," said Morris. "He might rise up and issue one more nasty opinion."

"Every writer in the press tent has been calling our room," said Sullivan, "looking for you for information."

"I just typed out what Detective Fannin is prepared to say, and gave it to AP's man from Atlanta. He was sitting at his computer. I didn't even have to wake him up. He's going with 'probable suicide,' quoting a 'reliable source.' That's me, kid." He handed back her empty glass. "Funny thing," added Morris. Then he told her about the president's private telephone number in Newton's business calendar.

"I bet Melvin wanted a favor," said Sullivan.

"My idea exactly," said Morris. "But the president denied knowing him at all. He did say he'd met several members of Augusta National over the years. But he hadn't given his private number to any Melvin Newton in recent days. Fannin showed me Newton's calendar. The number was scrawled, not composed between the lines like the other entries. It made me think, he might have jotted the number down in the dark . . . before he was killed—but I didn't say it to Fannin."

"And whoever gave him the number . . ." Sullivan let the implication hang in the air, then asked, "Is the president a golfer?"

"Yes. And not a shabby one. In fact, he's better than he'd care for the voting public to know."

"So. He might have been in touch with any one of the players in the Masters field. Maybe about a golfing date here . . . or somewhere else."

"Very possible, Sullivan. I'll pass that idea along to Detective Fannin. You're thinking one of the golfers might have shared the number with Newton . . . maybe to get his attention . . . and to get him outside in the dark . . . and then killed him over some old—or new—grudge."

Sullivan beamed her satisfaction at that analysis.

"I'll have to start paying you more attention," said Morris.

"Beginning tonight," said Sullivan. "In fact, you can begin right now . . . by refilling my glass."

Morris could see Edgar Benefield winding his way between tables and members, stopping to speak to this one and avoiding that one, all the time making his way in their direction.

Sullivan loved the way Edgar took her hand, as if it were more valuable than trees and sky. She looked at Morris without speaking, but written in her eyes was. "Do you see how a gentleman treats a lady?"

"I see," said Morris.

"What's that?" asked Benefield.

"Sorry. Thought Sullivan had something in her

eye there." He bent forward as if perhaps to look for a fallen tree limb in her sea-blue iris.

"Behave, Morris," said Sullivan, grinning at Edgar's puzzlement.

"Tell me, Edgar, what have you learned, if anything, from Phyllis?" Morris enjoyed getting his own question in before Benefield could quiz him about the detective.

"Well, actually, I was in her room when she called the family lawyer. I didn't catch his name. Larry something. It was obvious he didn't believe in Melvin's suicide. Phyllis had to persuade him *not* to hire an independent investigator into Melvin's death. I got the feeling he was dead, and that was all she needed to know."

Benefield signaled a waiter and ordered Scotch for the three of them.

"I tried to leave the room when they began to talk about Melvin's will," said Edgar. "Phyllis wanted me to stay. I can't imagine why."

"What did you hear?" asked Morris.

"Seems, from her end of the conversation, Melvin had recently updated his will, leaving quite a sum of money to her directly, and huge holdings in trust to be passed to his two sons as they reach age thirty. A complicated will. Tax considerations. That sort of thing. I didn't try to follow the details. In any event, Phyllis will be a wealthy woman all of her life."

"Then she won't be back in the secretarial pool," said Sullivan.

"I think not," said Benefield with a forced smile, just as their drinks were delivered.

They all touched glasses.

"What did you learn from the detective?" Edgar asked, not concealing his curiosity.

"Probable suicide," said Morris.

"Do you think that will be the end of it?"

"Probably," said Morris, pronouncing the word with just the proper irony.

"Can't pretend I will miss Melvin Newton," said Benefield. "Though I have not been too proud to avail myself of his cottage."

"Nor have any of us," said Sullivan.

"Well, to happier times. And to the tournament," said Morris. "May the new champion be a deserving one."

They all drank to that.

CHAPTER FOUR

Pressure descended over Augusta National like an unnatural element, seeping down through the pine needles and insinuating itself over the grass into the spikes of the players, threatening their precarious grips on a certain immortality. Gone were the easy swings of the practice rounds. Every breath was an intentional act. Clubs swung for a lifetime rested strangely behind golf balls that seemed as alien as grounded stars.

Morris and Sullivan breathed in the tension and the deadly beauty of the spring morning.

"'April is the cruellest month, breeding lilacs out of the dead land,'" Morris quoted in her ear as the former champion Seve Ballesteros paced the first tee, his great athleticism trapped in the moment, his eyes as dark as fate.

"You may not be a writer, Morris, but you know some good ones," Julia Sullivan whispered back.

"Hey, that's my line," croaked Morris.

"Just teasing you, old man."

"Yeah. But with the truth. It's against the code."

"You write like a dream, Morris. A dream by Fellini." She giggled in his ear.

Ballesteros, with his power and his balance, made a one-piece swing through the ball, but he was too quick in his eagerness and hooked it into the trees.

Now Morris could speak above a whisper. "A man's career takes a turn into the trees, and maybe he never wins his third Masters. But he's still young."

"And beautiful," said Sullivan.

"You noticed that."

"It just struck me. Right—"

"Don't tell me where," whispered Morris as David Berganio, Jr., an amateur, swallowed his fear and struck the ball exactly down the middle of the fairway.

So it went as champions and old friends teed off into the morning or the twilight of their careers: Palmer and Player, paired together like a warp in time; Watson, the gentleman stylist, and Calcavecchia, with his huge hip turn; Tommy Aaron and Chip Beck—two Georgians of separate eras, both winners of the one golf title on earth they most coveted; Gay Brewer and Doug Ford, with their own inexplicable styles; and the modern mechanical god, Nick Faldo, his swing as carefully in place as his youthful shock of hair—and Nicklaus. *Jack shouldn't be paired with anyone*, thought Morris, *for no man who ever played the game could equal him.*

Morris and Sullivan lingered at the first tee until Eddie Hayward stepped nervously up to defend his Masters championship. He pulled a new glove out of the bag his caddy held upright on the tee. He fumbled with it once, then twice.

"So, who's the wise guy?" Hayward accused his caddy, a thin white kid new to the Tour, who did not know what he was talking about. Heyward threw the glove into the crowd, and an elderly lady next to Morris picked it up. She turned it this way and that to see what was wrong with it. Morris saw immediately, it was a left-handed glove. He had to smile. Hayward was steaming. He snatched another, a right-handed glove, out of his caddy's hand. Twice his ball fell off the tee, to a smattering of snickers. Eddie set his sagging jaw and pushed a drive that took a fortunate kick off a pine tree into the fairway.

Speaking only with their eyes, Morris and Sullivan agreed to follow the inevitable disaster that would come to the unsavory Mr. Hayward. Funny thing: he parred the first hole and the next eight holes that followed; twice with miraculous putts, and once with a sand wedge improbably into the tough No. 5 hole on the fly. Hayward's game had always fed on his nasty resolution.

Morris found himself grudgingly admiring Hayward's determination in the face of his soft, dissipated talent.

"I'm sorry. I don't like anything about this man," said Sullivan, as if again reading his thoughts. "Let's leave him to the gods and see what's happening on Rae's Creek."

"Good idea, mate," said Morris, in his best Australian drawl, which brought the great absence of the Shark, Greg Norman, again to mind. His artillery shots would be missed across the back nine holes. And his gambles, which had turned so often to disaster. And his unsinkable spirit, in the best tradition of The Masters. How could one of the greatest players in the world not qualify for the tournament? A good question for the invitation committee. Morris remembered Doug Sanders once telling him, "If you aren't in Augusta on the first weekend in April, you might as well be off the face of the earth." And he remembered Sanders himself, long gone from the tournament he sadly never won, and the missed three-foot putt on the Old Course at St. Andrews that once cost him the British Open, which still lingered in the memory. Every fairway and green, even the openings in the trees, seemed to speak to Morris from out of the past, of tournaments played here and on other continents.

They caught Lanny Wadkins in his quick, quick steps down the steep 10th fairway into the dark shadows covering the first hole of the back nine. Wadkins hardly stopped, then flashed his lightning swing, sending the ball into the air like a "Message to Garcia." It found the green, and he holed the second putt in one quick stroke. All of his nervous energy carried him to the 11th tee in quick, quick steps, stopping only inside a flash of a swing and then another, and this time rapping home the first putt, and he repeated the Charlie Chaplin steps and the flashing action at the precarious, par-3, No. 12, and just one, sudden putt, and now he was quick-stepping around the bend of the land through the par-5, 13th hole, again home in one putt, and he had sounded his own birdie-birdie-birdie prayer through Amen Corner that had buried his chances so many tournaments before.

"My goodness," said Sullivan.

"I was thinking of the year Art Wall birdied six of the last holes coming in to win everything," said Morris. "But this is only Thursday, lassie. It's as far from Sunday as one man might live if he golfed his whole life."

"I won't have to buy the *Atlantic*. I'm getting a spoken draft of everything." She bumped against his vast chest with her shoulder.

"Ought to be a fee for that," said Morris. "I mean, you have to pay the lending library. The True Source ought to get something."

"The 'True Source' gets his share," said Sullivan with a laugh.

Morris borrowed their binoculars from around her neck, not missing the chance to nip an ear.

"Scandalous," said Sullivan.

Tom Watson came to the 12th tee, still in his Hogan cap, reminding Morris of the man himself, Hogan, and his last, legendary nine holes across The Masters landscape. The "Wee Ice Mon," they called him in Scotland when he won the only British Open he ever entered. But the year Morris was remembering, Hogan was fifty-five. His four U.S. Opens and all his honors were behind him. He'd not won The Masters in fourteen years. His knees were a ruin from the car wreck that nearly killed him. His icy nerves were shattered. He stood over every putt as if it might pass into time unstruck. And yet, that afternoon at Augusta, his swing, in all its lethal economy, was intact; every drive split the fairway and every approach found the pin. He turned the front nine even par. And then began the back. He played it in 30 strokes. And no man has ever played it in less. Under the familiar cap, which never swerved in his progression, Hogan limped toward each green. And rising to meet him were the thousands, in voluntary homage, and the currents of their applause filled the great pines as a wind sweeping through history, and Hogan's own lips, famous for their grim resolution, thinned, maybe into a smile, at this remarkable standing ovation, this consecutive salute to his greatness.

"What are you thinking?" Sullivan asked, of his silence.

"Oh. Of the Old Man, Hogan."

"And the day he played the back nine in thirty strokes."

"Yes."

"How old was he?"

"Fifty-five," said Morris.

"See how young we are," said Sullivan. "Our best game is in front of us."

Morris wrapped one big arm around her shoulders, as if to keep the moment timeless.

Lanny Wadkins got home with his 65, tying wee

Jeff Sluman for the first-day lead, three strokes clear of the field. But first days are for headlines, as perishable as Friday's newspapers. Ungallant Eddie Hayward, defending champion, hung surprisingly tough, with a two-under-par 70, to stay in the hunt.

CHAPTER FIVE

Drinks and an early dinner. They were Morris's only thoughts as he came out of the shower, shedding water like some beast in a rain forest.

"Was that you singing?" asked Sullivan, her nose in the bathroom door.

"Indeed."

"I thought it might have been a traffic accident."

Morris's wet towel smacked into the narrow opening of the door.

The first Scotch was like a miracle. Exceeded in its powers only by the second.

Morris was glad to prop his stiff leg under the long table. It had labored many a mile over the Augusta National. Thank God he had no deadline to meet. Others from Newton Cottage had arranged themselves at the long dinner table in the club, as if organized there by a tragedy out of the distant past. It seemed impossible that Melvin Newton had been dead only four days.

His widow, Phyllis, at the far end of the table, lifted her glass and sipped her wine, nodding with pleasure at its bouquet—or was it her new freedom that she was tasting? She'd put the funeral off until next week, so "Melvin's many friends from the Augusta National club might attend." They could go up on a two-man motorcycle, thought Morris. Edgar Benefield, erect and tanned and in his green blazer and rip-stripe tie, might have been back at his university for homecoming. His wife, Jerusha, was a painting by Da Vinci, her green eyes smiling at what? . . . Morris could not imagine. Sullivan stepped on his tender left foot until he looked at her and saw her laughing. "Oh, no," whispered Sullivan, measuring his admiration for Jerusha, making a tight fist with the hand not holding her glass. Jerusha caught the gesture and laughed, warning him with her own elegant finger.

The chairman, Michael Compton, found his way among the separate tables to join his wife, Aeriel, taking her hand, as fragile as a bird's. Compton's absolutely silver hair was mussed, even a bit ragged, as if the burden of responsibility for the tournament was driving his fingers through his scalp.

Louise Acton, just to the right of Morris, smiled under her own short, friendly haircut and asked Compton, "Where's Gerald? Are the players holding him prisoner for where the pins were placed?"

"I was about to ask you," said Compton. "I saw

his chair was empty. We have committee meetings right after dinner."

"Not some trouble out on the course with the machinery, I hope," Louise said with a laugh. "Gerald can't plug in an electric toothbrush."

"Not that I know of." Michael frowned his concern. "Perhaps we had better call your room. You don't know of any emergency?"

The fun went out of Louise's eyes. "No. I don't. He dressed early for dinner. Said he would join us here in the dining room." She began to rise from her chair, and Morris helped her to her feet.

"Anything I can do?" asked Morris.

"Thank you, but I'll just be a minute. I'll call the room. I can't imagine what's keeping him."

"I will check with the club staff and other members," said Compton, careful to keep the level of anxiety in his voice down.

Morris, not sure what he should do, sat awkwardly back down. He had finished dressing before Sullivan and had gone ahead to the clubhouse. He'd been standing on the terrace, watching the dusk gather, relishing a fresh Scotch, when he'd seen Gerald Acton, ungainly even in a fresh tie and coat, walking toward the big scoreboard near the 18th green. It must have been about 7 P.M.. Morris watched him meet up with a younger woman. Morris knew her face but not her name. She was a technician for CBS, with a variety of tools around her waist. But an attractive waist it was, the opposite of Acton's own billowing waist. Morris could not know what Acton and the woman were saying. It had struck him at the time that they were standing rather close in conversation. They might have been talking about anything, most likely some problem CBS was experiencing. Whatever they might have been saying, Morris could not imagine even Gerald Acton would have the gall to meet her for dinner, leaving his own chair empty next to his wife's. Morris bit his lip, considering what he should say to Louise, if anything.

Tom Spears, ever the athlete, and alert, even sitting down, read the concern on Morris's face.

"Maybe we should go help her," he said to Morris, who was relieved to be back on his feet.

When they were steps from the table, Spears said, "I saw them too. Just under the scoreboard."

"Do you know her?" asked Morris.

"I've met her. At a CBS party, a couple of years ago. I can't remember her name. I do remember she's an electrical engineer. From Auburn. Even has the hair to match the name of the school. I kidded her about it."

"Do you think . . ."

"Gerald? He would if he could. It always amazes me what attractive women see in some men."

"Money and power don't hurt," said Morris.

"Yeah. I've never been in a situation money would have made worse."

"I swear you stole that saying from Sullivan."

"Probably. What do we do, Morris, if he doesn't show?"

"We don't do a damn thing. We finish our dinner

and carry on. Louise will know how to handle it. She's had plenty of practice."

"But not here...at Augusta National," said Spears.

"No. And maybe the bastard is sick in his room. Or he had some emergency call."

"Without telling Louise?"

"Doesn't make sense," agreed Morris.

They found Louise talking with the club manager.

"No answer in the cottage," she said to Morris. "No message for me. And no one left a message for Gerald. It's strange, Morris."

"It is. Maybe I should check the pressroom. Some guys will be working late."

"Please," said Louise.

"I'll check the locker rooms," said Spears.

"I thank you both. And I'll meet you back at the table," said Louise.

Nothing. None of the handful of writers still working had seen Acton. Nor had he been seen in the locker room.

Morris knew Acton parked his rented Lincoln behind the cottage, and it was there, its doors locked. *What the hell?* thought Morris.

Louise was back sitting at their table. But neither she nor anyone else was eating.

Compton, his face even more strained than before, stood behind his own chair. He'd tracked down every committee chairman and a large number of members, and none of them had seen Acton since he was on the terrace early in the evening. Nor had any of the employees of the club seen him. The bartender said Acton got a phone call . . . maybe it was just after seven o'clock . . . but he didn't seem upset.

Morris didn't ask if the phone call had been from a man or a woman. He got no hint from Compton's expression that anyone had seen him with the woman from CBS.

"Morris, would we be foolish to call the police?" asked Louise.

"No," he said without hesitation. "Not to alarm you, but he might have fallen ill somewhere. Even if he was just called away to help one of the players and his car broke down, calling the police is the prudent thing to do. I'll call Detective Fannin, if you like, Louise."

"Please do. I'll wait in my room."

"And I'll go with you," said Sullivan.

"I'll see you both in a little while," said Morris, uncomfortable with his knowledge of Acton and the woman engineer and keen to talk with the bartender.

CHAPTER SIX

The unmarked police car slid to a stop and Detective Fannin stepped out in one motion, as if to confront bad news in the driveway.

"He hasn't turned up?" asked Fannin, holding on to the door, expecting the worst.

"No," said Morris.

"Shit!" The detective slammed the car door.

"That's about where we are," said Morris. "If Gerald Acton left the grounds, he left with somebody else. His own car is parked and locked behind Newton Cottage."

"Terrific," said Fannin.

"I think I may have been among the last to see him," said Morris. "Tom Spears and I both saw him talking with a winsome electrical engineer—a red-head—just below the big scoreboard at the 18th green."

"Did you know her?"

"Her face was familiar to me. Quite attractive, actually. She was wearing a ring of tools around her waist. The kind of waist that separates female engineers from male engineers."

"That kind," said the detective.

"I've seen her before at The Masters. But I don't know her. Spears said he met her a couple of years ago, at a party. He can't remember her name, but he's sure she's an engineer with CBS. And that she's an Auburn University woman. You Georgia boys know about them."

"Yeah," said Fannin, rolling his eyes. "What time did you see them together?"

"Must have been about seven P.M. Maybe a little before. He was supposed to have been headed to an early dinner and then a meeting of the Tees and Pin Placement Committee. But he never showed up for dinner."

"Could you hear anything Acton and the woman said?" asked Fannin.

"No. I was way over on the terrace, concentrating on my first Scotch of the day. But it struck me they were standing one beat closer together than two people talking about business."

"Nobody saw him after that?"

"Nobody we can find. Except Spears, who saw the two of them together at about the same time I did. Michael Compton ran down every tournament committee member, and a number of the other Augusta National members. Nobody has seen Acton.

Nobody left a message for him with the switch-board. He did get a phone call at the bar."

"From whom?" asked Fannin.

"I don't know. I haven't talked to the bartender. I was waiting for you. But Michael Compton spoke to him. The bartender said Acton was not upset by the call."

"Was it a man or a woman calling him?"

"I didn't ask. Didn't want to upset Louise. We can ask the bartender privately."

"Did the call come before or after you saw Acton with the young woman?"

"I'm thinking it must have been after I saw them. I left for the press tent to say hello to a couple of old friends. Acton must have gone to the bar. Then he just disappeared. Several of us were sitting at dinner, waiting to order . . . with Gerald's chair looming up empty next to Louise. It must have been seven-thirty before we began to look for him."

"When was the last time Louise saw him?"

"She said he left for the clubhouse while she was still dressing. Louise has gone back to her room. Sullivan is with her."

"I could never understand why a woman as attractive and as bright as Louise Acton would put up with Gerald," said the detective.

"And as rich as Louise," added Morris. "No. It's the mystery of the age: the large, ungainly, round-faced bastard and the beautiful, generous, fifth-richest woman in America. *He* uses *her* money to chase *his* women. A terrific fellow. Do you think he's the second Augusta National member to kill himself this week?"

"Oh, shit. Don't even think it," said the detective. "But the man may be lying out there in the night with a heart attack."

"Impossible," said Morris. "Acton has two spleens. He doesn't have a heart."

"Nevertheless, we'd better mount a search party."

"There are a number of Pinkerton men on the grounds, even at night," said Morris. "And I expect you can raise others on short notice."

"Compton's the club chairman. I'll ask him to round up some help. I expect he'd prefer to have his own people searching . . . rather than a van-load of deputies."

The detective was right. Compton sent for a dozen more Pinkerton men to report for overtime duty—and to do it quietly, reporting to no one but him.

Henry knew the golf course as well as Compton did. Together they split the Pinkertons into pairs to search the course and the grounds. Their huge, six-cell flashlights sent beams cutting through the trees like space weapons.

Detective Fannin nudged Morris. "Let's talk to the bartender."

They eased back into the clubhouse. The bartender was a large, friendly black man named Jack Walker, who had been with the club for twenty years. Morris could remember him as a young man. He introduced Jack to Henry. Jack remembered

Henry's face, even his name, and had once slipped him a beer before he was of drinking age.

"Man, I needed that beer," remembered Henry. "Cliff Roberts had been on my ass all afternoon."

"Mr. Cliff could do it," said Jack. "He was a hard man, but he was a fair one."

"Do you know that Gerald Acton is missing?" asked Henry, careful to keep his voice below the general hum of conversation in the bar. Members were not yet generally aware of the search of the grounds that was going on in the dark.

"Yessir. Mr. Compton spoke to me. Nothin' bad has happened to him, I hope?" Jack kept a carefully blank expression on his dark face, offering no hint of what he personally thought of Gerald Acton. Morris was sure he despised him, as did everybody who was around him enough to know him.

"We have no specific reason to think he's in trouble," said the detective. "But we're concerned. The phone call Acton took in the bar . . . What time was that?"

"Just after seven P.M., I believe. Maybe a few minutes after. My helper was just comin' on. And he was late, got here ten minutes after seven."

"Was it a man or a woman calling him?"

Jack rubbed down the bar with a damp rag. "I been thinkin' about that. I ain't sure. It was a *whispery* voice. Low in the throat, if you know what I mean. Just asked for 'Mr. Acton, please.' That's all she said."

"Why do you say *she*?" asked Morris.

"Well, I ain't sure," said Jack.

"Was Mr. Acton already in the bar when the call came through?" asked Fannin.

"He was just comin' in the door," said Jack. "I held the phone up so he could see it was for him."

"How long did they talk?" asked Morris.

"Not long. A couple of minutes."

"Could you hear anything he said?"

Jack shook his head. "No. I didn't listen. Mr. Acton turned his back. Just nodded his head up and down a couple of times. I couldn't hear what he said. Then he hung up. That was it."

"Did he leave immediately?" asked the detective.

"He said he didn't want a drink. He stood there a minute. And then he walked out toward the terrace. A whole bunch of members ordered drinks, and I didn't look up for a long time."

"Can an outside line ring this number?" asked Morris.

Jack nodded his head yes.

"And any phone on the grounds can ring this one?" asked the detective.

Jack nodded yes again.

"Was it an old voice or a young voice?" asked Morris.

Jack thought about that. "I didn't think it was a kid. But I really didn't think much about it. Wouldn't've thought anything about it if it hadn't been for that whispery kind of voice."

"Sexy voice?" asked Morris.

Jack made a face. "No. Just whispery."

"Thank you, Jack," said the detective. "If anything comes to mind, I'll be around."

"What do you think of that?" asked Morris, when they were alone in the front of the clubhouse.

"I don't like it," said Henry. "Why would someone disguise his or her voice?"

"She wouldn't . . . if she weren't afraid of being known."

"Why do you say *she*?" asked Henry.

"Because Jack inadvertently said *she*. Let's see if we can find a 'she' we know about."

Morris dialed a number for a private Augusta house that was rented every year by his old friend, CBS announcer James Carlton. The network rented several private houses for the tournament. Morris had partied in them all.

"Morris? Oh, no! I'm not partying with you guys! In fact, I'm already in bed. Unhappily, alone," said Carlton, working the phone with his famous voice.

"Your public would never believe it," said Morris. "Anyway, I'm not looking for you. I'm looking for one of your woman engineers."

"Shame on you."

"I just want to talk to her, Carlton. I know her red hair, but I don't know her name."

"What do you want to talk about?"

"I thought you were on the way to sleep," said Morris.

"I smell a story, old man."

"*Smell* is the right verb. Gerald Acton is missing."

"Who gives a damn?"

"Louise."

"Yeah, explain that one."

"Indeed."

"You don't think the bastard . . ." Now Carlton sounded entirely awake.

"All we know is he missed dinner and can't be found. No reason yet to get excited. Maybe I was the last person to see him. About seven o'clock. He was talking to your engineer."

"Angie Martin."

"Yes," said Morris.

"Bright young woman. Been with us five years. She's worked The Masters every year. Tough. Never panics. But she's recently divorced, still touchy about it, so go easy, Morris. She's staying in the house next door." Carlton gave him her number. "You'll call me if Acton's done a Melvin Newton?"

"I will."

"You swear?"

"I swear. Tell me, are Angie and Acton more than friends?"

"You'll have to ask her," said Carlton.

"Okay."

"Morris . . . should I come over to the club?" Carlton sounded more concerned than enthusiastic.

"No. I'll call you tonight, if it turns out to be . . . newsworthy." Morris settled on that word . . . in lieu of *murder* or *suicide*, either of which still seemed preposterous in the well-lit clubhouse. "Good night."

"I hope so," said Carlton.

Morris hung up and handed the receiver to Detective Fannin. "Her name is Angie Martin." Morris handed him her number. "It's a private house, one of several CBS rents. She and Acton may be more than friends. She's recently divorced. Carlton says she's still touchy about it."

Fannin nodded, and shook his head again. "The unlovely Gerald Acton, boy lover."

Morris said, "Look, there's no reason—at the moment—for her conversation with Acton to go any further than right here. It might have been as innocent as hell. Even if there's something going on between she and Acton, it's their business. Be sure she understands you're only trying to find out what happened to him."

"Agreed," said Fannin.

"Mind if I listen in?" asked Morris.

The detective shook his head while he dialed the number.

Fannin identified himself and described the curious absence of Gerald Acton. He told her straight on that she had been one of the last people seen talking to him. Did she have any idea where he might have disappeared to?

Angie Martin took refuge in silence. Finally she said, "No." Then, "Could I ask you who saw us?"

Morris nodded, yes.

"John Morris, the former AP writer—you know the old-timer . . ." Henry Fannin could not resist saying.

Morris shook his fist at him.

"Morris saw the two of you talking. Out by the scoreboard."

"I believe Morris is a friend of Jim Carlton's," said Martin. "Is that how he got my number?"

Morris shook his head.

"Morris has been around long enough to know everybody and their telephone numbers," said Fannin, shaking his own fist back at Morris.

"There's no mystery," said Angie. "Gerald told me he was going to an early dinner with his wife. After that, he had a committee meeting."

"He didn't give any hint of what other plans he might have?"

There was a distinct silence.

"No," she said.

"What else were the two of you talking about?"

"Listen"—there was a new directness in her voice—"does this conversation have to be made public?"

"Not unless something has happened to Mr. Acton, and your conversation can shed light on it," said Fannin. "He may be perfectly all right. We are more than a little jumpy after the death here of Melvin Newton. Acton, in fact, is staying in Newton Cottage."

"I know he is," said Angie. "To be blunt, Gerald was asking me to meet him tomorrow night. We've seen each other a few times in the past year . . . when I was on location here and other places." She added, quickly, as if about to be interrupted, "I know he's married. I was going through a divorce. It was pretty heady stuff, a man sending a private jet for you. But it's over."

"What did you tell him this evening?"

"That's what I told him, that it's over. I didn't intend to see him again. I've been through a patch of rough time. But I'm divorced now. And I have my life back together. And to be honest, I wouldn't want to upset his wife. I recently met her. I liked her very much. In fact, a lot more than I care for Gerald. He was a port in a storm, I guess. Good for my ego. Hard to explain it."

"I understand," said the detective, who was shaking his head at Morris that he did not understand. "But you have no idea where he might have gone tonight?"

"No," she said. "I have no idea at all. Please keep my name out of it, if you possibly can."

"I'll do my best," said the detective. "Tell me, what time were you talking with Acton?"

"Must have been about seven o'clock."

"Did you call him in the bar, just after that?"

"No," she said without hesitation. "I haven't spoken to him since we were talking at the 18th green."

"If he should call . . ."

"I'll tell him to go home. But you'll keep this off the record?" said Angie.

"I'll do my best." The detective hung up the receiver with a shake of his red head.

"Old-timer, am I?" said Morris.

"I meant it as a compliment," Fannin insisted with a large grin.

"Sure you did."

"I don't understand it, Morris. The slob is married to a rich, beautiful woman who puts up with him, and he catches the attention of this—apparently—attractive engineer."

"Shows what you can do if you send a private jet after a beautiful woman. Don't the beautiful women know they should keep their attention focused on the old-time writers and the young detectives? I don't think she's lying, Henry. She didn't have time to put together such a complete story."

"No," said the detective. "I believe her. So what the hell happened to the bastard? Maybe he ran off with Miss America."

"Somehow, I don't think so," Morris said, drawing imaginary circles on the floor with his walking stick.

"We'd better check on the bloody Pinkerton men. They may be stepping on holy ground," said Detective Fannin.

"Better there than on the golf greens," said Morris.

As they walked out of the clubhouse an older Pinkerton man came toward them out of the darkness, his six-cell flashlight cutting the night into long cylinders. He walked directly to the detective standing with Morris, under the terrace lights.

The Pinkerton man's face was white with concentration. He took a minute to get his breath, as if he had run the length of the course. Then he switched off his light as if it violated their confidence.

"We found him, Detective." The older man— Morris remembered him, Percy Malone was his name—caught his breath again. "He's dead. Stabbed to death, right in the heart. In a Port-o-let. By No. 10 green." Now Malone was breathless again, as if the memory of the corpse was after him.

"Shit!" said the detective.

"No accident this time," said Morris, whom the Pinkerton man also recognized from over the years.

"Not where it's stuck, it ain't an accident," said Malone. "Unless he was openin' his mail in a Port-o-let."

"Stabbed with a letter opener?" said Detective Fannin.

"Yeah. With the Augusta National name on the handle. I looked at it careful . . . but I didn't touch it."

"Shit!" said the detective again. "I'd better call my bloody crew. Then we'll go down there." He said to Morris, "We'd better tell Compton. He'll have to break the news to Louise. But not to the press. Not yet. We'll have reporters running in the dark like field mice."

Morris had to smile at the image of himself, a 230-pound field mouse, running on one good leg in the dark.

When Michael Compton joined them, Morris thought he might fall down with the news. In fact, he clutched Morris's thick arm.

"Oh, God. Not another one." He might have been speaking of the latest victim of a modern plague, *and maybe he was*, thought Morris.

"I'll have to tell Louise," said Compton.

"But only her . . . for now," said Fannin.

Compton nodded.

"Sullivan's with her. She'll be good support for Louise," said Morris.

"Do I tell Louise any of the awful details?"

Compton smoothed his silver hair, as if touching the source of his wealth.

"Better tell her everything we know . . . which is precious little," said Morris, aware the detective had not mentioned the CBS engineer to Michael. "Louise will want it straight." Morris realized neither he nor Compton had felt any need to say Gerald Acton's name aloud.

They started down the steep fairway to the No. 10 green, following the detective's own modest flashlight. The silence and the dark rose up around them, the great trees moving shadows in the night wind.

The Pinkerton men had jerry-rigged a floodlight from the TV power lines. A clutch of Port-o-lets was lit up in the trees like a small camp for displaced persons. The door to one of them was open. Morris could see a man's shoe and then a leg, twisted against itself in the doorway.

Detective Fannin shined his light directly into the tortured face of a very dead Gerald Acton, his eyes fixed open at the horror of his exit. He sat, crushed by his own weight into the floor of the Port-o-let, his left arm trapped behind him, his right arm folded over his chest, his hand fixed open in a gesture of rigor mortis, just under a gold letter opener sunk into his chest.

"Oh, my," said Morris.

The detective waved the Pinkerton men back from the door, then looked at the body for a long time. "I believe death came as more than a small surprise to Mr. Acton."

"Odd," said Morris.

"What?"

"Couple of things. If he was trying to pull the blade out, why is his hand under it, his thumb facing out, as if he were driving it in himself? And what the hell is he doing in a woman's Port-o-let?"

"I hadn't noticed." The detective stepped back and looked at the sign outside the door. "Meeting some lucky lady inside, do you think?"

"Now, there's a spot for romance," said Morris. "In the trees, in the near dark, in a Port-o-let."

Detective Fannin felt the dead man's rigid hand. "He's been dead a few hours, all right. You think he came straight down here after the phone call?"

"He had to. Somebody will turn up who saw him walking this way. Question is, who was he walking to meet?"

"How about Angie Martin for starters?"

"Not the worst guess you could make. Although her voice doesn't strike me as 'whispery,'" said Morris.

"Then maybe she hasn't whispered to you," said the detective.

"She's used to working with tools," said Morris. "But why wouldn't she use a screwdriver? Why risk lifting a letter opener from the club?"

Morris could read the crisp logo, AUGUSTA NATIONAL, on the gold handle of the letter opener.

"A screwdriver? Jesus," said the detective.

"Do you prefer the more delicate-type woman?" asked Morris. "And who says it was a woman anyhow? Wrestling his fat ass into a Port-o-let was no easy feat."

"You don't think he was killed inside there?" asked Fannin, looking again at the corpse crowded onto the floor.

"Oh, hell, no. There's hardly room in there for him. Where the hell would you put the other guy?"

"His pants are buckled and his zipper is zipped," said the detective. "He wasn't doing his business."

"Maybe . . . his monkey business," said Morris. "He didn't come down here representing the Tees and Pin Placement Committee."

"What did he come down here to do?"

"He was following his dick. It was his profession," said Morris.

"Then you do think he was meeting the engineer?"

"I don't know. He gets a phone call. Either it's a woman or a 'whispery voice' that sounds like a woman," said Morris. "Then again . . . only the bartender, we are sure, heard a 'whispery voice.' The same caller might have used her, or his, real voice with Acton."

"Why do you say that?" The detective's red hair took on a fiery, unholy reflection in the blast of the spotlight.

"The voice would have to speak with some authority to haul Acton, big, horny man that he was, off into the trees. You can bet one thing, it wasn't duty calling."

"If he wasn't killed in there, where was he killed?" The detective shook his head at the crushed grass, pounded into the ground by the heels of hundreds of anxious women waiting their turns in the Port-o-let.

"That's a first-string question," said Morris. "I absolutely believe he came down here expecting to meet a woman. Maybe just for a conversation leading to later. Maybe the dumb bastard was going to take her in the trees, with security men and ground crew and maybe even a few lingering golfers wandering over the course. But I doubt it. Acton was dressed for dinner with his wife, for God's sake. And maybe he came down to meet with the woman from hell. And she killed him and sat his big ass in that Port-o-let. Some woman," said Morris.

"Thank God I'm safely married," said Fannin.

"And maybe it was a man who was waiting for him. . . . " Morris leaned over with his hands on his knees and looked at the corpse as if it could express its regret. "Some man whose woman he had violated."

"That narrows it down to the country's living population," said the detective.

"But how would the man get near enough to do the job, without Acton's seeing him, if Acton was expecting to see a woman . . . ?" Morris let the thought roll around in his head. "Well, *maybe the man was waiting in the Port-o-let*. And sprang out and drove the letter opener *down* into Acton, and spun him around and shoved him inside where he sits." Morris was absolutely sure that was what had happened, as sure as if he had been there to see it and hear the shocked grunt of the dying man. "Get your crew to check his clothes and the back of his head and the walls and floor of the Port-o-let . . . for the possibility of that having happened," said Morris.

"Hell, you're sure it did happen that way," said Detective Fannin.

Morris did not deny it.

"How did the man beat Acton down here? If he called him on the phone?"

"Easy. He called from a cellular phone."

"Then there'll be a record of it at the telephone company," said the detective.

"Oh, yes. If you can find the number of the phone."

"How the hell can we do that?"

"The club has several cellular phones. My guess, ten-to-five, he used one of those. Just as he used a club letter opener. You have to say our man is true to the club colors."

"You're so sure, you're ruling out a woman killer."

"No," said Morris. "There might have been a woman waiting in that Port-o-let. But if so, it wasn't the woman he came down here to meet. Or there was a side to her he never met before."

"What about Louise?"

"She said she was still dressing when Acton left the cottage. It would have been easy to slip from the cottage through the trees to the No. 10 green, without being seen."

"What happened to the cellular phone? A man, or a woman, wouldn't call him to his death and then come walking up through the trees carrying the phone they called on?"

"Maybe the call was made from up the hill. . . ." Morris thought about that. "No. It was made from here. I'd bet on it. Had to be, if Acton hurried straight here. And he *had to hurry*, because he was expected for an early dinner. If I were you, I'd tell my crew to search the trees . . . and the green trash bags that haven't been picked up today . . . even those that have been picked up, if they haven't been dumped. . . . You're right, Henry. That phone was left down here with the body."

"And the killer just emerged from the trees by the 18th green, strolling under the scoreboard as if nothing had happened."

"Maybe," said Morris. "Or, if it was a member, he caught a ride on one of the security carts, or one of the CBS carts, or one of the carts used by the ground crew, or maybe he caught a ride on a CBS truck. A well-known face wouldn't be suspicious."

"But it would be remembered," said the detective.

"Ah, you have your work cut out for you, Henry. Lucky man."

"My ass," said the detective. "Tell me this, Morris. Did the same person kill Melvin Newton?"

"Oh, yes. Unless we are supposed to believe that in one week, one club member shoots himself and another club member stabs himself to death."

"Couldn't we have had one of each? Someone with a perfect alibi when Newton kills himself . . .

then that same someone kills Acton ... makes it seem like the work of a double murderer?"

"It's possible," admitted Morris. "We'll have to see how many people can account for where they were between seven P.M. and eight P.M. Almost nobody can prove where he was when Gerald Acton was killed. Including myself and Sullivan. It's not going to be easy. Some of us were dressing. Some were on the way to the club. Some were in the bar. I was on the terrace and then in the press tent. And I didn't even see Tom Spears, who saw Acton and the engineer about the same time I did. Or he says he did. The clubhouse and the grounds were a frenzy of people coming and going."

"And dying," said the detective.

"Yeah. There's that," said Morris.

A crisscross of flashlight beams moved down the hill toward them, as if by some mad code.

The angelic face of Karen Moseley shined in the hot spotlight, her fine blond hair standing out from her high forehead.

"Hello, Morris," she said.

It pleased him that she omitted his first name as naturally as had the past generation of golfers.

"Hello, Doctor. You're going to have to open an office here in the trees."

"Where is he?" She might have been asking after a deceased specimen of butterfly.

"In the Port-o-let," said Morris.

Dr. Moseley stood back while the scene-of-the-crime photographer, seemingly taller and thinner and more morose, aimed his video camera and his hooked nose into the Port-o-let. He switched to his 35-mm still camera and started all over again. He was careful where he stepped and where he put his hand in opening the door to the Port-o-let. Finally, he was satisfied with the harsh images he had caught in the cruel spotlight.

Dr. Moseley examined the beaten-down grass in front of the Port-o-let. Then she leaned inside to push and poke at the corpse in the same way she had probed the body of Melvin Newton. Finally, she stepped away.

"What do you think?" asked Detective Fannin.

"Only been dead a few hours. I'd guess three to four. What time is it now?" She looked at her watch. It was 10 P.M., exactly.

"Morris saw him alive about seven P.M." said Fannin.

"That ought to be about right," said Dr. Moseley. "We should get a pretty precise understanding of when he died. . . . His body is well protected in there. We don't have the problem of his head and one arm under water."

Now the same two middle-aged policemen who had scoured the earth around Melvin Newton's body were going over the ground outside the Port-o-let, with their plastic bags in their hands, as if they were engaged in some nighttime scavenger hunt.

"Morris has a theory," said the detective. He explained Morris's idea that the killer had waited inside the Port-o-let, and Dr. Moseley listened without speaking.

"If the killer was waiting inside," asked Morris,

"would his clothes have picked up identifiable dust or lint?"

"Not likely. These things are entirely plastic. And you must realize, they've been used by hundreds of people. Possibly we can tell if the body was thrust into that position after he was stabbed. It will be tricky, proving it—if he was pushed in there immediately after he was stabbed. We'll have to see what we can find out. But it sounds like a reasonable theory to me."

"If the killer was friends with Acton, why would he have to hide?" asked Fannin. "Why not just walk up and stab him?"

"Maybe that's what happened," said Morris. And maybe the killer was a young engineer, who had not dropped Acton but had been dropped by him. She would know Acton well enough to understand all his weaknesses. Morris considered it, but he didn't say it.

"Who would want both Melvin Newton *and* Gerald Acton dead?" asked Dr. Moseley.

"Remember, we are calling Newton's death 'accidental,'" said Detective Fannin.

Dr. Moseley nodded but did not withdraw her question.

"Plenty of people hated them . . . separately," said Morris. "Maybe we can narrow down who hated them both. But maybe the list doesn't narrow that much."

"You're dead sure it's a double murder," Fannin said quietly, so only the three of them could hear it.

"*Dead sure* is the correct expression," said Morris.

"And every writer and sportscaster in Augusta will come to the same conclusion. Acton's death ought to get just slightly less publicity than the assassination of a president."

"Oh, God," said the detective.

"I wouldn't count on divine intervention," said Morris.

Detective Fannin could only shake his head.

When Morris arrived, Julia Sullivan was sitting within easy reach of Louise Acton. Neither of them had been crying.

"Louise . . ." he began.

"Fix yourself a drink, old man. I could use another one myself." She held out her empty glass with a firm hand. She was wearing her familiar jeans and her short, dark hair shone healthily. . . . She sat on her couch, an impossible distance from the dead man in the Port-o-let.

Morris gave her a hug as he took her glass. Then Sullivan hugged him as if with a double squeeze against mortality.

Louise took the full glass to her lips. "Was he murdered, Morris?" Her voice was thick but not with grief.

"I don't think there is any doubt about it."

"Stabbed?"

He nodded. "Directly in the heart. He died quickly."

"Gerald had much to answer for, but nobody deserves a messy death," said Louise.

Morris nodded again.

Louise reached over and touched Morris's shoulder. "Morris, I hate that he was killed. But I'm not practicing a fake grief. And I don't intend to."

"Gerald was not famous for his generosity," said Morris.

"Except with my money," said Louise, with a sharp laugh uncharacteristic of her friendly style. "That's a nasty thing to say . . . since I have little interest in my money."

"Louise, throw me out if you don't want to answer this . . ." began Morris.

"Why did I bother staying married to Gerald Acton?" Louise anticipated his question, running her fingers throught her short hair.

Morris nodded.

"We have a son who is retarded. He's twenty-five. And profoundly retarded. Can't speak or sit. I don't know if he recognizes anybody. Not even me. Gerald Acton was a bastard, Morris. You know that as well as I do; he taught himself to be one. But he visited our son every week of his life, and he cried every time he saw him. Gerald hated the world for what he accused it of doing to his son, who has his name. Gerald was not the same man I married, Morris. You didn't know him then. He married me for my money. No doubt about that. But he was a free spirit. He was fun. I know that is impossible to believe, knowing what he became. We haven't lived together in years. But I couldn't bring myself to throw my son's father off the payroll. And I had no reason to. I have more money than a small civilization could spend. And the man I see doesn't ever want to remarry. And neither do I." And now the tears were flowing from her dark, friendly eyes. Sullivan held her like a small child.

"I'm sorry" was all that Morris could say.

She didn't cry long. "There's just the one question," said Louise. "Who hated him enough to kill him?" She blew her nose and went on to offer an answer: "The husbands of many wives might be angry enough. And he was a rude man to almost everybody."

"Were he and Melvin ever close?" asked Morris.

"No. They resented each other. And they deserved each other," said Louise, her old, unsinkable self.

"Did they share any business deals?" asked Morris.

"No. I didn't keep up with Gerald's business life"—she actually smiled—"but I don't think he saw Melvin Newton anywhere but in Augusta. I think this club was the only thing they had in common."

"Did you know about the CBS engineer, Angie Martin?"

"Of course. I knew about many of his women. I had no interest in them."

"The police promised they wouldn't make her name public, unless they had to," said Morris. "I saw her talking with Gerald about seven P.M. They were standing under the big scoreboard near the 18th green."

"I'm not surprised. Gerald and I had an agreement. He would be reasonably discreet. And so

would I. I imagine he and Ms. Martin were practicing their discretion."

"She says she's now divorced. That she was
breaking it off with Gerald."

"I do not doubt it," said Louise. "Sooner or later
they all tire of his money and power when they find
out those don't come with him."

"Louise, how did Melvin's death affect Gerald?"
It was the first time Sullivan had spoken since Morris entered the room, and it was a damn good question he hadn't thought to ask.

"Odd thing," said Louise. "He was frightened.
That was unusual for Gerald. He could be a bore
and a bastard, but he was not a timid man. He dug
his own handgun out of his suitcase. But he wasn't
carrying it when he was killed. It's in his room, on
his bed."

"Be damned," said Morris. "I wonder what he
suspected about Melvin's death?"

"We didn't talk much, Morris. Here at Augusta
National is the only place in the world we kept up
appearances. Gerald liked the glory of the tournament. And I liked the golf. And seeing old friends
like you and Julia. Gerald said one strange thing
about Melvin's death. He said, 'I guess it proves we
were right.'"

Morris spilled a bit of Scotch on his chin.

"Right about what, for God's sake?"

"I wonder," said Louise. "That's all he said. It
didn't make any sense to me."

"In what context did he say it?" asked Sullivan.

"We'd just heard of Melvin's death. We were

walking up the steps in the cottage to our separate rooms. I asked him, 'Do you think Melvin killed himself?'

"Gerald said, 'Don't be ridiculous.' And then he said, 'I guess it proves we were right all along.' And finally he said, 'By God, I've got my own gun, and I know how to use it.' "

"Those were his exact words?" asked Morris.

"As near as I can remember them. I didn't understand what he meant. I asked him. But he went on to his room without answering. I asked him again later what he meant, but he just shook his head and wouldn't answer."

"And maybe his suspicion cost him his life," said Morris. "Or maybe he was going to lose it anyhow. Odd, he didn't have his gun with him when he was killed. But I suppose he didn't expect to be killed at the dinner table."

"It had to be a woman that drew him into the woods," said Louise. "Gerald had all the money he could want. It was women he couldn't get enough of."

"I think we need to talk with Ms. Angie Martin," said Morris. "First, we'd better intercept Detective Fannin and Dr. Moseley. Fannin will want to talk with you, Louise. Probably tonight."

She nodded that she would expect him.

The detective trudged out of the night toward his automobile. Dr. Karen Moseley walked beside him, her hands in her pockets. Morris realized she was whistling, for God's sake. He introduced Dr. Moseley to Sullivan, who took her slim, fragile hand in her own.

"Did you learn anything?" asked Morris.

"A bit," said Dr. Moseley, her fine hair floating in the reflection of the detective's flashlight.

Morris waited.

"You were right. He was stuffed into the Port-o-let . . . almost immediately after he was stabbed."

"How could you tell?"

"The back of one trouser leg caught in the door hinge, just above the calf. It was torn. And there were threads caught in the hinge."

Detective Fannin said, "He couldn't have caught *the back* of his own pants leg stepping in the Port-o-let. Unless he lifted himself in with his hands, with his butt on the floor. Doesn't seem likely."

"No chance the killer could have left anything of himself in or around the Port-o-let?"

"There are enough fingerprints in there to populate Richmond County. We've packaged all the dust and hair and fiber we could find, but it will belong to hundreds of people."

"The Pinkerton men did find *this*," said Fannin, holding up a clumsy package of green plastic.

"What is it?" asked Morris.

"A trash bag, with a cellular telephone at the bottom. I have it all wrapped inside a second bag."

"Son of a bitch," said Morris.

"It belongs to the club, all right," said the detective. "It's got the Augusta National logo on the bottom. I'm not holding my breath expecting to find any prints. We would never have found the phone, Morris, if you hadn't imagined the whole scheme."

"Not the whole scheme," said Morris. "There's the small matter of who the killer might have been."

"There's that," said Fannin. "We won't tell the press we found the phone. The killer will think it was picked up with the hundreds of other trash bags. It almost was. Another fifteen minutes, and it would have been gone."

"You can find out if a call was made just after seven P.M. to the club bar . . . from this cellular number?" asked Morris.

"Oh, yes. And I'm giving odds of one thousand to one that the call was made. Now, who made it is another matter. It would have to be someone with access to the clubhouse."

"So now we need to find one 'whispery voice,' " said Morris, "and you can strap this voice in the electric chair. Are you going to change the official speculation about what happened to Melvin Newton?"

"That's up to the chief of police. But I think we have to say we believe Acton was murdered. And we are looking into any connection between his death and Melvin Newton's."

"Oh, hell. I've got to call James Carlton of CBS. I promised him I'd call when we learned what happened to Acton." Morris then told the detective what he and Sullivan had learned from Louise Acton.

"So that's why she stayed with him," said Fannin. "You never know another person."

"Hard enough to know yourself," said Morris. "Louise is waiting, if you want to speak to her."

"I'll do it now," said the detective. "I won't be able to go to sleep anyhow. What the hell do you think Acton meant . . . *'it proves we were right all along'*?"

Morris said, "You have to think the *it* means the death of Newton. And the *we* means he and Newton. That they were *right* about something *all along* that caused the death . . . the *murder* of Melvin Newton. And so Acton got his own handgun out of his suit-case to protect himself."

"Too bad he left it in his room," said Sullivan. "Maybe we could have had *A Shoot-out at the O.K. Port-o-let* that settled the whole matter."

Morris listened while the ringing telephone woke James Carlton.

"John Morris here. You're awake?"

"No. I always sleep with the phone in my hand. What the hell's up?" He was more awake with every word.

"We found Gerald Acton. Dead. Stabbed in the heart. In a Port-o-let by the No. 10 green."

"Jesus!" Now Carlton was totally awake. "What do the police say?"

"They say he was killed. They say they are look-ing into all possibile connections between his death and Melvin Newton's."

"I thought they were calling Newton's death ac-cidental."

"They *were*," said Morris. "But this is now."

"Who's on the case?"

"Detective Henry Fannin. But he's about to leave here. You'd better catch him at police headquarters downtown."

"Thanks, Morris."

"Yeah, for ruining your night's sleep."

"And for putting my ugly face on the morning show. How is Louise taking it?"

"Okay. But that's another story. See you on TV."

"Morris—"

But Morris hung up the receiver.

"Are you awake?" Sullivan was curled into a tight ball, but sleep wouldn't come.

"Somebody woke me up, snoring."

"I wasn't snoring. I wasn't even sleeping." She punched his thick shoulder.

"You would've been if you had'a been."

"What kind of English is that? The *Atlantic* will have a heart attack."

"Oh, no, they won't. They can't afford a heart attack."

"Morris, do you think Gerald's death is the end of it?"

"No."

Sullivan fitted the length of herself into his wide frame, as if to escape the thought of another death.

"Who will be next?" she asked, shivering.

"I don't know," said Morris, caught somewhere between asleep and awake. "But I'm betting he will be an asshole."

"Because . . ."

"Nobody's crying for the two he's killed already."

"Don't be so sure it's a he. Any thinking woman would have killed the two of them a long time ago. I know—" Sullivan said, as if interrupting herself . . . "you can't believe I said that."

"The hell I can't." He was almost awake. Then he was drifting back toward sleep.

"Nobody will kill you, Morris." She kissed his ear. "You are the sweetest man in my bed."

Morris was already snoring.

CHAPTER SEVEN

There was James Carlton's ugly face up on the screen on CBS's morning show. He was giving a report on the "stabbing death" of an Augusta National member. Carlton did not offer any new facts. He did not mention the CBS engineer or her role in Gerald Acton's life. But he closed with a flourish: "An unimpeachable source tells CBS that the recent deaths of two Augusta National members are closely linked. . . . "

"I think I may be the new, unpaid, unimpeachable CBS source," said Morris, propped up in bed.

"I told you, you need an agent," Sullivan said with a yawn.

"Well said. You're hired. You will now get ten percent of everything I have." Morris trapped her wrist under the cover.

"That's no bargain," said Sullivan, putting a pillow over his head with her free hand.

The large Augusta National pressroom was packed by 7 A.M. The mood had nothing to do with early starters getting ready for the second round of play. Nervous golf writers were talking on telephones, but not to their old cronies on the sports desk. Morris drifted among the writers, listening shamelessly to one end of their conversations and imagining the other end.

They were fielding unfamiliar questions from news editors they'd never had a drink with: "*Who the hell was Gerald Acton?* . . . Nobody. But his wife, Louise, is the fifth-richest woman in America. . . . *The hell you say? What did this Acton have to do with the dead publisher Melvin Newton?* . . . He was staying in his bloody cottage. . . . *Why?* . . . He needed a room, asshole. They won't let you sleep on the grass at Augusta National. . . . *What the hell is going on down there?* . . . *A bloody golf tournament.* Whadda you think this is, the Persian Gulf? . . . *No. Nobody gives a shit about the Persian Gulf.* . . ."

Morris stopped by the desk of Walter Edwards.

"I'm having breakfast with Louise Acton in her room in thirty minutes. She's a dear woman. I'll talk with her, but I don't promise what I'll file. . . . Listen, her husband is dead. But Louise is *not charged* with killing him. ("Of course, she should have killed him years ago," whispered Edwards to Morris.) . . . "No, I'm not writing that Louise is a suspect. *You* write it. Just remember, she spends weekends at the Long Island estate of the publisher of this newspaper. . . . I know you don't give a damn about that. . . . I predict a great future for you in journalism. . . . ("Bastard," whispered Edwards to Morris, stretching his long, lean legs under his desk and closing his eyes, not listening to whoever was instructing him on the telephone.) Finally, Walter put the receiver down without so much as a good-bye.

"Aren't you lucky?" said Morris. "Nothing like a little human compassion from the news desk to get the heart started in the morning."

" 'All the news that's fit to print.' " Walter quoted the slogan of the good, gray *New York Times*. "Where's my crime writer when I need him? He's sick in bed, that's where. The Georgia grits got him. Things have changed, Morris. We'll print any rumor that titillates the Upper East Side. I don't dare write he was stabbed to death by an alien creature in a Port-o-let. They'd print it with an illustration of an alien outhouse. Tell me, what happened?"

"Somebody called Acton in the clubhouse bar just after seven P.M.. Acton must have agreed to meet him, or her, or a third party in the woods by the No. 10 green."

"The bartender doesn't know if a man or a woman called?"

"A 'whispery voice' called," said Morris. "The 'Unisex Murderer.' They'll love it in the *Times*."

"Oh, God, will they. What can I write without fouling you up? You are helping the police?"

"Yes, but don't write that. I just happen to know Newton and Acton and the detective."

"Henry Fannin is still on the case?"

"Yes."

"You don't doubt somebody killed them both."

"No."

"Of course somebody did," said Edwards, his long hands and arms folded behind his gray, aristocratic head. "We never thought Melvin killed himself. Somebody must have it in for bastards."

"I said the same thing to Sullivan. Surely there's a better reason than that."

"Wives and husbands have long considered being married to a bastard reason enough to commit murder."

"Gerald was a bastard, all right. And who doesn't love Louise?" said Morris. "But I might be able to tell you something about Gerald Acton you didn't know. Then again, I doubt it."

"Try me."

"They had a profoundly retarded son. He's twenty-five. Can't walk or talk and maybe isn't even aware of who his mother is. Louise said Gerald went to see him every week. And wept every time he went."

"Be damned," said Walter. "I didn't know it. So our boy was a bastard, but he wasn't altogether a bastard. I'm glad to know it."

"It's why Louise never dumped him," said Morris, "though they haven't lived together in years."

"I'm having breakfast with Louise. I'll let you know what she tells me."

"Good. Ask her if Gerald and Melvin were involved in anything together. Anything that somebody else could resent. Maybe she'll be more forthcoming with you than she was with me."

"I'll do it," said Edwards.

Walter was a master at getting people to tell him about themselves. And he never wrote an ungraceful sentence in his life, always reason enough to assassinate a fellow sportswriter.

"What are you smiling at?" asked Walter.

"Fate," said Morris.

"Now, there's a villain. What else can you tell me?"

"Nothing . . . at the moment. I'll be in touch," said Morris.

Detective Fannin, looking smaller and younger than ever, his freckles standing out on his face like teenage embarrassment, addressed the writers and broadcasters in the pressroom. He gave them the straight facts, leaving out the cellular telephone, the "whispery voice," the torn trousers and threads in the hinges of the Port-o-let, the suspected sequence of events at the death scene, the Augusta National letter opener as murder weapon, and the CBS engineer.

Well, thought Morris, *the 'whispery' voice will be on page one of the* New York Times *soon enough*. He'd been careful to clear it first with Henry before telling Walter Edwards. The killer, however confident, would be sweating a bit about the sound of his voice on the telephone to the bartender. Or maybe it was "her" voice. *Let our killer sweat*, thought Morris. *Nervous murderers don't live extensive lives.* Then again, he or she would be rocking in a certain false comfort, not knowing they had found the cellular phone the call was surely made from. The phone only helped them understand the sequence of events, but every understanding was a step closer to the killer.

Detective Fannin read to the reporters a written statement from Louise Acton, who declined to be interviewed.

But she was having breakfast in her room with Walter Edwards, thought Morris. *If she gave him a memorable quote, the other reporters would be cussed out by their editors. But who said life was fair? Nobody who ever played golf. And whatever happened to the bloody tournament?*

Morris found Club Chairman Michael Compton drinking a cup of coffee standing up, as if to sit down would somehow violate the massive responsibility he carried for the tournament.

"Of course we are going to play," said Compton. "The golfers and the public aren't in danger."

"How do you know that?" asked Morris.

"None of them have been killed," said Compton, the *killed* all but sticking in his throat. "What do you know, Morris, that I don't know?" Compton's hand was smoothing his silver hair.

"Not much. Nothing that ought to influence your decision to keep playing. I don't think one person now believes that Melvin Newton killed himself. I never did. But I was hoping the police would let it go as suicide. And maybe they would've."

"You're sure it's somebody we know who killed them both?" Compton set his coffee cup on the table under him, resignedly.

"I can promise you neither man was killed by a stranger."

"No." Compton had to agree. "Just for the record, Morris, I was in my room at seven P.M., going over my notes for the committee meetings. I know it's an easy hike through the trees down to the 10th green. But I walked across to the bar about seven forty-five, just before I joined you for dinner. I can't remember seeing anybody until I got into the clubhouse."

"It's the detective who will want to hear all that," said Morris.

"I already told him. He didn't seem impressed."

"Michael, can you think of any circumstances linking Acton and Newton that might have ended in bitter feelings?" asked Morris.

Compton again ran his hand over his silver hair as if it were a precious metal. He shook his head.

"No. They might have resented one another from time to time. That's not unknown among powerful men. You wouldn't put them on the same committee. There are many members of this Club who would not sit well on the same committee. But no one is murdering them."

"No," said Morris. Then he thought, *Tournament week is not over.*

* * *

Morris eased off the terrace toward the 18th green, surrounded this early by empty bleachers, ghostly in the morning light, hours away from the first-finishing twosome. Still, a lively crowd milled under the huge scoreboard, with Lanny Wadkins's name leading all the rest, at least until the first shot of the second day was struck in anger. Morris balanced his great bulk with his cane and let the fans flow around him in their bright skirts and plaid trousers, many of them wearing their own golf shoes. He held a fresh Coke in his hand without tasting it. And kept his eye on the main CBS tower, until the red-haired engineer, Angie Martin, appeared with the circle of tools around her slim waist. Morris eased over to her.

"I'm John Morris. A writer. Used to be with the Associated Press. Can we talk for one minute?" Morris offered her the Coke in its paper cup.

Angie Martin looked at her watch, then looked at him and took the Coke. She couldn't drink for biting her lip.

"Of course, you've heard what happened to Acton," said Morris.

She nodded. Her eyes were more fearful than regretful.

"Detective Fannin wants to talk with you again. He doesn't want to embarrass you. And he doesn't want to stir things up in the media."

"I told him, I don't know anything. I have no idea. . . . I didn't. . . ." She took a sip of Coke and choked on it.

"Nobody's accusing you," said Morris. "The detective just wants your help."

"What can I tell him?"

"How did you know to meet Acton right here yesterday"—Morris pointed at the ground they stood on—"just at seven P.M.?"

"I didn't. I was working. We had a problem on this tower. Gerald just showed up. I'd been avoiding him. He left a message at my house earlier. I didn't return his call."

"Did he leave the message in his own name?" asked Morris.

"Just, 'Gerald, call me.' I didn't. I told you. I was breaking it off."

"You didn't call him just after seven P.M. yesterday, in the bar?" asked Morris.

"No." Now she could swallow the Coke.

"That's a very huge question," said Morris. "Be sure you answer it with all the candor you have."

Now she was frightened.

"You don't believe me. This Detective . . . Fannin . . . won't believe me either. You'll both cost me my job. . . ." She was panicking.

Morris touched her hand. "Easy. None of those things is going to happen . . . if you tell the detective the truth. If you called the man, say you did. It doesn't mean you killed him."

The word *killed* caused her to step backward onto the foot of an elderly fan. "Sorry," she begged, as if she had committed a felony.

"Let me ask one more time: you're sure you didn't call Gerald in the bar," said Morris.

Now she was angry.

"Yes, goddammit, I'm sure."

"That's better," Morris said, for the first time believing her.

Her curiosity overtook her fear.

"Is it true? He was stabbed?"

"Yes. And left in a Port-o-let by the No. 10 green."

"Oh, God."

"Just after he was talking with you."

"Please, God." She was begging Morris, and not God, as if he could undo everything.

"Does it really shock you?" Morris asked, touching her hand again for support.

She considered it, leaning first on one foot and then the other.

"Yes. You don't expect anybody you know to be killed." Then she said, "He was a powerful man. He . . . could be a son of a bitch. He didn't ask. He demanded. I really didn't like him very much. I just got caught up in my own troubles . . . and he made it so easy . . . with his plane and his money . . . and— to be truthful—when he was alone in some city away from New York . . . he could be funny. You might not believe that, if you've known him a long time. But it's true. But those moods never lasted. He'd soon be his same nasty self. I wish I'd never gotten involved with him, but . . ." She left the wish unfinished.

"Did you ever overhear him on the telephone?"

"Oh, yes. He could be a bastard." She touched her red hair as if it were burning with the memory.

"Did you hear him speak to anybody in particular?" Morris kept his voice level.

"No. He just dialed numbers and would start in chewing somebody out. I never knew who he was talking to."

"New York numbers?"

"If we were in New York. When we were in other cities, the calls were long-distance numbers. I assumed he was calling New York. He would dial more than seven digits. He used a credit card."

Morris made a mental note to tell Detective Fannin to check Acton's credit card calls, but it was something he would do routinely.

"What kind of things would he say?" asked Morris.

She thought. "I can't remember any specific thing. Sometimes he might have been talking to his broker. About something he was buying or selling. He could get awfully angry. He often called about his plane. It was always needing repairs. He got furious about that. People left messages for him at hotels. But he rarely answered them. He usually threw them away. I never saw who they were from. I don't think I'm being much help."

"More help than you realize," said Morris. "Tell Detective Fannin everything you've told me. He's waiting in the living room at Newton Cottage." Morris pointed past the 10th tee.

"I can't stay long," she said. "I've got work to do."

"It won't take long," said Morris. "Tell me this, first: How well did you know Melvin Newton?"

She looked at him with gathering suspicion. "I'd barely met him. Here at the club. He wasn't a very friendly man—I don't mean that I ever tried . . ."

"I understand," said Morris. "You never heard Acton call Melvin Newton on the phone?"

Angie thought, pulling on a small wrench around her waist with her left hand. "I did . . . at least once. . . . We were at an NFL game in Chicago. Soldier Field is a bitch to work. I know it was Newton because after they fussed on the phone, Gerald slammed the receiver down and said, 'How can you expect a goddamned romance publisher like Melvin Newton to understand business?' I had met the man, but I didn't even realize he was a book publisher."

"What business?" asked Morris.

"I have no idea." She shook her head.

"What were they fussing about?"

"I don't know. . . ." She thought. "License. Something about a license. I don't know for what. It was nearly a year ago."

"Keep thinking," said Morris. "Let your mind drift back. Don't force it. Let your subconscious work. It might surprise you what you remember—when you least expect it. Let me know if you remember something else."

Morris touched her hand again and took back the empty cup. "Tell me, where were you between seven and eight P.M.?"

Martin looked down at her strong, surprisingly beautiful hands. "I was right here. I never left this area. I was working on the tower." Her chin defied him to doubt her.

She could have spun Gerald Acton into the Port-o-let with those strong hands, thought Morris. *And it was just a few steps into the trees and then down to the 10th green. Who would have missed her?*

Angie Martin made a pained face and started toward the Newton Cottage.

Morris felt a touch on the back and turned to look into the most beautiful green eyes in America. Soon to be in Paris.

"Friend of yours?" asked Jerusha Benefield.

"Not really. She's an engineer with CBS."

"More attractive than the programming they put on the air."

Morris didn't offer to explain what they had been talking about.

"Where's Edgar?" he asked.

"He's going to meet me here," said Jerusha. "He's over watching the players on the practice tee. He yearns to be young again, Morris, and to be playing golf here again."

"Don't we all?"

"Not me. I'm ready for a new life."

"Still heading for Paris?"

"Yes." Her smile lit up the grass and trees. Then she frowned, like a summer storm. "I've been visiting with Louise. Gerald Acton was a dreadful man. But nobody deserves to be killed."

"And especially not left in a Port-o-let," said Morris. "How is Louise?"

"Not as well as she wants us to believe. She's

having breakfast with our old friend, Walter Edwards."

"The last gentleman," said Morris. "Jerusha, was there any particular connection between Gerald and Melvin? Were they ever in business together?"

She hesitated. "Not that I know of. I wouldn't wish a partnership with either of those two on a dead man." She shivered at her own words, rare in their hostility. She made an effort to recover the gentleness of her true voice. "We normally saw the Actons and the Newtons only at Augusta National. It was the one thing we all seemed to have in common. To be honest, Edgar and I avoided both men, and Phyllis too. We loved Louise. We saw her often."

Morris was sure she did not realize she was speaking in the past tense. In her mind, she was already living on the Île St. Louis. Jerusha was a tall, elegant woman, but Morris knew she worked out in a gym in New York three times a week. And she had the strong hands of an artist.

She seemed to read his mind. "I was slow taking my shower yesterday evening. Edgar had already left for the clubhouse. I just dawdled until nearly eight o'clock. I know I could have slipped through the trees from the cottage, Morris." She kissed him on the cheek. "I'm flattered you think I might be tough enough to have done it."

Morris blushed. She was the only woman in the New World who could make him blush. He couldn't help but wonder, for the first time in his memory, if Jerusha was being entirely honest with him.

Morris felt a strong hand on his wide back.

"Do you always hang out with the beautiful women, Morris?"

"What kind of question is that? Of course I do. Especially those with emeralds for eyes." Morris and Edgar Benefield knew each other too well to have to shake hands. "Who looks sharp on the practice tee?" asked Morris.

"Raymond Floyd," Edgar said, without hesitation. "And he still has the touch around the greens of a young man." He did not hide his envy of that lingering, youthful gift.

"I expect to say the same thing about you, when you play in your first Senior tournament," said Morris.

Benefield only frowned at the possibility. "Tell me, what do the police say?" Edgar had yet to acknowledge his wife. They stood separately, as if already an ocean was between them.

Morris told him about the "whispery voice" calling Acton to the No. 10 green. How he was stabbed with an Augusta National letter opener—a fact, he cautioned Edgar, the police hadn't released. Morris slipped him the detail about the murder weapon almost before he thought about it; it would be interesting to see if he passed the detail on to anybody else. Benefield accepted the information without wincing.

"Acton took the call in the bar, just after seven P.M.," said Morris. He did not ask Edgar where he had been at the time, but let his silence ask the question for him.

"Morris, for the record, I had dressed before Jerusha, and gotten a drink at the clubhouse, and at seven P.M. I was standing outside, looking down the 18th fairway, remembering all the good times," said Benefield. "We had our share of good times, Morris."

Like his wife, he was speaking of his life in the past tense. Morris thought for a minute the man might weep. Jerusha must have sensed the same possibility and took Edgar's arm.

"I saw you standing out there," Morris said, almost to himself. He suddenly remembered Edgar, looking very much alone in the swarm of spectators coming up the 18th fairway as the first round of another Masters tournament passed into time. Benefield hadn't been thirty feet from the conversation between Gerald Acton and Angie Martin.

Edgar said, "I stood there a long time, Morris. I remember speaking with Payne Stewart; he was looking for his wife. I couldn't tell you the time. Maybe seven-thirty, seven-forty, I'm not sure. I was just drinking my Scotch and drinking in the past."

"The man you need to account to for your whereabouts is Detective Fannin," said Morris. "I'm sure you'll hear from him. He's over at Newton Cottage. He's interviewing us all again."

Edgar breathed a sigh of resignation. "Where did all the good times go?" he said, as if to the golfing gods. Jerusha held to his arm as though she herself was suddenly reluctant to let go of the past.

Morris meant to ask him about the relationship between Melvin Newton and Gerald Acton, but decided to wait until they were alone.

* * *

Morris made the rounds of the pressroom and then the clubhouse. He ran into one happy face: Sid Norton's. He couldn't keep the smile off his whiskey-shattered mug.

"Why so happy?" asked Morris.

"Look," said Sid, "I'm at the age when I don't want to see anybody dead. The next corpse may be my own. But with that bastard Gerald Acton gone, the club may keep me around."

"Are you hoping? Or do you know something?" asked Morris.

"I asked the chairman, our man Michael Compton. He said he would take it back up with the board. With the shit Acton gone, and the shit Newton gone, I think I'm back in." Sid pushed a shock of absolutely white hair out of his traveled but unrepentant eyes.

"Careful how you say that to Detective Fannin," said Morris. "He just might think you dusted the two of them to keep your job."

Norton did not suppress his grin. "Whoever did it, did the world of golf a fuckin' favor. And you can quote me."

"I wouldn't quote you to Louise," said Morris.

And now the grin was gone. Norton shook his large head. "No. I wouldn't hurt Louise for the world of golf, or any other world. Why did she ever keep a shit like Acton around, Morris?"

Morris elected to ask a question rather than answer him. "Tell me, was he always a bastard? I only knew him the last seventeen years."

Norton thought. Then said, "I knew him when he was a kid. That was a long time ago." Norton made an obvious effort to remember. "To be honest, he wasn't a bad kid. He didn't have a dime. But he always hung out with money. I was an assistant pro at Winged Foot, outside New York. One summer he actually worked at the club, waiting tables. Played a decent game of golf. Then, years later, he married Louise. Became a full-time asshole. I think he hated me for remembering him when he didn't have shit. After Mr. Roberts died, I was gonna be hung out to dry here . . . sooner or later. Now, maybe not." Sid was smiling again.

"Whatever you do, Sid, don't neglect to tell all that to the detective. It's what you try to hide that the police will hold against you."

Morris waited until the silence provoked Norton to speak. "Look, old man, at seven P.M. I was changing a goddamned tire on my car. Around behind Newton Cottage. In the shadows of those trees, I couldn't see the lugs on the wheels. It was a mess. Finally got it changed. Took me damn near three-quarters of an hour. Went inside and washed up. Then came on over to the bar. Hell, I don't know if anybody saw me. I can tell you nobody offered to help me." He held up his big, square hands that ought to have been able to change a tire in fifteen minutes.

"Sid, what do you think of when you think of

Melvin and Gerald together? And I don't mean that they were both assholes."

Sid thought a minute. "They both liked to play the Big Man down here. That's for sure. I don't know if either of them gave a damn about golf. Acton, as I said, had played a decent game as a kid. They were both rich. Or married to rich women. I don't think they could stand each other."

"You ever hear of them being in business together? Or chasing the same woman? Anything, together?"

"They both wanted to be chairman of this club," said Sid, "perish the fuckin' thought. Newton didn't make any secret about his ambition. Acton politicked for the job, but not out loud. It would never have happened. The club didn't have two bigger bastards. And women?" Sid speculated. "Acton chased everything with a body temperature. Newton . . . I think he just wanted to own the United States. He liked himself too much to worry about women. I gotta get back to the shop, before somebody accuses me of being drunk in the bar."

"What the hell's goin' on, Morris?"

He turned toward the harsh voice and soft face of Eddie Hayward.

"It looks like the club has to bury another member," said Morris.

"I'm just surprised somebody didn't stab that son of a bitch Acton ten years ago."

"How about you?" said Morris. "Where were you at seven P.M.?"

"Don't give me that shit, Morris." Hayward swelled up inside his softening midsection.

Morris kept looking him in the eye until he said, "I was in the locker room. I'd stayed around to hit balls—I was pushing every damn thing I swung at all day—and then I got stomach cramps. Cheap food in this overrated dining room was killin' me; I must'a been in the head the better part of an hour. Thank God for Jack Daniel's. He saved my life again."

Morris didn't smile. "An hour? That's a lot of stomach cramps. Are you pulling out of the tournament?"

"What are you, crazy? I'll shit my pants first. I get it goin', I'll win this son of a bitch again. I shot 70 and didn't birdie a par-five hole on the golf course."

Morris admitted, "I followed you several holes on the front. You hung in there tough."

"Damn right I did. I been hanging tough out here for twenty years. Seen plenty of fancy kids who could hit it out of sight disappear, and their sponsors' asses with 'em. I still got it in me to ruin a few more." His soft-hard smile was not a pretty sight.

"You didn't *ruin* Newton and Acton, did you?" asked Morris.

"You spread that around, I'll sue your ass," said Hayward, swelling up again, but not enough to challenge the man standing a head taller and a half foot thicker than himself.

"You do that," said Morris. "Maybe I could put together a little series for one of the *Hard Copy* television shows about your days on the tour . . . during and between marriages."

Hayward was too angry to breathe. He meant to live off his Masters title into a licentious old age. He didn't need any scandals out of his past showing up on television. He forced himself to swallow his spit.

"Look, Morris. I didn't kill the bastards. I ain't cryin' over them either. They can't arrest me for that."

"Did those two, Acton and Newton, ever cut any deals together?" Morris found himself approximating Hayward's own gutter English, expecting nothing for his effort.

"Oh, hell, yes," said Hayward. "They wanted to open a gambling casino up in Reno, Nevada, if they could get a license. Wanted to have a golf course. Talked to me about being the goddamned club pro. What do you think of that shit? Me in Reno fuckin' Nevada."

Morris was amazed. "When was that?"

"A couple of years ago," said Hayward, pleased that he had shocked Morris with his knowledge. "It all fell through. The bastards couldn't trust each other to light a cigarette off a match. And the state of Nevada didn't trust either one of 'em. Then I won The Masters, and they could both drop dead, as far as I was concerned." He laughed at his accidental slip of language. "And I guess they both did . . . with a little help from one of their friends, you think?" His laugh was uglier than his smile.

"Who else knew about this Nevada deal?" asked Morris.

Hayward thought. "Compton knew. He told 'em both they'd have to get out of the club. They wouldn't stand for two members who owned a gambling casino. I don't know what the big deal was. Members own racehorses, and they bet plenty on them. And they mostly lose their asses," said Hayward, pleased that it was true. "But nobody is kicking those bastards out of the club."

"True," admitted Morris. "Detective Fannin will be talking to you, to all of us, over in Newton Cottage. Don't edit the truth out of what you tell him, is my best advice."

Hayward didn't so much as nod. He turned without speaking and walked toward the sanctuary of the players' locker room, off-limits even to detectives.

Morris hunted up Tom Spears. He was having a Bloody Mary in the dining room.

"Kinda early for you, old man," said Morris.

Spears lifted his glass.

"I've drunk to better times."

Morris agreed.

"So what's happened?" asked Spears, one fist under his darkly handsome face.

Morris caught him up on the details that had been made public, saying nothing about the letter opener. Tom already knew about the "whispery voice" calling Acton on the telephone in the bar.

"You ever know of a deal between Newton and Acton?" asked Morris. "A business deal of any kind?"

"I'd be the last person on earth to know," said

Spears. "I couldn't stand either of those two guys, and the feeling was mutual. But they couldn't take my two Masters titles away, bastards that they were."

"Maybe with those two gone, especially Newton, the board will give you permission to make your TV commercial on the grounds," said Morris.

Spears looked at him to see if he was implying something. Morris's eyes offered nothing.

Spears said, "I've tried not to be a nuisance . . . with all that's happened. I did speak to Michael Compton this morning. He felt it would be okay. In fact, he promised me it would be okay. That there had been enough bad blood this week at Augusta National for a lifetime. But the board still has to approve it. Morris, I don't feel any guilt about it. I just want to make some honest money that I think I deserve. I didn't kill either of the bastards." Spears drank from his Bloody Mary. "But you think the same person killed them both, don't you?"

"Oh, yes," said Morris. "Tell me, old man—"

"Where was I between seven P.M. and eight P.M.?"

Morris nodded.

"I was stirring around in the bar and on the terrace, stuck my head in the locker room. Palmer wanted to see me about something. I never did catch up with him. Still haven't. I didn't see any one person; I saw *everybody*."

"Did Detective Fannin ask for a list of them?"

"Oh, yes. I told him ten or twelve people I *think* I spoke to. You know how it is in a bar."

Morris asked, quite directly, "Tom, did you ever have an offer as a teaching pro in Nevada?"

The question caught him off balance. "I'll have to think. I pissed away nine jobs in I don't know how many states. I can't remember all the offers I had when I first left the tour. Nothing in Nevada comes to mind. That's not to say I never got an offer there. Why, Morris?"

"Just asking." Something stirred in Morris's memory; he even closed his eyes and couldn't capture it.

"You okay?" asked Spears.

"Yes. I was just trying to think . . . but I can't."

"Sounds like my golf swing," said Spears.

Morris put his arm around Spears's shoulder. "Speaking of not forgetting, you were going to show me the sketches you've done over the years of Sullivan."

"I haven't forgotten. Let's slip off before dinner, and I'll show them to you. It's just a few minutes' ride to a warehouse on the river. But don't expect too much, Morris. I was a professional golfer. I'm an amateur painter."

"I like the subject so much, I'm sure to like the sketches," Morris said. Then he laughed. "Just so you are a better artist than you are a club pro."

Spears laughed harder than Morris. "I'm not much of an artist, but I'm not that awkward."

Morris warned, "Our Detective Fannin will be looking for you. He's interviewing all of us over at Newton Cottage. Don't hold back what you remember, Tom."

"No." Spears rubbed his arthritis-ruined hands.

"Tell me," said Morris, "have you seen Sullivan?"

Spears shook his head and went back to his Bloody Mary.

Sullivan was in their suite, taking a mid-morning shower, singing in her sexy contralto: " 'Isn't it rich . . . isn't it queer . . . losing my timing this late . . . in my career . . . send in the clowns . . . there ought to be clowns . . . don't bother . . . they're here.' " She knew only those several phrases and kept repeating them. Morris reached through the shower curtain and turned off the water.

"What!" Sullivan's light brown hair was thick with shampoo. With her eyes closed, she was feeling the air in front of her for the water that had disappeared.

"Isn't it gay . . ." sang Morris, badly. "Isn't it dear . . . you with the suds in your hair . . . me without fear . . ."

Sullivan flicked a double-handful of soapsuds all in his face and down the front of his shirt and trousers. There was nothing to do but join her in the steamy shower.

"Beats golf," said Morris, "even with a deranged woman and soap in my eyes." He was unable to speak again for a while.

Morris toweled off Sullivan's thick hair as if he were working the corner of a promising lightweight. She sat on the edge of the bed with her eyes closed.

"It's wonderful having a love slave," she said, tossing her head with the delicious feel of the towel.

"Don't think this is free; I get paid, big time, for this kind of stuff," said Morris, himself a huge, half-dry catastrophe.

"I can believe it. It's like being toweled off by an exotic sea creature."

"You mean by a whale," said Morris, threatening her with a snap of the towel. She looked at him as if he were a truant little boy. He was not fat. He was just a great chunk who would, she hoped, never grow up.

"So, what did you find out?" she asked, stepping into her clothes, loving the intimacy of the moment.

"You tell me," said Morris. He scrambled into his own clothes, summing up, as he dressed, all the loose ends of information he had searched out, some of it contradictory.

Morris wasn't sure when he was thinking, and when he was talking. "Walter Edwards was having breakfast with Louise. . . . I want to know what she told him. Walter, of course, said she should have killed Gerald years ago. . . . But something he didn't know . . . none of us knew about the Actons' retarded son."

Sullivan said, "I didn't know whether to cry or be angry with Louise for not having told us years ago. But who can be angry with Louise? I'll always think of Gerald Acton differently, Morris, though I couldn't bear to be around him."

Morris nodded his agreement, and resumed his summary: "Angie Martin swore she did not call Acton out of the bar. She swore it twice. But this is an athletic engineer, Sullivan, with hands strong enough to wrestle a dying Gerald Acton into a Port-o-let. She also said it was hard to believe, but Acton could, at rare times, be a funny guy . . . but that the happy moods never lasted . . . that he quickly went back to being a son of a bitch. I can believe that. Louise also said Gerald could be a lot of fun when she first met him as a young man . . ."

Sullivan straightened his vast belt. "I'm sorry he couldn't have stayed a human being, instead of becoming the bastard we knew so well."

Morris said, "He was about as funny to me as a coral snake. Angie Martin said Acton would dial New York phone numbers and start in chewing out whoever answered. I can believe that too. Martin said he once hung up after a particular call and said, 'How can you expect a goddamned romance publisher like Melvin Newton to understand business?' She had no idea what kind of business he meant. She only knew they were arguing about some sort of license. That's a serious point, Sullivan. Louise told me she wasn't aware of *any* business connection between Gerald and Melvin. Jerusha—"

Sullivan stopped buttoning her blouse to hold up one warning fist.

"I only interviewed her in the line of duty," said Morris, smiling.

Sullivan cocked her head in disbelief.

"Jerusha said she didn't know of any deals between Acton and Newton. She said any business between those two would be a partnership in hell.

Which is where the corporation is now headquartered, if they had one."

"I can't believe you said that," said Sullivan, in mock horror.

"Me either. It sounds so much like a sexy friend of mine."

Sullivan yielded to the adjective *sexy*.

Morris continued, "Jerusha said she and Edgar saw the Actons and Newtons only at Augusta. She said they avoided both men and Phyllis too. But that they 'loved Louise' and saw her often. Jerusha said all that in the past tense. She's already moved to Paris in her mind. Edgar Benefield came up—"

Good," said Sullivan, coming over to run a comb through his damp hair and kiss him on the lips.

Morris soldiered on: "Edgar said he got a drink in the bar and at seven P.M. was standing outside, looking down the 18th fairway, remembering the good times we once had. . . . Everybody is living his life in the past tense—everybody except us, Sullivan." Morris wrapped a large arm around her fresh blouse.

"You're mussing me. . . ."

"Sorry."

"I didn't say stop," said Sullivan.

Morris could only shake his head. "You are . . ."

"I know the word . . . incorrigible."

"At least. Anyway, it came to me—when Edgar described where he had been standing—that I did see him yesterday, doing exactly what he said he was doing . . . holding a drink, looking out over the 18th hole. I saw him at the same time I saw Acton talking to Angie Martin. They weren't thirty feet apart. Sullivan, it's a short hike through the trees from where Edgar was standing to the 10th green. Edgar swears he didn't call Acton in the bar. Sullivan, it must have been you. You can't deny you have a 'whispery voice.'"

"Oh," she whispered in her best recollection of Tallulah Bankhead, "if it had been me, darling, it would have been worth it, even if it cost him his life."

"Sullivan . . ."

"You can't believe I said that."

"I don't know why not. You are shameless."

"You can tell by the company I keep."

Morris just shook his formidable head.

"I'm going to ask Edgar, when I catch him alone, if he knew of any deals between Acton and Newton. Jerusha seemed to hesitate . . . I'm not sure she was being entirely candid with me. There had to be some connection between Acton and Newton and the killer; he didn't choose the two of them to murder by accident."

"And you like Walter Edwards's 'kill all the bastards' theory," said Sullivan. "If so, this is going to be the longest-running serial murderer since Genghis Khan."

"Sid Norton," said Morris, shaking his head again, "told me that with 'the shit Acton gone, and the shit Newton gone' he might just keep his job as club pro. He said Michael Compton told him he would take it up again with the board. Sid said Acton and Newton couldn't 'stand each other.'

Among other rivalries, he said each wanted to be chairman of the club. If Sid knew of any business they were in together, he was careful not to bring it up. Norton said he was changing a tire on his car behind Newton Cottage about seven o'clock last night, and it took him three-quarters of an hour. That's a long time for a strong man to change an automobile tire."

Morris shook his head at the tie he was tying, as if it could be coerced into a proper knot.

He continued, "I looked up Tom Spears. Never saw him having a Bloody Mary quite so early in the morning. Spears said he would be 'the last person on earth to know' of any deal between Acton and Newton. He 'couldn't stand' either man. No doubt, Sullivan, they are both worth more to him dead. Compton promised Spears this morning—now that those two men and their objections are gone—that he can make his TV ad for a Japanese automobile *on the grounds* of Augusta National. It's the first serious money Spears has made in years from his two Masters titles. Tom doesn't hide his relief—or pretend 'any fake guilt' about their deaths. I did ask him if he had ever had an offer as a club pro in Nevada—"

"That's a bizarre question, even for you," said Sullivan.

Morris smiled the smile of the true source, all the time collecting his thoughts; he would have to ask Arnold Palmer if, indeed, he had been looking for Tom Spears yesterday afternoon; Sullivan held his jacket, which was as large as a small blanket, and wrapped him in it.

Morris continued, "So these two men, Acton and Newton, *never got it on* in business together . . . except something Acton discussed—we don't know what—in a short telephone conversation overheard by Angie Martin. Right? *Wrong!*

"Eddie Hayward, our distinguished, lovable, asshole defending champion, told me, flat out, that 'a couple of years ago' Newton and Acton *planned to open a gambling casino in Reno, Nevada.* That they were going to have a golf course. *And talked with Eddie about being the club pro.* Eddie swears they gave up the idea because Augusta National's chairman, Michael Compton, told them they would have to get out of the club. That the membership wouldn't tolerate casino owners. This is the same Michael Compton who told me he was in his room alone from seven P.M. until seven forty-five going over his notes for his committee meetings."

Morris puffed up in indignation. "And what did our gentleman-chairman Compton tell me, when I asked him if he could think of 'any circumstances linking Acton and Newton that might have ended in bitter feelings'? He shook his silver head—a polite, unspoken, emphatic *no*. My ass! All these members and 'friends,' who'd known the two bastards for twenty years, even his wife—whom we love," he quickly added, "had no bloody idea the two guys were even gonna stage a garage sale together. And Eddie Hayward says they were planning to build a gambling casino, for God's sake, for millions of dollars. Somebody is lying, Lady Sullivan."

"I'm shocked. Lying, you say? And in a gentle-man's club?" She added, seriously, "I talked a long time last night with Louise. Mostly I listened. She told me about their retarded son. And how nasty Gerald Acton was faithful to him as he never was to her. Louise said she didn't know of any circumstance involving Gerald and Melvin that might have led to their murders. I believe her, Morris."

"I believe her, too, and I wasn't even there," said Morris. "Louise Acton, Michael Compton—I haven't spoken with his wife, Aeriel, and I haven't spoken with Phyllis Newton—Tom Spears, Jerusha and Edgar Benefield, Sid Norton, even Walter Edwards . . . *nobody* admits the two bastards were partners to-gether in anything . . . not even in raising money for the United Fund; even Angie Martin is terribly vague about what 'business' she heard them discus-sing on the telephone. And here Eddie Hay-ward says, straight out, that a couple of years ago they were planning what had to be a massive investment in a gambling casino. I can't wait to run that proposition around Newton Cottage and the old clubhouse . . . in my own time," Morris cautioned himself.

"I'll not breathe a word, except possibly to the handsome *New York Times*," said Sullivan, advancing one memorable leg and foot toward the door to the downstairs and the nearly forgotten golf tournament.

Morris took on the expression of a martyr at the moment of martyrdom.

Then he smiled. "To hell with murder . . ."

"That's the place for it." Sullivan grinned.

"Let's go where the only crime is against par."

CHAPTER EIGHT

Julia Sullivan took one brief look at a pairing sheet and was off toward the delicious par-3 6th hole. Morris poled along behind her, swinging his stiff left knee.

"I don't have to ask who you are keen to follow," said Morris.

"Hush, and walk faster."

They were taking a shortcut past the No. 2 tee, through a multitude of fans, ebbing and flowing, like an undecided civilization.

Sullivan pushed her way, unladylike, through the circle of spectators around the top of the sloping sixth green. Morris followed her, leaving a wake of faint apologies behind him.

Sullivan leaned on him while he leaned on his cane. She took his binoculars from around his neck.

Fred Couples, hatless, his hair blowing around his

handsome forehead, stood high above them on the tee with a six-iron in his hands. He seemed to barely swing the club and the ball fell from an improbable height, nearer and nearer the flag until it struck *exactly* in the hole, spinning a bare six feet backward. After Couples drained the putt he smiled directly at Julia Sullivan, who threw her small white cap in the air like a new graduate from the naval academy.

The crowd seemed to swell around them with the very greatness of the tee shot. Sullivan, a sorceress to the bone, led them all to the 7th tee.

The unflappable Couples struck a mid-iron into the narrow fairway and gathered his well-appointed separate parts over a wedge shot.

Sullivan sighed into the binoculars.

Morris whispered in her ear, "Careful, don't break your eyes."

"I can't see a thing. The lenses have fogged over."

Morris followed the high flight of the wedge, the ball stopping precariously on the tilted slope of the green.

Couples, with his wide shoulders and narrow waist and beautiful eyes, stood over his putt.

"Don't breathe so loudly," Morris whispered into Sullivan's ear.

She patted her heart with her hand . . . and jumped in the air with an obscene shout when his putt dived into the heart of the cup. Two birdies in a row. And Sullivan led the charge to the 8th tee, an uphill par 5.

Couples, with his double-jointed upper body, made an astonishing shoulder turn and delivered the

clubhead into the ball with the speed of sin, which
was just what Sullivan had in mind. The ball escaped
gravity until it fell of its own volition some 300 yards
from the tee. Morris, riding his cane—and Sullivan
in the lead—fled up the hill with the gypsy-caravan
of fans, the same looks on the faces of all the women
among them. Couples, with a bare three-iron, struck
the innocent ball with a fierce draw that carried it
high over the hill and onto the green in the manner
of a young Nicklaus, who could have matched the
shot but not the sex appeal. There was the matter
of two simple putts, and Fred had covered the 535
yards in four strokes. Sullivan, giggling and cheer-
ing, pulled them all, like a sensuous, magnetic field,
toward the 9th tee.

Grown men fell back from her resolute progress,
and they saw young Fred Couples—who might
have been young Tom Jones to the women in the
gallery—detonate a ball down the fairway to within
a bare sand wedge—for a boy god—of the 9th
green. The wedge he stopped, with all his art, *one
foot* from the hole. Sullivan was shameless in her applause.

They fought their way to the 485-yard 10th hole.
The mass of humanity around the first tee and the
18th green and the 10th tee had no slight chance of
staying Sullivan from her appointed round. She
stood within arm's reach of Couples as he obliter-
ated the ball with his tee shot, sending it into the
air like a heat-seeking missle a full 350 yards from
where even Sullivan stood speechless. Couples
needed no more than a seven-iron to spin the ball

fifteen feet from the cup, and he used one bold sweep of the putter to drop it in the hole. Five birdies in a row in the broad daylight.

"I think you might be arrested in Georgia for what you just hollered," Morris whispered to Sullivan, who did not answer for the glaze over her eyes. Morris did not miss the police tape guarding the Port-o-let in the trees by the 10th green, but he did not speak of it either, not wanting to break the spell for either of them. Sullivan would not have noticed if the letter opener had been descending into the victim's last cry.

What? A mortal par on No. 11? But Sullivan clapped her hands as if it had been a feat unknown to golf. Now they sat on the grass, Morris lowering himself with his cane like a pilgrim come from a hundred miles. Sullivan knew to watch the tops of the great pines, to see them shake against the winds they could not feel on the surface of the earth. Fred Couples watched with her for the secret of the tree-tops. He was tied for the lead in the 56th playing of The Masters. He drew out a six-iron and returned it to the bag. Then he pulled out a seven-iron as if unlocking a magical sword from a mythic rock, and without hesitation struck the ball high into the air toward the most famous, most treacherous, par-3 hole in all of golf. He was safely on the 12th green and then in the 12th hole in two putts for a par of three. Sullivan led a sea of applause.

They did not have to move from the ground they sat on to watch Mr. Couples lash a monstrous drive around the ancient trees along the par-5 13th hole to within a mere six-iron of the green, which rolled through deep shadows without mercy down to Rae's Creek. Couples flowed through the six-iron shot, sending the ball onto the green, and in two bold putts he made his sixth birdie in eight holes and temporarily took the lead in the tournament he seemed destined to win.

After finishing his round of 67, and after 137 strokes in 36 holes of play, Couples was one shot behind the wee, strong men from Australia and Wales: Craig Parry and Ian Woosnam, defending champion. Improbably, Eddie Hayward, as nasty as ever, turning up his nose at the polite applause from the gallery, eagled No. 15 to shoot 69, keeping the defending champion in the hunt.

Morris sneaked Sullivan into the pressroom, wearing Walter Edwards's badge, a grievous sin at Augusta National. The sportswriters from the larger papers had been reinforced with hard-nosed crime reporters. They asked "friendly" questions, such as: "How does a small-time, bush-league police department hope to catch a serial murderer?" Detective Fannin stood up to it better than Morris had imagined he would. Fannin surprised him by telling the reporters that Acton and Newton had planned to build a multimillion-dollar gambling casino. This caused a feeding frenzy among the press, now wanting to know if these were "mob killings."

Morris recognized the tall, thin, first-string crime writer from the New York *Daily News*, who asked Fannin if the Augusta National club had considered stopping the golf tournament to save lives. Club

Chairman Michael Compton answered the question himself: "No." But he added that "all writers are free to leave as they choose."

The questions grew more hostile until Detective Fannin made his escape.

Finally, Fred Couples appeared at the microphone to answer legitimate golf questions. Couples denied knowing anything about a gambling casino. "I'm just here to play golf, and to try and win one of the four great tournaments in the world. My heart goes out to the families of the victims."

"We could follow your progress around the course from here," said *Sports Illustrated*'s golf writer, famous for never leaving the press tent. "It sounded like a lot of birdies."

"It's nice to hear the people scream and yell," admitted Couples.

"That wasn't 'people,' " Morris whispered to Sullivan, "that was *you* he heard."

"What do you mean?" whispered Sullivan. "He's just a nice boy with a beautiful golf swing. That's all I came to see."

"My ass," said Morris.

"There's that," she said with a laugh.

They didn't hear another word Mr. Couples had to say.

Morris returned the press badge to Walter Edwards. And filled him in on what Detective Henry Fannin had said.

"Thank God the *Times* flew in a crime reporter," said Edwards. "I can concentrate on the golf tournament. You two followed young Mr. Couples; he must have played very well."

"Ask Sullivan," said Morris.

"He did everything a golfer can legally do in the daylight," said Sullivan.

"Oh, my," said Walter. He added, "I had a long visit with Louise Acton."

"How was she?"

"Sad. I think not just over what happened yesterday, but over all the lost, bitter years of her life with and without Gerald. She blames herself for not having done something about it. Even officially leaving him would have been a healthier thing . . . she feels."

"He was lucky she didn't throw him out on the street broke," said Sullivan.

"He told Louise he was sure somebody was out to harm him," said Edwards.

"After Melvin was found dead, he told me he was afraid," said Morris.

"Louise said he slept all week with his gun under his pillow. The maid apparently found it one morning and was too scared to touch it. She asked Louise to come get it. Louise put the gun back in his suitcase."

"What did he say to her . . . specifically?" asked Morris.

"He told her at one point, 'Nobody can hate like an old friend who turns against you. . . . ' Then he apparently said, 'Well, hate can work both ways.' "

"Did Louise ask him who, or what, he meant?"

"Yes. He just stuck his chin out and put his gun back under his pillow. He didn't answer her."

"Maybe he'd still be alive if he'd carried the gun to the No. 10 green," said Morris. "I guess he didn't expect to be attacked in the middle of the golf course . . . in the last daylight."

"Did he warn Louise to protect herself?" asked Sullivan.

Edwards shook his head.

"Louise said he only seemed to fear for himself. She urged him to go to the police. He said, 'Fuck the police. I'll take care of myself—like I always have.' "

"Yeah," said Morris, "Big Shot to the very end. So, it was an 'old friend' he feared. That's more than Louise remembered just after Gerald was killed. Not surprising. The shock of it. Well, it also had to be a 'friend' who got close enough to Melvin Newton to stick a gun in his ear." Morris tapped his cane on the firm grass. "Maybe—it's entirely possible—Gerald Acton feared the *wrong* old friend."

"You mean . . . maybe he guessed wrong who killed Melvin?" said Sullivan. "And he wasn't afraid to meet whoever telephoned him in the bar?"

"Yes," said Morris. "Or he wasn't afraid to meet whoever the voice on the phone told him to meet. Or why would he have agreed to meet him, or her, anywhere *without* his gun?"

"He was too cocky," said Sullivan. "Or too sure of his opinion . . . of who killed Melvin."

"I think you are right on both counts. And maybe he was horny, to boot," said Morris.

"I'm shocked," said Sullivan.

"It's a well-known condition," said Morris.

"Can we see some proof?" asked Sullivan.

"We'll have to ask the medical examiner—did the boy have it up in the Port-o-let?"

"Nothing like a knife to the heart to calm the libido." Walter smiled, tipping his old Hogan cap and moving toward the blank, impatient screen of his word processor.

"Let's stir among the patrons and see who we can make uneasy," Morris said to Sullivan.

Standing on the edge of the terrace with a Bloody Mary in his hand, as if saluting the day, was Edgar Benefield. Jerusha was not in sight.

Sullivan gave him an elaborate hug for old times' sake.

"Good try, Edgar," said Morris. "But you can't compete with young Fred Couples."

"We saw him make five consecutive birdies," said Sullivan.

"I played with him once," said Edgar. "He hit the ball all the way to the horizon . . . with no effort. And very much a gentleman."

"Speaking of the opposite of gentlemen," said Morris, "were you aware that Melvin and Gerald had been involved in a potential multimillion-dollar deal?"

Edgar looked down as if the answer were in his glass. "No." He shook his head. "Not that I was around them that much . . . except here at Augusta National. I wasn't aware they cared for each other . . . or even trusted each other."

"You never heard them speak of a common business interest? Specifically, arguing about a license?"

Edgar took a sip of his drink, thought, shook his head again. "No. They sometimes argued about the club's business, petty stuff, it seemed to me. The years the membership considered new tees on No. 10 and No. 13. I heard them argue about that. Not that either one played enough golf anymore to justify an opinion." He paused. "Any particular kind of license?"

Morris shook his head. "Strange," he said, enigmatically. He didn't offer to explain what he meant.

Benefield spoke into the silence: "I've tried to imagine what common purpose the killer might have had . . . if, indeed, Melvin and Gerald were killed by the same person." Benefield drained the last of his drink. "Neither of them was an attractive man. But that's hardly the stuff of murder."

"You are the fifth person to hit on their unfortunate personalities as a possible motive for murder." Morris did not identify himself or Sullivan or the detective or Walter Edwards as having shared the thought.

"It's a bit of a stretch," said Sullivan. "But not unknown. Oscar Wilde probably had it backward: We always kill the one we *hate* is the more likely result."

"It's a thought," said Edgar, holding up his glass, which was in need of a refill. He nodded and walked toward the open door of the clubhouse.

"Let's catch Payne." Morris pointed to the handsome Payne Stewart. Sullivan smiled her willingness.

"You can't have him. I just want to ask him a question," said Morris.

Stewart, in his plus-fours in the dark colors of the Atlanta Falcons, was sitting in a lawn chair with the expression of a man waiting for his wife who was not in sight. He also had the defeated look of a 75 written on his face, a score made on a course he should dominate with his great length.

"Sorry about your round," said Morris, as Sullivan kissed him on his cheek.

"I need the kiss. But any sympathy is wasted," said Stewart. "I earned all 75 strokes. I can't believe I don't play this course better, Morris."

"Oh, you will. Your time will come. One year you will be nailing your irons to the pins and your putter will be hot and you will dominate the tournament."

"Will you please call me when that year comes around? At the moment, I'm missing the cut." Already he was smiling. He was not a young man given to depression, which would extend his career in championship golf.

"Tell me," said Morris, "did you speak with Edgar Benefield late yesterday? About seven-thirty or seven-forty P.M.? He said you were looking for your wife."

"Benefield? Oh, yes. The old amateur . . ."

Morris winced at the description.

"Just like today. I was looking for my wife. I don't blame her for hiding out. If I saw my husband shoot 74-75 . . . I'd be in the bar somewhere having a double Scotch. Or applying for a day job. We'll starve to death with me missing the cut in every tournament."

Morris laughed. "Sure you will. You could finance the Bank of England—and God knows they need it—with your winnings these past two years alone."

Stewart lifted his cap and lowered it on his blond hair. "The police aren't suspecting Mr. Benefield . . . ?"

"No. No," said Morris. "They're just trying to establish where we all were when Gerald Acton was killed . . . those of us who knew him."

"Well, yesterday Mr. Benefield was standing not ten feet from here, when I asked him if he'd seen my wife." Stewart thought a minute. "Maybe it was closer to seven forty-five than seven-thirty. My wife didn't show up until nearly eight P.M. Morris, it's a nasty thing, murder."

"At least no one is killing the players," said Morris, ". . . yet."

"You don't expect them to, do you?" Stewart was alarmed.

"I've seen it done," said Morris. "Remember the U.S. Open in Atlanta a number of years ago?"

"I wasn't in the field. But I remember reading about it." Stewart waved his long arm to his wife, who was coming around the corner of the clubhouse. He stood up to catch her attention.

"Thank you, Payne . . . good luck the rest of the year," said Morris.

"If I keep hitting it like I hit it this week . . . I'll

need more than luck. I'll need a loan." He tipped his cap to Sullivan and was off to join his wife.

"Well, Edgar didn't lie," said Sullivan, seriously.

Morris nodded that he hadn't. Edgar, like Walter Edwards, was among the last gentlemen. But the deed might have been done, he thought, between the phone call and seven forty-five.

Sullivan pointed. "There's Arnie. Didn't you want to ask him a question?" Palmer was bending over his putter on the practice green, though he had also missed the halfway cut of the tournament he had won four times.

Sullivan leaned over the protective rope to kiss Arnie straight on the lips.

"That does ease the pain," he said.

"You've won your share around here," said Morris, who had enjoyed writing about each of Palmer's four Masters championships.

"I'm still greedy," said Palmer.

"Good. You belong playing, right here."

"Tell me, Morris, what do the police know about the murder of Gerald Acton?"

"Not much. Somebody called him on the phone in the bar . . . about seven o'clock. And he immediately went down to the No. 10 green. And somebody killed him."

"Took some guts," said Palmer, "to kill him with people still moving all around the course."

"Or some desperation," said Morris.

"What about the golfers? Are they in danger?" asked Palmer. "Then again, maybe the killer is a player. . . . I'll never forget what happened at the

Open in Atlanta. Why do these things always happen in Georgia?"

"I don't know who might be in danger," said Morris. "Whoever killed the two of them knew them both well."

Sullivan said, "Morris didn't answer your question, 'Why do these things always happen in Georgia?' He didn't answer it because he was born in Atlanta, and that city 'is entirely surrounded by Georgia,' as a drummer in a swing band once told us. All things ghastly are capable of happening in Georgia, Arnold. You know that."

He laughed his deep laugh, almost a croak of a laugh.

"Tell me . . ." said Morris, "and speaking of players—were you looking for Tom Spears late yesterday?"

"Yes. I wanted to borrow his old blade putter, the one I gave him years ago. The one he won this tournament with twice. I never did catch up with him. I had to leave to meet some people for dinner. I guess I left here just after seven P.M. Why? You know Tom Spears is as fine a man as ever played the Tour."

"Indeed," said Morris. "And a great friend of ours. But the police are checking where each of us—who knew Gerald Acton—were . . . when he was killed. Tom said he was no place in particular: just walking on the terrace and through the bar and sticking his head in the locker room, looking for you. . . . He didn't know why you were looking for him. And I believe him. Too bad you didn't catch up with him to borrow the putter."

"I don't think any putter in existence could have helped me . . . but I'm still looking." He grinned his famous grin.

"Putt it quicker," said Sullivan, pointing to the practice green. "Don't take so long over the ball. You know what Monty used to say: 'Putt it quick . . . before you have time to fuck it up.' "

Palmer dropped his putter laughing. "That was Monty, all right. I promise I'll remember it. It won't help me, but I'll remember it." He picked up his reluctant putter and stroked another ball . . . quickly.

Morris took Sullivan by the elbow.

"Let's go check on our boy detective."

The living room of Newton Cottage was empty. They found Detective Fannin getting himself a cup of coffee in the kitchen.

"So, what have you found out?" asked Morris.

"The whole world of golf was afoot yesterday between seven and eight P.M. Not one damn person was sitting down in the presence of another damn person. They were getting dressed, changing tires, standing alone in crowds of people on the course or in the goddamn bar—"

"Or hoping to get laid," said Morris.

"Amen," said Sullivan.

Morris and Fannin compared notes.

"Palmer confirmed he was looking for Tom Spears," said Morris, "wanted to borrow his putter.

Never caught up with him. But Arnie said he left the grounds by seven P.M."

Fannin shook his red head.

"They all have the same story. They saw *nobody* or they saw *everybody*. I checked Sid Norton's car. The spare tire is still on the left front wheel. But it could have been changed anytime."

"We spoke with Payne Stewart," said Morris. "He did remember seeing Edgar Benefield by the 18th green, and asked him if he had seen his wife. But Payne thought it was nearer seven forty-five than seven-thirty. His wife didn't show up until nearly eight o'clock."

The detective could only run his hand through his red hair.

"Your electrical engineer admits to speaking with Acton—about seven P.M. Angie Martin swears she did not call him afterward, on her CBS cellular phone. And she didn't," said the detective. "At least, not on that particular phone."

"You've had the call to the bar traced already?"

"Sure. It's amazingly easy in this computer age, as long as you have the number the call was made *from*. The call was made from the Augusta National cellular phone we found in the garbage bag near the No. 10 green. . . . It was made at seven-eleven P.M."

"Where was the phone supposed to be?" asked Sullivan.

"It was checked out to the chairman, Michael Compton," said the detective, letting the information settle in the silence. "I spoke with Mr. Compton. He last remembers having the phone in his possession in his official golf cart . . . which he parked by the practice putting green. He last used it while checking on crowd control at the 15th hole. A number of fans crashed the ropes at No. 15, crossing the fairway with a tee shot dangerously in the air. Luckily, nobody was hurt. Mr. Compton fired one of the marshalls on the 15th fairway and called the clubhouse to get a volunteer replacement. We've checked. That call was made at five twenty-four P.M. He insists he did not use the phone after that."

"It would have been a gutsy move for him to call Acton to his death on his own phone," said Morris. "But then, it was a gutsy murder."

"He volunteered to let us take elimination prints," said the detective. "His fingerprints are all over the cellular phone, as you might expect."

"But there were no strange prints?" said Morris.

The detective again shook his red head, like some new police ritual.

"I forgot. . . . Where was Michael Compton after seven P.M.?" Morris thought about it, and then answered his own question. "He says he was in his room, going over his notes for the committee meetings, until seven forty-five, when he walked over to the clubhouse."

The detective slapped his thigh with exasperation.

"There was three-quarters of an hour out of every life at Augusta National yesterday . . . starting at seven P.M."

"Yes, and one life went out forever," said Morris. "Angie Martin swears she never left the area around the CBS tower at the 18th green. That's where she was talking to Gerald Acton. I, for God's sake, saw them. Spears said he also saw them under the scoreboard. That's where Edgar Benefield was standing. I saw him too. They should have put up a fuckin' traffic light...." Morris got his breath, while searching his memory. "Sid Norton was changing his tire.... Michael Compton was studying· his notes in his room.... Jerusha Benefield was careful to tell me she was 'slow taking her shower' and didn't get over to the clubhouse until about eight P.M."

"If she is the killer," said the detective, "I'm going to volunteer to be the next corpse."

"Don't say a word, John Morris," warned Sullivan, threatening him with her right fist.

"But the big zinger," said Morris, raising his own trigger finger, "was Eddie Hayward. Insisting that Gerald and Melvin, a couple of years ago, were planning *to build and operate a gambling casino in Reno, Nevada*! He says they talked to him about being the club pro! Did he tell you that?" asked Morris.

"Jesus Christ!" said Detective Fannin. "I haven't spoken to Eddie Hayward. He never came by here. I sent word I wanted to see him."

"I also told him you were looking for him," said Morris.

"Tell me exactly what he said." Fannin sat down, as if to reinforce his concentration.

Morris went over Eddie's words verbatim.

"And Louise Acton insisted to Sullivan and to me that she knew of no business deals between Gerald and Melvin," said Morris. "We believe her. I haven't spoken with Phyllis Newton."

"It's astonishing, if it's true," said the detective. "It's a more astonishing lie, if it's not true."

"Nobody else claims to know anything about *any* deal between Acton and Newton," said Morris. "Not Tom Spears. Not Sid Norton. Not Edgar Benefield, or his wife, Jerusha. Not Compton—who Eddie says told the two of them *they would have to get out of Augusta National* if they built a gambling casino. Now how could Michael forget a controversial thing like that?"

"It's possible," said Sullivan. "It's possible, too, that it was an awkward question he didn't want to go into again."

"Murder is the most awkward question of all," said Morris.

"And I plan to go into it with Mr. Compton with all guns blazing," said the detective. "Maybe you could sit in, Morris. Since it was you Eddie told about the deal."

"I'd be glad to. I'd love to hear his explanation."

"And where does Eddie claim to have been after seven P.M.?" asked the detective.

"I hesitate to tell you," said Morris.

"Go ahead. I'm prepared to hear anything."

"He was in the locker room, in the toilet, with stomach cramps . . . for the better part of an hour."

Henry Fannin looked to the ceiling for a sign from the gods.

"Of course he was."

"Well," said Sullivan, "the man was killed in a

Port-o-let. Maybe Eddie just got his toilets con-
fused."

The detective laughed in spite of himself.

"I'll send word to our defending champion, Mr.
Hayward, he'd better get his ass over here or he'll
be playing tomorrow's round with a deck of used
cards in a city cell," said the detective.

He also sent a separate deputy running to fetch
the club chairman, Michael Compton.

Phyllis Newton, in a dark sea of formal black,
stepped into the cottage as if she, too, had been sum-
moned. She recognized the detective immediately.

"Tell me, is this madman still loose? What have
the police found out?" She waved at Morris and Sullivan without taking her attention from the detective.

"We haven't made an arrest," said Fannin. "We
do believe the same person killed both your husband
and Gerald Acton."

Phyllis made an angry grunt. "*Accidental death*. I
told you it was rubbish. Melvin would have been the
last man ever to kill himself."

"You did tell me exactly that," said Detective
Fannin. "And you were exactly right. When did you
hear about Mr. Acton's death?"

Phyllis looked directly at him. "I believe that is a
polite way of asking me where I was when he was
killed?"

Fannin did not deny it.

"I was here in the cottage. In my room. I made
several long-distance calls, around seven P.M. I ordered my dinner sent to my room. I wasn't up to

all the commotion in the dining room. But that would be preferred to the 'poor thing' pats on the hand and the fake sad remarks. Melvin Newton was not a much loved man. Not by anybody in this club. And we all know it. Why practice hypocrisy?"

Morris had to fight off a smile, remembering the first, dramatic moments practiced by the new widow in her "bereavement." She seemed to have made a hard-shell recovery.

Phyllis continued, "They brought my dinner . . . at maybe a quarter after seven. I went directly to bed after eating it."

Phyllis looked strong enough to lift an ox out of a ditch. Morris didn't doubt she had the stomach to drive a knife into Gerald Acton and then slip through the trees and eat her dinner, as evidence of her presence, and go soundly to sleep. A slight shudder ran down his right arm into his hand, resting on his walking cane. He could see the same frightened look in Sullivan's eyes.

"Tell me," said the detective, "were you ever aware of any multimillion-dollar deal being considered by Mr. Newton and Mr. Acton?"

Phyllis Newton looked at him as if he were demented.

"Melvin was a major American publisher. I don't believe Mr. Acton was involved in any business whatsoever, except that of spending his wife's money. If he spent any of it with my husband, I am not aware of it."

"You never heard Mr. Newton speak of building

a gambling casino in Reno, Nevada?" asked the detective.

She was too taken aback to answer immediately.

"I didn't realize the police were allowed to drink on the job," she said. "That's the most ridiculous question I have ever been asked."

"One of the older players in the tournament told me it was entirely true," said Morris. "He said Gerald and Melvin were in the deal together . . . and offered him the job as club pro of the golf course they were going to build with the casino."

"You better arrest the man who said that," Phyllis said to the detective. "The man is a liar, and most probably a killer."

"Why do you find it so unbelievable, Phyllis?" asked Sullivan. "Melvin has made multimillion-dollar deals before."

"The man abhorred gambling," said Phyllis. "He wouldn't bet more than a dollar on a round of golf. He was entirely too tight to gamble."

"Owning a gambling casino is not the same as gambling in one," Morris said, quietly. "If it has a good location, and excellent management, a casino can be enormously profitable."

"It's bullshit, Morris. And you know it. Who is this golfer? He must be an all-time idiot, and golf has produced some huge ones." Phyllis looked at Sullivan as if she were responsible for the entire insane idea.

"Eddie Hayward," said Morris, without asking permission of the detective, even with his eyes, to reveal Eddie's name.

"That ignorant son of a bitch," said Phyllis. "Melvin once refused to so much as give him a ride from the airport to the club. He would never on earth have offered him a job. He is too, too common. And an enormous liar. You have your man, Detective." Phyllis stared, as if she expected him to pull his handcuffs out of his coat pocket. She started in again: "Melvin was appalled at the way *Eddie Hayward*"—she said his name as if it were a social disease—"sold the Masters title 'as if it were dog food,' Melvin used to say. In fact, the man was in a dog food commercial. And that's where he belongs. He's a goddamned liar." She paused. "You didn't listen to me before . . . when Melvin was killed. And I have no reason to believe you will listen to me this time. I'm going to my room to rest."

They watched her climb the stairs.

"She has a point, Morris," said the detective. "She couldn't have been more adamant that her husband would never have killed himself. Maybe Eddie Hayward is lying his nasty head off. The question is why?"

"I can't imagine," said Morris. "But Michael Compton is the man to break the tie."

They were on a second cup of coffee when the club chairman, Compton, came through the door. He looked like a man who had just been drafted into an unpopular war. His silver hair was neglected into every direction.

Detective Fannin did not allow Compton to sit down before asking, "Why didn't you tell us that Mr. Newton and Mr. Acton planned to build a multimillion-dollar gambling casino? In Reno, Nevada?

And that you threatened to have them thrown out of the Augusta National club if they did it?"

Compton sat down as if the questions were too heavy to field standing up. He buried his hands deep in his hair.

"That was two years ago," said Compton. "The deal never went through. I never believed they were serious about it. It was just some pipe dream that a developer brought to Gerald Acton . . . some guy he was on a board of directors with. Gerald asked several Augusta National club members if they were interested. Only Melvin expressed any interest. He said he liked 'the greedy sound of it.' They came to me together. I told them the club would not tolerate members who owned a gambling casino." Compton stopped talking. He said it all so precisely, Morris thought, he must have rehearsed it all in his mind.

"But you didn't think that was a 'circumstance linking Acton and Newton that might have ended in bitter feelings'?" reminded Morris.

Compton shook his head, seemingly more in despair than in defiance. "I'm afraid I misled you, Morris. And I apologize for it. But the only person I know Gerald and Melvin blamed for the deal falling through was me. And I know I didn't kill them. And, besides, the whole thing fell through two years ago. The developer couldn't get a gambling license."

Of course, thought Morris. *That's what Angie Martin heard Acton arguing with Newton about on the phone . . . a license . . . a gambling license!* But that wasn't two years ago. Morris was sure Angie Martin told him she had been seeing Acton only for the past year.

"How is it Phyllis knows nothing about this proposed deal?" asked Morris. "She just gave us a tongue-lashing . . . insisting it never existed."

"It's not my place to speak for Phyllis," said Compton. "But I'm not sure how familiar she was with any of Melvin's business activities. As far as I could see, he kept an iron hand on everything he did."

"Mr. Compton," said Detective Fannin, "think carefully . . . then tell me again why you failed to tell the police about the casino deal between Mr. Newton and Mr. Acton. Let me caution you to be entirely truthful."

Now Compton buried both hands in his shattered hair. He seemed to wait for a pool of resolve to fill before speaking.

Finally, he said, "I overstepped my responsibility as club chairman in discouraging it. I admit that. There is nothing in the articles of the club to keep a member from owning a gambling casino. But the old chairman, Cliff Roberts, with the sheer force of his personality, would have thrown a member out for even suggesting such an enterprise. I hated the idea myself. It's against everything the club stands for. I killed it, or did my best to kill it. I'm still nervous about my legal exposure for having done so—if the estates of either man were to take legal action. That's why I didn't mention it to you. That, and the fact the deal has been long dead . . ." The word *dead* gave him pause. But he forced himself to finish his thoughts. "I still can't see how the failed casino proposal could have affected either man's death." This time he didn't flinch at the word *death*.

"What if one of them was suing you?" asked Morris. "What if they were both suing you? You are a wealthy man. Would that have been enough reason for you to have killed them?"

Compton stood up from his chair.

"Morris . . . I'm shocked. You've been a friend of mine for twenty years—"

"And I can't remember your ever having lied to me before," said Morris.

Compton sat back down.

"There is a deeper truth. . . ." Compton faltered. He seemed to breathe out what faint youth was left in his face. "Gerald did recently threaten to sue me. He found out I had made the unfortunate mistake of calling the head of the gambling commission in Nevada. . . . I tried to discourage his allowing the casino. I'm sure it's not the reason the state of Nevada ruled against it. But I might have a hard time proving that. . . ." Michael couldn't seem to get enough oxygen. Morris found himself unable not to sympathize with an old friend. Compton suddenly admitted, "My own finances . . . at the moment . . . during this recession . . . are rather tight. Nothing we can't weather. But a large damage suit against me might be . . . awkward."

"Not so awkward as murder," said Detective Fannin.

"No," Compton whispered, shaking his head in despair. "I do apologize, Morris. I simply hoped the casino controversy would not have to come out."

"It may have had nothing to do with their deaths," said Morris, "but people have been killed for a lot less than millions of dollars. What did your lawyers advise you to do?"

Compton bit his lip. "I haven't turned it over to my lawyers. No suit has been filed against me. Lawyers complicate everything. And they are hellishly expensive in New York."

Morris asked, "Did you know Melvin and Gerald once asked Eddie Hayward if he would be interested in the club job at the casino golf course?"

"No," Compton said firmly. "And while I am confessing my indiscretions . . . I have another one to admit. I can't bear the son of a bitch . . . defending Masters champion Eddie Hayward." For the first time, he almost smiled.

"You are standing at the end of a long line," said Morris.

"What more can I say, Detective Fannin?" Compton asked, his hands too nervous to release each other.

"I want to talk with you much more extensively. After I talk with the head of the gambling commission in Nevada."

Compton could only agree with a nod of his head.

"I would also like to speak with your wife," said the detective.

"Is that truly necessary?" Compton was able to get to his feet.

"Yes."

"I'll send her down," he said, reluctantly. He made his way up the stairs, a very lonely figure of a man.

Morris waited until he disappeared into his suite of rooms.

"You remember Angie Martin overheard Acton fussing on the phone with Melvin Newton over a license. Angie said she and Gerald had only been seeing each other *for the past year*. Compton says this casino deal has been dead for *two years*."

"Shit, I didn't catch that," said Detective Fannin. "But I find it difficult to believe Mr. Compton would kill them both over a potential lawsuit. There just doesn't seem to be enough *passion* in his motive. When you put a gun directly to a man's head, and when you drive a letter opener into a man's heart . . . you don't only want to kill him, you want to *annihilate* him."

"Well said." Morris nodded his agreement.

Sullivan said, "I think a large elephant just ran through the cottage . . . but we'd better be careful not to chase him and step on a silent asp."

"Spoken like the true dragon lady," said Morris. "And sound advice."

Aeriel Compton, tall and thin and entirely in control of herself, came down the stairs without so much as touching the banister. She nodded to them all and sat without being asked.

"May I tell you what I know about the matter?" she asked Detective Fannin.

"By all means, Mrs. Compton."

"In September . . . I remember it very well, for we had just come home from London . . . Michael advised me that Gerald Acton was threatening to bring a very large suit against him. Michael was concerned. The recession has ravaged the real estate market in Manhattan, and that is the essential core of our family holdings." Her hands settled on her thin lap without so much as a twitch between them. "Michael advised me that he had, indeed, discouraged Gerald Acton and Melvin Newton from financing a gambling casino in Nevada. That he had, on one occasion, called the gambling authorities in Nevada to discourage the project. And that he had certainly overstepped his authority as chairman of Augusta National. I was concerned. I was not alarmed. I *am not alarmed*. My husband did what he thought was correct. If there are to be legal repercussions . . . let them come. To imagine that Michael would kill two men over such a matter is the depth of absurdity."

"Did either of the two men—or their wives— ever bring up the matter with you?" asked the detective.

She quickly shook her head. "No. Absolutely not."

Her voice was pleasantly soft, but Morris did not doubt the steel resolve behind it.

"Aeriel," asked Morris, "did Michael mention the golfer Eddie Hayward . . . that he might have been a party to the deal?"

She made no expression while she thought.

"No. Decidedly not. I would remember it. Michael does not have much respect for Mr. Hayward, even as the defending champion of this tournament."

"He is not alone," admitted Morris. "Do you

have any opinions about what might have happened to Gerald and Melvin?"

It was an unexpected question, and Morris could not imagine where it came from.

Aeriel Compton thought for as long as a full minute.

"I doubt that business matters were significant to what happened. I would imagine the motive for both murders—" she did not falter over the word *murders*—"was extremely *personal*. It would not have been difficult to despise either man. I can tell you that Michael and I are only staying in Melvin Newton's cottage while our own cottage is being renovated." She added, quickly, "There is not a more lovely person in New York City than Louise Acton—or one whom I admire more."

Aeriel Compton stood in one graceful movement.

"Thank you," said the detective. "If you or your husband should remember some further details that might affect this investigation, please—"

"We will certainly do that, detective." Aeriel Compton mounted the stairs without looking back.

"So, what do you think?" asked Detective Fannin.

Morris could only shake his head. "You'd better get a full accounting of the Comptons' financial status. It might be far more precarious than he suggested. New York real estate is on its ass. Just ask Donald Trump."

"I'll do that immediately," said the detective.

"It's illogical, but possible . . ." said Morris. "Michael first threatens to throw them out of the club, which is overstepping his authority. Then he helps persuade the state of Nevada that the casino is a bad idea. . . . Better check and see if the Comptons have any real estate in Nevada . . ."

"You don't mean a gambling casino in Reno?" said Sullivan.

"Possibly. Or maybe they have enough other holdings in the state—enough to give them serious clout."

"I'll check it out," said the detective.

"Excuse me if I don't buy it," said Sullivan. "This powerful man from an old, powerful New York family, so fears a lawsuit . . . and a pretty tenuous one, it would be my guess—and I've been the object of a few lawsuits—that he kills two members of his own club? I don't think so. I bet he has his own lawyers from here to Rockefeller Center. He could keep it in the courts until everybody was dead."

"Maybe his entire empire is coming down around his ears," said Morris, "and any scandal within this club would reverberate all over New York City. Maybe Acton and Newton were tight with the banks holding Compton's notes. A good man might kill to keep his family empire."

Sullivan raised one eyebrow in absolute skepticism.

"So who killed them?" the detective asked her.

"I agree with Aeriel . . . somebody who hated them," said Sullivan.

Morris said, "Maybe Michael has hated them

for a long time . . . for an entirely different reason."

"Now you might be onto something," said Sullivan.

"And the lawsuit was just the last brick on the load of malice," said Morris.

"Could be."

"Could be," echoed Morris.

"You two can run down all the old feuds you can dig up," said Detective Fannin. "I'm going to put a match to the Compton empire and see if it burns."

"I'm for taking a nap, John Morris," said Sullivan. "Are you game?" She stood on one smart leg.

"I promised Tom Spears I'd meet him in the bar," said Morris. "He has something he wants to show me."

"Nothing like a better offer," said Sullivan, with one raised brow.

Morris turned the rental car through the allée of magnolias.

"It won't be long—I'll be driving that Japanese car right between these babies . . . for a solid bunch of money," said Spears. "They say they'll run the ad all over the world . . . during next year's tournament. I can't wait. I'm tired of being broke, Morris."

"I know the feeling," said Morris. "Where's the warehouse you keep your paintings in?"

"Down by the river. It was a nineteenth-century textile mill. But it's getting gentrified. Luckily, I have a cheap, long-term lease. The developers keep trying to buy me out. Now I'll be able to hold them off . . . until I find myself someplace on this planet that's home."

The warehouse stood like a fortress overlooking the Savannah River on its way to the Atlantic. All but the north end had been turned into condos. Spears led the way up an old, ugly flight of stairs and opened a door on the top landing into one long room with a very high ceiling. The peeling walls and scarred wooden floor had been ignored throughout this century. All along the walls stood blank backs of stretched canvases, crowded together like forgotten passengers on a ghost train.

"It was a turn-of-the-century towel factory," said Spears. "I hate to think how many lost souls worked themselves into eternity in this room." He walked the length of the room and pulled open a high curtain to an astonishing view, even through the filthy glass panes, of the Savannah River far below them.

"Good lord," said Morris.

"Oh, yes," said Spears.

Morris turned back to the room, now flooded with the light of late afternoon.

"I have no idea where to find our Ms. Sullivan," said Spears. "I made sketches of her over the years. But a couple of years ago I did pull all of them together; the question is where?"

"I'm glad you don't know," said Morris. "Now you'll have to turn all the paintings around. I want to see everything."

Spears stopped with his hand on the top of a large canvas. It was trembling.

"A few people have seen one or two of these

drawings and paintings, Morris. But nobody has ever been in this room before. Just look. Don't give me any bullshit."

"No," agreed Morris.

Spears turned the canvas around. Morris could not have imagined the scene . . . or the deft cross-hatchings of his style, in pen and ink. The men in the narrow room, which ran into darkness, were sitting on benches in varying stages of undress, careless of the eye that had caught them; Morris could almost hear the murmur of them, feel the tension among them; one with his head down was pulling on his golf shoes. The work was rough, deliberately unfinished. Morris opened his mouth in astonishment, but did not speak.

Most of the first canvases Spears turned were in pen and ink, or in pencil or charcoal, but then came one and then others in acrylic, and then there were many paintings in watercolor, all of them with the same bold draftsmanship, painted with great freedom and rawness, none of the fake, insipid stuff of so many modern sports illustrators, with their splashes of color across famous jerseys in lieu of true emotion. Morris loved the great, open, wind-blown links of Scotland, sun-shattered and undominated, with the dark ghosts of old men in their tattered sweaters, carrying the burden of other men's clubs all their lives, and not a line of sentimentality on the surface of the paintings.

Morris said, "Did you ever meet a wonderful artist—he did early work for *Sports Illustrated*. Had a tiny little walk-up studio off Fifty-seventh—"

"John Groth," said Spears, with a great smile on his face. "He painted me when I won my first Masters. Got me interested in trying it myself."

"Shit, I remember the painting," said Morris. "It went with a terrific profile by Herbert Warren Wind."

"A wonderful man, John Groth," said Spears. "And of course, you're right. I imitate him with every stroke of the brush."

"No . . ." said Morris, looking at the face of a thin old bartender in a pub he knew in St. Andrews; he knew it by the unfinished sign over the bar, and he knew the bartender, too, but the painting carried the dark joy of all the great pubs of Scotland. "You owe John Groth no more than John Groth owes Honoré Daumier."

"Morris, you fucking amaze me. Do you know painting?"

"Oh, hell, no. But I loved to have a drink with John Groth. *Sports Illustrated* has never known his equal, and he's a greater painter than he is an illustrator. I don't know a damn thing, Tom, but I know that to be true. I loved going up into Groth's tiny studio and making him poke through the great accumulation of canvases he never tried to sell or do anything with. He just threw them in rolled-up piles, unequaled drawings of Hemingway in Cuba and in Spain that ought to be hanging in museums. He painted an elephant race in India. He painted bloody stick games between American Indian tribes. He's been everywhere. Seen everything. Tiger hunts. Cliff divers in Mexico. He's a kind and generous man. He introduced ignorant me to his own heroes: Daumier, who also started out as an illustrator, in France; and Thomas Eakins; and Eakins's great American contemporary, Winslow Homer; and George Bellows with his wonderful drawings and paintings of hellish boxers and dream tennis parties at Newport; and Bellows's teacher, Robert Henri; and William Glackens and John Sloan, and that's about the limit of what I know very little about, old man. I know this: you are damn good. I can't tell you why I know. But I do."

"Goddamn," said Spears. "I should have brought you up here years ago. Even if it's all bullshit, I love it."

"You've never tried to do anything with your work?" asked Morris.

"I gave one or two things to friends, old caddies in Scotland. They liked them."

"I don't know beans about the art world, Tom. But I know somebody who does. And she would help you: Jerusha Benefield."

Morris could have sworn he blushed. There was no doubt Spears cleared his throat before saying: "She's a real painter, Morris. I was in their apartment once, in New York. They had a party for Augusta National members in the city. I was passing through and was invited. I couldn't believe the quality of her work. I didn't even know she was a painter until I asked about an unbelievable painting of the ocean . . ."

". . . At night," said Morris.

"Yes."

"I've seen it. It's unforgettable."

"I'm not in that league," said Spears.

"You're in a different league. But I'm telling you, it's a major league. You must know it. You wouldn't have kept after it so many years."

"I seemed to be able to get better . . . even with these hands," admitted Spears, holding up his arthritis-stricken right hand.

"I don't mind asking Jerusha for her advice about what you should do with your work," said Morris. "You know she is leaving New York to live in Paris?"

"I didn't know," said Spears, more alarmed than he meant to reveal.

"Edgar is in a state about it," said Morris. "She's going to take up her painting again. She says she can't do it in New York, that she needs a life for her work."

"Edgar's a fool not to go with her," said Spears.

"He says he can't live anywhere but New York . . . that he's an Easterner to the last."

"He's a fool," said Spears.

"I'm not sure any man can look at her . . . and then get to know her . . . and not be half in love with her. If you tell Sullivan I said that, I will set fire to this warehouse."

Spears reached back for a canvas he had carefully passed over. The green of her eyes took Morris's breath away. She was wearing a green, formal, off-the-shoulder dress, and yet the painting was wildly raw and swirling and the delicate beauty of her face seemed to be whirled about by the sea of colors.

Morris looked at it for a long time.

He said, "Nobody could have painted that paint-ing who did not love her."

Tom Spears did not deny it.

"Someday, somewhere, she has to see that paint-ing," said Morris. "It will happen. One day."

"You have to promise me, Morris, you won't say anything about it. . . ."

"Reluctantly, I promise. I was never the world's greatest journalist, but I've always kept my prom-ises."

Spears breathed his relief. Then he walked to the far corner of the room.

"I remember where I put Sullivan. It just came to me; I gathered them up from various spots along the wall, from over the years . . ."

There were eight of them. And Spears turned them around suddenly, as if time had moved through the room in an instant.

Julia Sullivan was a kid with her long hair, her head swung to one side, laughing at the damn world. The pen-and-ink face seemed almost able to speak. Spears had caught her eyes and her brows and the play of her lips, all of it free and laughing in the rapid pen-and-ink cross-hatchings. Then she was looking over Monty's head, her chin resting in his hairline, which was wildly Irish. They seemed to be singing some drinking song, as Irish as his dark hair. Morris laughed aloud to hear them. She was sitting on the terrace at Augusta National in one of the old wooden chairs, and she might have been the mistress of Baron Prosper Jules Alphonse Berckmans, looking over his nineteenth-century nursery. She was standing, her face caught in a great crowd surrounding a golf green below them, all of their expressions drawn to the moment, but hers bold and careless of the golfing gods. She was sitting alone in the bar at Augusta National and her hair mixed with the dark quietude of the room until they had the same quality of sadness. Morris saw her that way only once, the year Monty died. She was swinging a golf club in an improbable, hilarious way, imitating some poor chap to the glee of a semi-circle of writers, Walter Edwards among them, younger, laughing in spite of himself; Morris found his own great bulk at the back of the semi-circle. She was offering up a toast and all the others, old friends from the golfing/writing wars, were lifting their glasses to Tom Spears himself, with the hint of a trophy beyond him. And Sullivan was hugging Morris's own neck in the last scene, sitting on the front hood of her favorite antique automobile. Morris did not brush the tears from his eyes.

CHAPTER NINE

Morris walked the eight canvases into Newton Cottage. If he met Julia Sullivan, the game was up. The Georgia National Guard couldn't keep her from looking at the sketches under his arm. But the living room was empty.

I could have a body under my arm, thought Morris, and who would ever know it? No problem for a simple murderer to come and go in Newton Cottage. Where to put the damn things? It would be easier to catch the killer than to hide the sketches from Sullivan. He went up the stairs and through the door into their private suite of rooms. His luck held: no Sullivan. He poked into the closets and under the bed and behind the couch. Too obvious. There was a good space behind the refrigerator in the small kitchenette. Sullivan never went deeper into a kitchen than the front door of the refrigerator.

He was careful to see that no one had swept behind it in a generation. The sketches were safe enough there. Tom Spears had done his best to give the drawings to him. Morris would have none of it. He'd inflicted a check of five thousand dollars on Spears. Morris advised him: "You can either accept it or have your ass whipped." Spears looked down at his own two arthritic hands and laughed.

"It's nothing but a bargain," said Morris. "Never, ever, sell anything this cheaply again."

When would he spring the sketches of her youth, and of her former life with Monty, and of their own life together, on Sullivan? Morris grinned an evil grin. It was a great, unsuspected power to hold over her. She would breathe the air in the cottage and know something was up. But she could never guess what. He stepped into the bathroom and under the shower and sang even louder and more off key than usual.

Detective Henry Fannin was helping himself to a light beer from the downstairs refrigerator in Newton Cottage. "Caught in the act," he said.

"How about opening another one," said Morris. They touched bottles in a silent toast.

"So you survived the good bastards in the press tent?" said Morris.

"Barely."

"That's more than some presidential candidates have done. What are the boys writing?"

"The failed gambling license. And the Nevada gambling czar is having a tizzy with a crocheted tail.

What he doesn't need most is a double-murder among applicants for a gambling license."

"What else does he say?" asked Morris.

Fannin touched the cool bottle to the dark freckles on his face. "I talked to the Nevada man myself. He hesitated to say anything at first. Then I explained what we needed to know and why. Then he reluctantly admitted that Michael Compton had called him two years ago. He swears the call had nothing to do with the state's ruling against Acton and Newton's gambling casino. He said the local developer in the deal with them had been caught lying, twice, in applications for licenses. Both lies had to do with his silent partners, who were not acceptable to the state of Nevada. They had criminal records. So the state denied the gambling license."

"That ought to let Compton off the hook . . . for any legal damages."

"His lawyers should have been able to establish that with one phone call," said the detective.

"Remember," said Morris, "Compton never told his lawyers. No lawsuit had been filed against him, and he hated the complication and the expense of New York lawyers. He also thought the license issue was dead—until recently, when Gerald Acton threatened to sue him. Of course, we have only his word for all of that."

"It can be checked easily enough. I can't see Compton killing two men, if he wasn't worried enough to consult his lawyers," said Fannin.

"It doesn't make sense . . . unless he's not telling us *something else* that threatened him," said Morris.

"What did our splendid medical examiner, Dr. Karen Moseley, find out from Acton's body?"

"For one thing," said the detective, "Acton died quickly, but maybe not instantly. The blade barely caught his heart, and he could have lived several minutes." Detective Fannin held up a white golf tee with the Augusta National logo printed on it. "He was gripping one of these in his right hand."

Morris turned the tee between his thumb and finger. "Do you think he took it off the killer? Or was he carrying it himself? People finger golf tees, buckeyes, paper clips . . ."

"Did you ever see Gerald Acton fingering a golf tee?" asked the detective.

Morris thought. "No." Now who did, from time to time, finger a golf tee as a talisman? Somebody. He couldn't think who it was.

"It's possible Acton pulled the tee out of the killer's jacket," said Fannin. "He was stabbed and was being turned backward into the Port-o-let, and he was clutching for anything. Maybe his hand reached into the killer's jacket or sweater and pulled the tee out of his pocket. It was in his right hand."

"Maybe the killer now has a torn jacket," said Morris.

"We've already checked the clothes of those who knew Acton well, especially those of you in this cottage."

"Do I have a ripped jacket?"

"No. But your gray slacks could stand a cleaning."

Morris smiled, and said, "Maybe Acton pulled the tee out of his own pocket. To tell us something."

"What?"

"That the man who killed him was a golfer. Or a member of the Augusta National club."

"It's possible. With a knife in his heart, it's more likely he was clutching for anything, in his own pocket or in the killer's pocket, or in the Port-o-let. The sharp end of the tee was bloody; Acton squeezed it so hard before he died, he buried it in his own palm."

"Cheerful thought," said Morris. "Your people didn't happen to find a golf tee on Melvin Newton—or near his body?"

"No," said the detective. "And they left no square inch of ground unsearched."

Morris thought about that. He had an idea, but it was hardly worth mentioning. "What else did Dr. Moseley find out from Acton's body?"

"Acton's liver was in rotten shape. It could have failed at any time. He never met a drink he didn't like. Dr. Moseley couldn't believe he wasn't having liver problems. Louise confirmed it this morning. Doctors warned Gerald he had to quit drinking. He ignored them, bullyboy that he was."

"So, Melvin Newton's heart was pure, and he was going to live forever, and Gerald Acton's health was in serious decline," said Morris. "No pattern there." The idea of a pattern reminded him. "Does Dr. Moseley have an opinion on whether the killer was left-handed or right-handed?"

The detective shook his head in exasperation.

"The angle of the letter opener into his chest suggests *left-handed*."

"Hell, none of us is left-handed," said Morris, ticking off the suspects in his mind.

"It's a guess, at best," said the detective. "The angle of attack was from above . . . no doubt about that. But it was also slightly from the left. Now, we don't know at what angle Acton was standing. If he was, indeed, below the door to the Port-o-let . . . he could have had his left side turned slightly away, especially if he was looking back toward the 10th green."

"And the shot that killed Melvin Newton was fired from his right-hand side," remembered Morris. "But the killer could have held the gun in either hand."

"Yes," said Detective Fannin. "But statistics, past studies of similar gunshot wounds, would suggest the gun was held in the killer's *right* hand."

"Terrific," said Morris, "an ambidextrous killer."

Fannin turned his palms up, helpless.

"I suppose there is one pattern," said Morris. "Neither victim had a chance to defend himself. Each attack was premeditated . . . sudden and lethal."

"True," said the detective. "No signs of a struggle either time. No flesh, or fabric, under Acton's nails. No serious bruises, except where his legs were crushed into the Port-o-let. And then he was dead in a few minutes. But probably not before he knew who killed him."

"Must have been a double shock," said Morris, "knowing and dying."

"Yes. Dr. Moseley is sure he died sitting down, the way his blood pooled, and other 'cheerful' indications, as you like to say, Morris."

Morris imagined the open door of the Port-o-let, the killer stepping out and down, driving the letter opener into the heart of the startled Gerald Acton with his *left* hand . . . then spinning him with his right hand and arm into the open door of the Port-o-let. It would take a sure athlete, with confidence in a sure left hand. Right-handed golfers control the swinging of the club with the *lead, left* hand. A lifetime of golf can make for a strong left hand and confidence in it around the handle of a club . . . *or a knife*.

"What are you thinking?" asked the detective.

"How it happened. What the dying man must have thought," said Morris.

"What a fool he'd been . . . responding to the phone call."

"Or maybe his last thought was just the face of the man who was killing him. Or the woman. It wouldn't have taken brute strength, just a certain athleticism," Morris said. "I've forgotten. Was Acton wearing his Augusta National blazer?"

"Yes. But it was not buttoned. If it had been, it might have saved his life. Stabbing through the jacket would have been a tough go with the letter opener."

Morris thought back . . . tried to remember the sight of Acton talking with Angie Martin. Suddenly he could see his billowing waist, the opposite of the woman's trim one. "Acton's green blazer was unbuttoned, okay, at least it was when he was talking with the woman engineer. I remember noticing the vast difference in their waists. The killer must have noticed the open jacket too. Or he would have come with a helluva knife."

"This killer hasn't missed anything."

"Or anybody," said Morris. "I don't think there is any doubt he, or she, *came to Augusta* with the idea of killing the two men. There was nothing spontaneous about the way either victim was led to his death. Maybe the site of Acton's death was not planned. Maybe something else fell through, and killing him in the Port-o-let was invented. I have an idea it was. And if it was, we have a clever and gutsy killer on our hands."

Henry Fannin had a sudden thought. "Do you suppose he originally meant to shoot them both . . . at the same time?"

Morris considered it. "I wouldn't be surprised. A walk at night. Deep in the woods. A long way from a noisy party. And the end of a deep quarrel among old friends—if either of the two victims could have been said to have friends. It was just good luck for the killer that the shooting of Melvin Newton was first considered a suicide. It's possible he meant the shooting at the edge of Eisenhower Pond to be somehow symbolic of the old chairman's death. . . ."

Morris thought again of his idea—it would bear checking out. "But I don't believe the killer originally meant to fake a suicide. I believe he also meant to kill Gerald Acton all along. . . . You could be right. That he first meant to shoot them both at the same time . . . It would have been such a shock to the second victim, when he shot the first one. It would have been easy—if you are into cold-blooded murder—to also shoot the second man."

"One big question," said Detective Fannin. "Is it over? Settled? Will there be any more murders?"

Morris shook his head. "I don't know. I thought so—after the first one. I thought one of Melvin Newton's peers evened an old score. And that would be it. But this last, daylight murder . . . the aggressive way it was done . . . The killer meant to leave this man Acton dead . . . and a message with him— of revenge. And maybe he hasn't finished yet."

"Shit," said the detective, shivering in the air-conditioned kitchen. "You make it sound entirely too believable."

"No other news?" asked Morris.

"Oh, yes. The White House called," said Detective Fannin.

"And what did the former first baseman have to say?"

"His aide said a 'thorough search' of the president's personal telephone calls and written correspondence for the *past two years* revealed 'no letter, no telephone call, to or from a Melvin Newton.' With 'no possibility' of a mistake."

"Oh, hell, no," said Morris. "We may lose a submarine, or a portion of an aircraft carrier, or 225 Marines from time to time, but there's 'no possibility' our government could misplace even one telephone call. Oh, hell, no."

"Newton's own personal secretary can find nothing . . ." said Fannin. "No record of any correspondence or conversation with the president. She didn't have his telephone number or even the address of the White House. In fact, she was obviously startled by the question."

"Is everybody stonewalling? Augusta-gate?" suggested Morris.

"You're terrible," said the detective, looking over his shoulder as if expecting the Secret Service to come through the kitchen window.

Morris squeezed his own big hands into one mass of knuckles. There were small things he had forgotten to ask himself. They worried at his lapsed memory. All his life he had regretted not keeping a journal. And never more than this week.

"What's going on in here . . . a kitchen-cabinet debate?" Julia Sullivan patted Henry Fannin and hugged Morris as if she hadn't seen him in years.

"I don't know, but you should come into the kitchen more often," said Morris.

"Fat chance," said Sullivan. "My idea of a home-cooked meal is Chinese takeout." She looked at the grin on his face. "What are you hiding, John Morris? What are you two villians plotting?" She looked into the innocent face of Detective Fannin. "It's not you," she said, "it's *him*." She pointed a finger at Morris.

"We just have the modest problem of a double murderer among us. Nothing serious," said Morris.

She drowned him with the disbelief in her eyes, then looked around the kitchen as if she expected to see a long-hidden mistress of Morris's, baking bread.

Morris avoided her stare while telling her what Detective Fannin had learned from the autopsy and from the Nevada gambling czar. And about the detective's idea, that maybe the murderer had intended to shoot both men the first night.

Sullivan thought about it. "I like it. Remember, Louise Acton told Walter Edwards that Gerald feared an 'old friend' . . . that he said, 'Nobody can hate like an old friend.' "

"I remember," said Morris. "I also remember Louise didn't mention any of that when she was first questioned. She said then . . . that Gerald answered, 'ridiculous,' when she asked him if he believed that Melvin Newton had killed himself. She quoted Gerald as saying—curiously—'I guess it proves we were right all along.' What 'we'? And 'right' about *what* or *whom* 'all along'?"

Sullivan said, "I think two of the 'we' he meant had to be Gerald and Melvin. Melvin's death must have proved they—he and Gerald—'were right' about something . . . or somebody."

"Yes," said Morris. "Except they were—excuse the expression—dead wrong. Or Gerald would be alive. Remember, Gerald also said to Louise, 'I've got my own gun, and I know how to use it.' He just didn't know when to use it. Or against whom. What he thought he and Melvin were right about . . . they must have been wrong about. If that makes any sense."

"It does," said Sullivan. "No doubt Gerald Acton thought the wrong man killed Melvin Newton. Or he would never have trusted the killer on the telephone, and gone alone to the 10th green."

"All of that hangs on our trusting Louise Acton," said the detective. "Gerald might never have said any of those things."

"True," said Morris. "I should be able to doubt Louise. But I can't. That's dangerous business in a murder investigation. You'd better doubt even yourself."

Sullivan was shaking her head. "Louise wouldn't lie. Even to save herself."

"Excuse me while I hold on to all my doubts—about everybody," said Detective Fannin, putting down his empty beer bottle and easing toward the kitchen door.

"Something besides murder is going on in this cottage," Sullivan shouted after him, "and you detectives are not entirely off the hook." She turned around. "And you are very much on the hook, John Morris." She forced him to look into her blue eyes until he laughed.

Morris intended to follow up on his idea about Melvin's murder, but it could wait. He wanted, for a while, to get the hell away from death and dying. "Let's go see some golf, Sullivan. It's a game that can break your heart, but it's too cruel to put you out of your misery with simple murder."

"Okay." She took one of his large arms in both of her hands. "I think I am going to like whatever is going on in this cottage . . . if it doesn't kill me."

Morris bit his lip to keep from smiling.

The colorful fans strung out across the golf course, under rain-heavy clouds, were in no way concerned about murder. They were all sure they would live forever. Not just the college kids sitting in their jeans on the grass along the pond at the par-3, 16th hole, as they had done for a generation, but the old and the young followed their eyes up the fairways and through the trees and thundered their hands together to signal a birdie putt by a new or an old favorite player. Time, or death, did not exist for them on this Saturday afternoon in April.

Sullivan and Morris lost themselves in the deep affection of the crowd for the tournament. They grazed among the leaders. The solid, human fireplug of a Welshman, Ian Woosnam, began the day having to make a rare, left-handed pass at an iron shot when his ball came to rest beside a tree on the first hole.

"See," said Morris. "Golfers are an adaptable lot, from the left side and the right side; the detective says you can't say the same for murderers."

"You don't think friendly Ian Woosnam killed the two of them?" said Sullivan.

"Nope. He only murders the golf ball."

The Augusta course extracted further revenge from the wee Welshman when he hooked his drive into an unplayable lie on the difficult 5th hole and dropped two strokes to par.

In the twosome ahead of him, old Raymond

Floyd, with the touch of a lesser god, stroked a curling, fifteen-foot putt from the fringe into the cup for a birdie two, to go nine-under-par. Floyd then stopped a wedge shot ten feet from the hole on the lovely little No. 7, and Couples, for the second time, flew an iron shot directly into the hole only to have it spin back one foot from the pin. Both made their birdie putts, leaving Floyd one stroke clear of Couples and leading the field.

Morris and Sullivan enjoyed the sight of the two great American players in the same twosome.

Couples easily reached the No. 8 green and drew even with a birdie, only to have Floyd tickle home a treacherous ten-foot birdie putt on No. 9.

Once again Amen Corner had the last word, as Floyd attempted to recover from a bunkered shot on No. 12. His sand wedge came up short of the hole. Sullivan closed her eyes when he drew back his putter: it didn't help; he missed the putt for a bogie four. She kept her eyes wide open on the next hole, but that didn't help either; Raymond three-putted for another bogie on the always deceptive 13th green. Then Floyd chipped improbably into the hole on No. 14, and Couples and he left the green tied . . . but not for the lead.

"Here it comes!" warned Morris. Rain clouds rolled down over the golf course, sending sheets of water flying among players and spectators and TV towers.

"It's pretty cozy under here," said Sullivan, snuggling against his wide shoulder under their blue umbrella.

"Don't get any ideas, there are forty thousand people out here watching us," said Morris.

"All sissies; look at them run," said Sullivan of the masses of fans fleeing hopelessly among the trees.

The little Australian strongman, Craig Parry, with forearms like Popeye's, walked off the 14th green under the round shelter of his own umbrella, two shots clear of Couples and Floyd and the field. Woosnam, a hole behind Parry, suffered back-to-back double bogies, dropping to six-under-par. The four of them would have to finish their rounds in the morning before playing Sunday's final round in the afternoon. Another Australian, Ian Baker-Finch, with the classic swing and a British Open Championship, did finish at nine-under-par, with a splendid 68.

Sullivan and Morris, huddling together like displaced persons after a great calamity, walked toward the clubhouse along the 18th fairway, moving among the stream of fans as colorful in their rain suits and under their umbrellas as poppies blowing in a field. They stopped to check the great scoreboard by the 18th green.

"Look at 'your boy' Hayward. I don't believe it," said Sullivan.

"He's not 'my boy,' " said Morris, "but then, neither was Hitler, and he's in all the history books." Eddie Hayward had finished the third round before the rains came, shooting a gutsy 69, his six birdies wiping out three bogies, leaving him one shot off the lead in defense of his Masters title.

"The bastard may defend his championship yet," admitted Morris. "If he does, it will be absolutely impossible for anybody to inhabit the same planet with him. But you've got to give him credit for a helluva effort."

"Don't worry," said Sullivan. "He'll claim enough credit to break a small bank. Let's see what 'your buddy' has to say."

Morris tilted the umbrella from over her head, sending the rain momentarily in her eyes.

"Careful. There is room for one large man to sleep on the couch in our suite."

Morris quickly settled the umbrella back over her head.

Hayward had already met with the press. Walter Edwards told them that he stayed so long after the last question had been asked, they had to throw him out of the room. "You'll find him at the bar, all modesty," said Walter.

Sullivan led the way into the crowded clubhouse and spotted Eddie holding forth in the bar. Modesty was nowhere in sight.

Tom Spears rolled his eyes at them both.

Sullivan offered a wet cheek to be kissed.

Morris was careful not to squeeze Spears's arthritic right hand; Tom's left hand worked a golf tee through his tortured fingers with practiced ease.

"The bullshit is deeper in here than the rainwater is out there," said Spears. "But the guy shot an amazing round of golf. He birdied *all four* par threes. I don't think even Nicklaus ever did that. But I wouldn't bet on it. Nicklaus did every great thing that can be honestly done on a golf course."

Morris, unusually quiet, managed to get a pair of honest Scotches into his and Sullivan's chilled hands.

Eddie was saying, as if the world couldn't wait to hear it, and, indeed, the world couldn't: "Shortest putt I had on a par three was fourteen feet . . . on No. 13. Drowned it from forty bloody feet on No. 4. . . . Must've broke the length of this bar . . . straight in the damn hole. Ran it down the length of the green on six. Didn't even step it off. Had to be fifty goddamn feet. Ran it *up* the green on No. 16. Damn Nicklaus didn't make that great putt of his from that far out, the last time he won. . . ."

Sullivan whispered to Morris and to Spears, "Got his round in there with Nicklaus's. Next he'll be working in Hogan."

"If Hogan had ever putted like that," Hayward said in his next breath, "he'd have gone around this fuckin' course in nothin'."

Sullivan and Morris and Spears laughed so hard together, the crowd at the bar, even Eddie Hayward, hushed to see what the fuss was about.

"What the hell's so funny, Morris?" yelled Hayward. "You bettin' on some flat-bellied kid to win this thing?"

"I am," said Morris. "But you shot a very great round of golf."

"I don't-need-yore-ass to tell me that," Eddie said, slurring his words ever so slightly, after what must have been a quick blizzard of bourbons. He was lifting a fresh one to the unlovely smirk on his mouth. "Here's to everybody who didn't get struck by lightning . . . or killed in a Port-o-let." Eddie smirked more broadly into the embarrassed silence at the bar. Now members and guests were turning their backs on him and resuming their own forced conversations.

Eddie pushed his way through the crowd, but his elbow met solid resistance from Morris, who did not budge out of his way.

"We can always count on you to make an ass of yourself, Eddie," Morris said, his formidable bulk giving not an inch.

"What's it to you, Morris? You're no member around here. You're just another past-tense sportswriter."

"One thing he can't be is a jerk," said Sullivan. "You've got a copyright on that position." Her hot eyes dared him to answer her back.

"Why don't you just enjoy a great round, Eddie," Morris said, not wanting to deck the defending champion of America's favorite golf tournament.

Eddie said, "What's the big deal? A guy gets hisself offed in a Port-o-let. It's damn funny. He was a nasty bastard, anyway."

Morris could only shake his head in disgust; it was a bush league thing for Hayward to say, but it was true enough.

"I wonder if it was funny to the man who killed him?" Sullivan asked seriously. "Maybe he did it for kicks."

Hayward turned to stare at her. "You accusing me . . . you . . ."

Morris put his big forearm across Hayward's throat, cutting off his words. "Better hush and go along, Eddie. I'd hate to see you playing the last round with your throat in a cast."

Eddie pasted on his best smirk and pushed away from Morris and out through the crowd.

"We former champions are a swell lot," said Spears.

"I know one who is," said Sullivan, giving him a full hug around the neck.

"Do you think it's possible, Morris," asked Spears, "that someone killed them for sport? Someone out of his mind?"

"No," said Morris. "Someone had a deep hatred. Someone came here to kill them both. I only hope he—or she—has gotten enough satisfaction."

Sullivan shivered, from the damp and from the thought, spilling a bit of Scotch down the side of her glass.

"Excuse me, you two . . . I see my agent," said Spears. "He's been dodging me for two years, and now that I have an okay to do my commercial, he comes looking for me." He eased his way through the crowd, holding his glass as high as his head.

"Let's get out of these wet clothes," Sullivan said, tugging at Morris's sleeve.

"Is that an invitation?"

"If you're up to it, old man."

Morris said, "Let's take a short rain check—if you'll excuse the expression. As long as we're already wet . . . are you game for a scavenger hunt in the dark?" Before she could say no, he added, "How are you fixed for a flashlight?"

"You want to go back out in this?" She pointed at the rain falling against the window.

Morris smiled, as if offering her a chance of a lifetime.

"Why not?" said Sullivan, squashing one soaked-through shoe with a wet foot. She moved through the crowd and stuck her nose against the window. It was plenty dark out, but the rain had tapered off to a drizzle.

"I don't suppose you would entertain the question, Why?" said Sullivan.

"It's a crazy idea," said Morris. "I'm not even sure what it will tell me if I find it. Any sane person would wait until daylight. But it's bugging me."

"We can't have that. I bet we can borrow a flashlight from the club. What are we looking for?" Sullivan forgot the damp and the chill with the excitement of the search.

"I'll tell you as we walk along," said Morris.

Sid Norton was still in the pro shop and had one of the big six-cell flashlights, which he lent them.

"What the hell did you lose out there, Morris? I'll have the ground crew find it for you." Sid seemed more than slightly curious.

"It's too small for them ever to find it," said Morris. "And I know right where it is," he lied, "if it's still there. Thanks for the light. We'll bring it right back."

"Just drop it off in the morning. I'm about to call

it a night." Sid looked old and tired and in need of a drink.

Morris led the way with the light. The drizzle slid off the umbrella and around them, as if they were finding their way in the gloaming across a links course in old Scotland.

"What, Morris? What are we looking for?"

He told her.

"Good Lord, man. You're insane. There must be a thousand of them left on the course."

"We're not going on the course." Morris led the way, with the round shower of a light cutting through the rain, toward Eisenhower Pond.

"It's creepy," Sullivan said as they moved under the great dark shadows that were pines. The going was slow. It seemed the pond was miles away.

They stepped onto fairwaylike turf, and there was a soft splash in the night, and Sullivan grabbed Morris's arm, sending the beam of light jerking berserkly over Eisenhower Pond.

"The geese," Morris said as the beam caught the pair of them on the water like dancers on a moving stage.

Morris swept the light along the near shore, stopping on the yellow police tape that still cordoned off the low site where Melvin Newton had lain facedown in the pond.

"I don't think we are supposed to disturb the ground here," Sullivan said as they stood over the low rectangle of yellow tape.

"We're not going to look on the ground," said Morris. "Even if it had been pushed into the turf, they would have found it. We're going to look along the edge of the water. It would float well enough."

"If it's there, we'll never spot it. It's too small. It might be all the way out in the middle."

"It's possible. I wouldn't be shocked if a bass swallowed it for a bug," said Morris. "Fishing in this pond is like fishing in an aquarium. Eisenhower liked it that way."

Leaning over the edge of the water, following the now shortened beam of light with their eyes, they forgot the rain drizzling off the umbrella.

Both of them shouted a word! "Damn!" . . . when a frog jumped into the water, from right under their noses.

"I think I'm wetter than I was," said Sullivan.

Morris caught his own breath. "You don't need a gun out here in the dark, you could scare a man to death."

He reached with his hand into the water near the edge, but it touched only the white tip of a quill, a float lost off some fisherman's line.

"Let's go back around to the other side of where the body was found," said Morris. He was wetter and colder and entirely out of confidence.

Not six feet from where Melvin Newton's head had lain under the water, Sullivan dropped to her knees and nearly scooped up the white object with both hands.

Morris stopped her. "I don't think there is any chance a fingerprint could have survived this long in the water. But we'd better not touch it."

Sullivan pulled a handkerchief seemingly out of

the night air and seined up the floating golf tee from the edge of the pond, where it was trapped by hanging leaves of grass.

Morris shined the light directly on it. The Augusta National logo was printed in green ink along the white stem.

"What does it mean?" asked Sullivan, holding it in the handkerchief like a precious stone.

"I'm not sure. But I'm betting it was placed in Newton's left hand before or after he was shot . . . and it floated to this spot." Morris lifted a small, broken stick out of the pond and stuck it in the ground to mark the place where they had found the tee.

"I don't suppose the police thought to look for anything floating in the water," said Sullivan.

"They had no reason at that time to be looking for a golf tee," said Morris. "If they'd found it here, it wouldn't have meant anything to them. But then an identical tee turns up in Gerald Acton's dead hand in the Port-o-let. Our killer, Sullivan, is trying to tell us something."

"What?" She handled the small, sharp tee as if it held the answer to the ages.

"I don't know. Something to do with this golf club? Or with certain of its members? Or with this tournament?"

Sullivan straightened up as if memory had lifted her by the nape of the neck.

"No, Morris!" She turned on him as though denying her own guilt. "He didn't do it! He would never kill anyone. Not cold-bloodedly."

"You saw the tee tonight—in his hand?"

"I should throw it back in," Sullivan said, lifting the handkerchief in both of her own hands.

"Don't jump to conclusions. We only know Tom Spears carries a golf tee like this one . . . and fingers it—maybe without even realizing it."

"Maybe—tonight—it was just accidental . . . that he was playing with a golf tee. Maybe he never does."

"Sorry to remember it . . . but at the party in Monty's honor, Spears had a white golf tee in his hand, working it between his fingers. It's strange what the mind remembers."

"You said it yourself, Morris. It doesn't mean a damn thing." Sullivan handed him the tee wrapped in the handkerchief, as if it had dishonored them both.

CHAPTER TEN

"Here I am, Morris. What is it you want to tell me?" Tom Spears sat on the banister of the back porch. The rains had blown away. It looked to be a perfect Sunday for the last round of The Masters golf tournament.

Morris opened the handkerchief. The golf tee lay absurdly in it.

"I don't think you have a one-of-a-kind there, old man."

"No," said Morris. "Gerald Acton died with one just like it in his left hand. We found this one last night, floating in the pond where Melvin Newton was shot to death. Know anybody who's always palming a golf tee?"

Spears opened his own left hand to reveal an identical tee, then shook his head at Sullivan. "I can't believe you two have decided I'm a killer, because I'm always carrying a golf tee. It's just a habit. And it helps keep my fingers active. I like to think it slows my arthritis. I doubt that it does." Spears shut his mouth, as if he heard himself talking too earnestly.

"The tees don't prove a damn thing," said Morris. "But I don't doubt how they got there. *Who* put them there is another matter. I wanted you to know we're giving this tee to Detective Fannin. And we'll tell him where we found it. And we'll tell him that you have a habit of fingering an identical tee."

Spears thought about that. "So, what do you want me to do, think up a phony reason for carrying a golf tee?"

"The true reason will do fine. We just want you to know what we're up to. Double murder doesn't respect even old friends," said Morris. "We also thought you might have some insight into the meaning of the tees."

"I have one insight: I didn't kill the bastards," said Spears. "There have been times I would have been tempted."

Sullivan touched his arm. "What do you think the tees mean? Why would the killer leave them behind?"

Spears thought about it. He spit over the rail of Newton Cottage's back porch. "It could be a coincidence. That tee could have been thrown in the pond by some innocent golfer. People throw things in the water for the hell of it." Spears thought again. "But you're probably right. It's not a coincidence.

And maybe the killer wanted me to have this conversation . . . not with you, but with the police. It's no secret I'm always juggling a golf tee. I do it without even thinking about it. But a killer might think about it."

"Very possible," said Morris. "But it's a thin piece of evidence. If it were more damning, we would have given it straight to the police . . . your being an old friend or not. Maybe the tee meant something else to whoever left it. Maybe there is a bitterness for the Augusta National logo we don't understand."

Spears thought about that. "Maybe," he said. "So you two aren't buying me as a double murderer?"

Morris shook his head. "How can you buy anybody as a killer? Much less an old friend. But then, murder is rarely logical."

Spears smiled. "So, I'm not *it* . . . yet. But you're not letting me off the hook?"

"The police just searched my own closet," said Morris. "None of us is off the hook until the killer is caught. You don't have any other thoughts as to what the tees might have meant?"

"Analysis is your line of interest, Morris," said Spears. "But isn't it typical of serial murderers to leave a signature at the scene? Maybe I've watched too many movies."

" 'Serial murderers'?" said Morris. "Jesus! I don't pretend to know their psychology. Maybe they do give each death a personal touch. Maybe that's even true for some ordinary, garden-variety, human killers. Which I believe is what we have here. I think somebody among us had a hate on for at least two old acquaintances."

"And maybe the golf tees help spell out the hatred in a code we don't understand," said Sullivan.

"Maybe," said Morris.

"I think it's true," said Spears, holding his own tee up as if it could speak to them. "Remember: you start the game with a tee in the ground."

"Indeed," said Morris.

Detective Fannin took the handkerchief as if it were wrapped around a gift for a crown prince. "How far was it from the body?"

"Oh, maybe ten feet," said Morris. "We marked the spot at the edge of pond with a small stick."

"It could have come from anywhere," said the detective.

"Oh, yes," said Morris. "But it hasn't been in the water long. The white paint, the green logo are still fresh."

"You don't doubt the killer put it in his hand . . . before or after he shot him," said Fannin.

"No."

"Why?" The detective peeled the handkerchief away until the golf tee was looking at him.

"That's the question. Sullivan's right. It's a code the killer laid down that we don't understand."

"There were no prints, except Gerald Acton's, on the other one. I doubt any hint of a print survived for days in the water on this one," said the detective. "I understand all members of the club have access to these tees."

"Oh, yes. And I expect anyone else who has access to the clubhouse could have picked them up in the pro shop," said Morris.

"We come back to the same question," said the detective. "Why?"

"Tom Spears made a good point: in golf, the game doesn't begin until you put the tee in the ground."

"And you say Spears is always fingering a tee just like this one."

"Yes. He's in his room. You can talk with him yourself. He says playing with a tee helps keep his fingers active. He hopes it slows the effect of his arthritis, but he doubts it. It's just a habit that, he thinks, maybe the killer noticed."

"To cast some suspicion on Spears?" said the detective.

"Possibly. But as I told him, that would be faint evidence. I think Sullivan is right: it's a code to the killer's hatred that we can't understand."

"You think the killer has to be a club member," asked Fannin, "for the logo to be that important to him?"

"Or her. But there are no female club members," said Morris. "The tee doesn't help much there: it's a member, or a player, or a former friend, or a combination of the three. The killer isn't a stranger. A stranger wouldn't have had the access . . . to the grounds or to the victims. Well, a stranger could have killed Acton, but that makes no sense at all."

"If only this tee were a tape recording," said Fannin.

"Then the world wouldn't need detectives," said Morris. "What more have you learned about the Nevada caper?"

"Nothing that helps," said the detective. "Melvin Newton's chief financial officer faxed me all the documents he could find on Melvin's attempt to open a gambling casino. Turns out there were a few. Phyllis didn't know about Melvin's idea for a casino. And she had no idea about any of his business plans. Gerald Acton's lawyer found a handful of correspondence in his files on the subject of a casino. Both the financial officer and the lawyer said they tried to discourage their bosses from any involvement in gambling. Turns out getting a license was just as tough as they predicted it would be. In fact, impossible. There was an official letter of application for a gambling license in Nevada from both men, dated *two years ago*. There were a couple of queries to banks from both men. There was one note from Newton to Eddie Hayward, setting up a meeting in New York. And a sizzling letter from Acton to Michael Compton, complaining of his flat rejection of the idea of a gambling casino owned by a club member. All dated two years ago. Acton didn't threaten a lawsuit, but he hinted at it. There was no correspondence on the subject later than two years ago in either man's file. No names were mentioned of fellow club members, other than Michael Compton, or of golfers, other than Eddie Hayward. Nothing in any of the material we didn't already know.

"Oh, yes," said Detective Fannin, barely getting his breath. "There is no record of any gambling property in Nevada owned by the Compton family. Michael Compton does have powerful friends in the state. But no one is accusing any of them of using undue influence to kill any gambling license application."

"Terrific," said Morris. "Tell me, how do you explain the fact that Angie Martin overheard Gerald Acton arguing on the phone with Melvin Newton about a license . . . and she had only been seeing Acton *in the last year*? How do you explain it if the casino deal had been dead two years?"

"I can't," said the detective. "I interviewed Ms. Martin again. She never heard the word, *gambling*. Maybe they were arguing about a liquor license."

"Maybe so," said Morris. "I've never believed in coincidence."

"I know," said the detective. "Look, I'm going inside to talk with Tom Spears. I would hate it, Morris, if he turns out to be our man." Fannin ran his freckled hand through his red hair.

"So would we all," said Morris. "Tell me . . ."

Fannin stopped with his hand on the handle to the porch door.

"Do you think it's over?" asked Morris.

The detective held the doorknob as if he could feel the answer. "I don't know. I'm scared to think about it. I won't rest easy until the tournament is over."

Morris started through the living room of Newton Cottage. Sullivan was meeting him over at the

clubhouse for breakfast. Sitting under a lamp, reading the *Atlanta Journal*, was Jerusha Benefield.

"I say, it's against all nature for anyone to look
so beautiful so early in the morning," said Morris.

She smiled, looking up with her emerald eyes.
"Morris, you will have to come to see me in Paris.
Who else can help me feel good when I haven't slept
all night?"

"It's a deal. Any country that lives on wine is my
kind of country."

"I saw the detective," said Jerusha. "Is there anything new about the murders?" She breathed the
word *murders*.

"Not really," said Morris. "A golf tee turned
up in the water near where Melvin was killed. And
there was a similar Augusta National tee in Gerald's
hand. Nobody can figure why. Do you have any
ideas?"

"A golf tee. One of the small, wooden tees." She
measured a small space between her long artist's finger and thumb.

Morris nodded.

"Surely it wasn't a weapon?"

"No," said Morris.

"Then you think it was . . . sort of a . . . calling
card," said Jerusha.

"Possibly," said Morris.

She folded her arms as if against the cold. "It
makes it all even more . . . deliberate," she said.

"Exactly," said Morris. "Have you and Edgar had
breakfast? I'm supposed to meet Sullivan."

"Edgar got up ages ago," said Jerusha. "I haven't

eaten yet. I'd love to join you. I was reading your old friend, Furman Bisher."

"How is he this morning?"

"Amusing."

"Bisher's serious, even when he's being amusing," said Morris. He had a sudden thought. "Before we eat, would you mind looking at something for me . . . a series of sketches, actually."

"Oh, really? Something you are thinking about buying?" Jerusha smiled her interest.

"Something I've already bought."

"I'm not very good at appraisals," said Jerusha.

"I doubt that," said Morris. "But I just want your thoughts about the work. No bullshit."

"Nobody would dare bullshit you, John Morris. You've got me curious. Let's see what you've bought."

Morris reached behind the refrigerator.

Jerusha laughed in spite of herself. "A lot of art-work would best be hung behind the refrigerator—especially my own," she said.

"Remember, no bullshit," said Morris. "I've seen your stuff. I bet it hangs in all the right places. I put these back here so Sullivan wouldn't find them. You'll see why." He began to prop the pen-and-ink sketches on the kitchen counter.

Jerusha Benefield stood in front of the first one with her hand over her mouth, and looked at it as if she were memorizing it. She did the same for each of the eight sketches before she said a word.

Morris would look at the sketches himself and then at her, not daring to speak.

"They are splendid, Morris," Jerusha said with no false sentiment in her voice. "I should think Julia Sullivan will faint when she sees them. I would. Who in the world made them?"

"Did you spot yourself in the crowd at the bar?"

"Of course I did." She put her hand again to her mouth. The sketch had caught her out of time, exactly, just the tilt of her head, her eyes all but green in the dark ink, lifting her own glass to touch Tom Spears's.

Morris had to bite his tongue, so as not to tell her about the extraordinary painting of her in the old Augusta warehouse.

She pushed against his shoulder. "Who did this work, Morris? It's taken years. And the artist has gotten stronger with every year. To catch sadness in pure ink is genius."

"I think you must be right," said Morris. "You know the artist: Tom Spears."

She put both of her hands on the kitchen counter in surprise. "Our Tom Spears?"

"The same," said Morris. "You wouldn't believe his work. He keeps it in an old warehouse here in Augusta, overlooking the river."

"I would kill to see it," Jerusha said, then caught herself. "I don't suppose that is an appropriate verb."

"We've got to make Tom show it to you. I want to see it all again myself . . . hundreds of sketches and watercolors. It's like one man's lifetime show. He's never sold any of it—until yesterday—and I had to twist his arm. He's never even exhibited one of them."

"What he has you can't teach. . . ." Jerusha said, looking at the sketches again with heightened interest. "To catch a person alive . . . without faking it. Oh, Morris, you will have to let me be there when you show these to Sullivan."

"It's a deal. Maybe we'll do it before we leave Augusta. You think his work is strong enough—"

"Yes," she interrupted him. "I don't have to see another thing he has done. I'm amazed. The strength of it gives me a chill. Any number of dealers would love to handle him."

"Help me convince him of that. Tom's hands, you know, are ruined for golf. Arthritis. Doesn't seem to bother his painting. He's knocked around. He was a very great player. He wasn't meant to be a club pro. I think he was meant to be a painter."

"Oh, yes. I'll take a selection of his work back to New York. I'll make him let me." She lifted the sketch of Sullivan sitting on the old wooden chair like a mistress of Baron Prosper Jules Alphonse Berckmans.

"Yes," said Morris, "I think you can do that."

"What do you mean?" She was more than curious at the conviction in his voice.

"I mean exactly that; I believe you can convince him to do it. I know he thinks your own work is wonderful and far beyond anything he could imagine doing." Morris offered no other indication of what he truly meant: that Tom Spears had been in love with her for years. If she ever saw his painting of her, she would know it immediately.

"What are you two hiding?" Sullivan asked before they had even sat down to breakfast.

Morris looked at Jerusha Benefield as if he couldn't imagine what she meant. Jerusha kissed Sullivan on the cheek, as she might have kissed a favored sister who was about to inherit a vast fortune.

Sullivan was puzzled, but pleased, and didn't try to understand it further.

Morris and Sullivan sat in the stands around the 18th hole, taking in the welcome sun, watching the six leaders complete their third rounds after yesterday's rain delay, all of them trembling for the championship, yet pleased to be alive and playing golf in Augusta in April. Fred Couples birdied two of his last four holes for a 69. He seemed almost to go to sleep under the lazy rhythm of his swing. It was odd to see him holding the club without a glove, Ben Hogan being the last man to win The Masters playing in his bare hands. Couples walked casually up the 18th fairway as if he were back home playing in a Sunday-morning foursome. He holed his second putt on the 18th green to stand eleven-under-par for three rounds. His mentor, old Raymond Floyd, completed his own third round in 71 strokes, to stand ten-under-par. Raymond climbed the hill to the 18th green with his short, short little steps like a postman making his rounds. He was all confidence and did not stand over the ball like a man with forty-nine-year-old nerves. The great Australian Ian Baker-Finch, and his talented young countryman Craig Parry, and the great English players Nick Faldo and Ian Woosnam, and Nick Price of Zimbabwe, were playing with resolution and were very much in the running to keep an American from winning the country's most beloved tournament for the fourth year in a row.

"Let's take a short nap and catch these boys when they tee it up after lunch," said Morris.

Sullivan gave him a slow stare. "Is that a proposition?"

"Well, I don't know," said Morris. "I'm not responsible for my actions when I'm asleep."

"Good."

The sun never shone brighter. The crowds seemed to have grown younger. Murder might have been banished from the planet. Morris leaned on his cane on the clubhouse terrace and felt superior to time.

"You're good, Morris, but not that good," whispered Sullivan.

"They say memory is the first to go," said Morris.

"I thought it was the *second* to go," she said with a laugh.

Morris ignored her. "A ham sandwich and a Bloody Mary and we'll tackle this course with our bare hands . . . just like young Mr. Couples."

"Maybe two Bloody Marys," Sullivan said, already one bite into her ham sandwich.

* * *

Young Mr. Couples, paired with Craig Parry, stood on the first tee, testing the wind with a patch of grass flung in the air. The game was on.

They could see Floyd bogey the first hole in front of them.

Sullivan held her hands over her ears as if to protect them from artillery fire as Parry bludgeoned his drive on the second hole. He easily reached the green in two shots, and took, for the moment, the tournament lead. But the oxygen went out of the air for Parry, and he gasped for his breath, and Morris gasped with him, while he missed his first and second putts on holes No. 3, No. 4, and No. 5, falling into a tie for the lead with Couples, who laid down pars as sure as railroad ties.

Old Raymond Floyd, up ahead, briefly took the lead himself with a stylish birdie on the par-5, 8th hole.

Couples played a brilliant bunker shot to save par on No. 7. Sullivan, on her best behavior, only smiled seductively.

And now Couples, America's "8-by-10 glossy," stood over a twenty-five-foot putt on No. 8 that was sure to break at least once and maybe twice, and it surely did, falling exactly into the hole for a birdie four. Sullivan gave Morris a high five, as if they had stroked it into the hole themselves. But that putt was only a preparation. Couples, ever hatless, his hair blowing in the light breeze, addressed a twenty-foot putt that was only impossible on the ninth green, which tilted like a destroyer in a high sea. Sullivan closed her eyes when he drew back his putter, but Couples stroked it up the steep incline, and it broke back nearly as far down as the twenty feet it first lay from the hole, curling impossibly into the cup for a birdie three. It was the first of several strokes that were to save the tournament for Master Fred Couples. Had the ball missed the cup, it might have spilled off the green into the fairway.

Sullivan opened her eyes at the explosion of cheers. "I can't believe he made it," she shouted.

"Believe it," said Morris. "It was easy. It only defied gravity. Game for the back nine?"

Sullivan was already gone through the hordes to the 10th tee. Morris took a moment to study the scoreboard. The defending champion, the unlovely Eddie Hayward, was still among the leaders, but had lost any hope of retaining his title by taking a quadruple-bogey 9 on the deceptively sinister 13th hole. Morris could imagine the rage on his face, but took no satisfaction from it.

The field was receding from the fair Mr. Couples. He seemed to yield to the pressure of the lead when he bunkered his second shot on No. 10. And his explosion from the sand left him ten nervous feet short of the hole. But he stepped up to the putt— of a length he had missed so often in other major tournament rounds—and drained it like a champion.

Sullivan clapped her hands above her head as if at an outdoor fiesta in old Mexico.

Fred Couples stood with his hands on his narrow hips on the 12th tee, as men have stood since Horton Smith won the first Masters tournament in 1934.

It was impossible to gauge the winds as they swirled over Rae's Creek among the great Georgia pines. And yet, Couples looked up as if the answer were written in the air. He threw a tuft of grass, which blew in every direction, telling him nothing. Finally, he pulled an eight-iron out of his bag, when the field to a man, excepting the human cannon, John Daly, would have needed a seven-iron. So often it had come to that moment at Augusta: Fred Couples, three shots clear of the field, and seven holes to play. And the first of them a bare 155 yards long, across Rae's Creek, as tame as the river Avon and as lethal to a man as "sin, the world, and the devil," this par 3, No. 12, a deadly interlude in the middle pew of Amen Corner, leading across Ben Hogan bridge, the one way to a certain immortality.

Tom Weiskopf, of the flowing swing and hot temperament, who four times finished runner-up in The Masters championship, once drowned three balls in this creek—which he could in places jump across—and with them his last hopes for a green jacket he would never wear.

Couples again tested the wind with a tuft of grass, and again it was blown to the four directions. Now he addressed the ball. And now he sent it into the air as high as a mortar shell. The ball was not ten yards from the blade of his club when Couples and Morris and Sullivan, and the ten thousand spectators standing in the trees and crowded in the bleachers, knew it would fall short of the green.

"Oh, shit," said Sullivan.

Couples watched, frozen in time and horror. No

ball since 1934 had landed short of the green on the steep incline and failed to spill down into Rae's Creek, provoking, most likely, a double-bogey 5 and the possibility of a fate worse than that. The drop zone was so dangerously near the green that a flip wedge could easily spin back again into the water, a memory Weiskopf would carry to his grave.

Morris watched the ball land and was amazed to see it settle, against all gravity, on the sharp incline. "I believe God knows something we don't," he said.

"Did anybody ever kiss God?" Sullivan asked, jumping in the air with animal delight.

"I don't think it's in the Scriptures," Morris said, shaking his head.

Couples kept staring at the white dot on the green slope, as if he could hold it there with his eyes. Now he took his time walking across Hogan Bridge to the green. He was too young to have seen the half-century of catastrophes on the hole. He walked to his ball, resting in midair, and addressed it with his wedge, over and over again, until Morris nearly screamed to hit the damn thing before it moved, and finally Couples lifted it gently to the green, where it rolled dead to the hole, leaving a tap-in for a par 3, preserving Couples's three-shot lead in the tournament.

Most every writer, and all the broadcasters, missed the truth of the miracle. The ground around the 12th green had been too wet from yesterday's storm to support a mower, and the grass on the incline had not been cut for maybe the only time in the history of the tournament. The two-day-old

grass tips had lived to save the momentum of a
would-be champion. Morris would look up the man
whose job it was to mow the grass, and he laughed
and wondered if the champion might want to split
the pot with him.

Couples, some of the casualness drained from his
stance, addressed his ball on the 13th tee. Tightness
crept into his swing, and he failed to draw the ball
around the dogleg, leaving it on the high side of the
fairway, behind a huge pine tree.

"Do you think he will go for it?" whispered Sullivan, as they leaned to see his exact lie in the light
rough.

"Not in this lifetime," said Morris.

Couples resisted the urge to draw a long-iron 225
yards to the green, over the same Rae's Creek, which
continued its treachery the length of the hole. He
pitched safely into the fairway and made his par 5.

"Let's skip No. 14," said Morris, "and watch
them play to the green on 15." Sullivan was game.

A spectacular roar erupted from the 14th green.
It was Old Man Floyd, they were to learn, hooding
a wedge and driving the ball into the steep slope of
the green, which it climbed and ran straight into the
hole for a birdie 3.

Couples, behind him, came away from the 14th
with a par 4. Length itself subverted Fred on the
500-yard, par-5 15th hole. Sullivan had to dance out
of the way of his ball, as his monstrous drive carried
the hill, only to run through the fairway and trickle
into the scattering of trees she and Morris had taken
refuge among.

"You might have kicked it back into the fairway," said Morris.

"What would he have done for me if I had?" asked Sullivan.

"Oh, no, he wouldn't," said Morris.

Couples walked back and forth where his ball lay, as if he could march the trees out of existence. This time there would be no laying up safely in the fairway. He pulled a long-iron out of his bag, and with no hesitation hooked the ball bravely around the trees and over the distant pond, only to see it roll off the green into the light rough of the collar. His pitch was not close. His putt was not good.

Sullivan made a terrible face. If it could have spoken, it would have been a scream.

Couples made his way to the 16th tee, holding to a two-shot lead. All of his practiced casualness had run down his arms and legs and through the spikes of his shoes into the still-damp ground, like an electrical charge. He bent over his ball on the tee, human and vulnerable, and pushed the iron into the upper right-hand bunker. In almost every Masters played since the lake was filled in front of the 16th green, it would have been impossible to explode the ball from that bunker and keep it within thirty feet of the hole, so steep was the incline of the green. But the still-faithful grass was wet and soft, and had grown longer since it was mowed in the morning, and Couples exploded the ball in the air with such touch, holding on to the club at the last with only his left hand, that it stopped innocently close to the hole.

"Oh, my," said Morris. Sullivan, for once, could only swallow her anxiety.

Two holes to play. And still Couples held to the two-shot lead over his old friend, Raymond Floyd, in the twosome up ahead. But he would have to summon his will one more time to save the championship.

Sullivan pushed their way among the fans on the high mounds behind the 17th green.

Couples left a wedge twenty-five feet below the pin. His approach putt was all fear and energy and ran four slippery feet above the hole. It was, again, the same length putt that had drowned all his previous efforts to win a major tournament. He gathered his will and ran the putt directly into the hole.

Sullivan breathed her last breath and fell against Morris, as if he would have to carry her up the 18th fairway.

The tournament was over. The 18th hole was a formality. Fred Couples, all youth, with his thick hair blowing to the four winds, walked into the standing applause, as had Horton Smith, and Sarazen, and Nelson, and Guldahl, and Demaret, and Hogan, and Snead, and Burk, and Palmer, and Player, and Nicklaus, and Watson, and Floyd, and Faldo before him.

Something about that list of names sent Morris's mind spinning, until it stopped on a name more famous than any of them . . . and then linked it with another, lesser name.

"Oh, shit!" he said, the pain as vulgar as the language.

Sullivan clutched his arm with both of her hands, fearful he had suffered some damaging insult to his health.

"It's just ... I always hate to see it end," said Morris. Now was no time, among all the cries and whispers of victory, to make a wild speculation, even to Sullivan. "All that's left," he said, "is the drinking and the singing." And the small matter, he thought, of a double murder.

There was plenty of drinking and singing in the clubhouse. Morris could almost hear the voice of Monty Sullivan, toasting the young champion and his spectacular wife; who could have known that Fred Couples's happiness would fade with the singing? But it was a popular victory. You could not tell that Couples's old friend and mentor, and one-time Ryder Cup captain, Raymond Floyd, had not won the cup himself, he was so happy for his protégé.

Club Chairman Michael Compton made a little impromptu speech. Even his reserved wife, Aeriel, followed the toast with a "Hear! Hear!" Sid Norton, his job as club pro once again secure, lifted a full glass of Irish whiskey, as much in defiance as in celebration; Morris was glad to see he was not drunk.

"The tournament's lucky," Tom Spears said into Morris's ear. "Fred's one of the good guys."

"Indeed," said Morris.

Edgar Benefield and his wife, Jerusha, waved at them from across the room; they might have been a couple celebrating a long, happy marriage, instead of preparing to take up separate residences six thousand miles apart.

The bartenders were heroic, filling the endless empty glasses, including their own. Morris looked over the crowd for the detective, but he was nowhere in sight. Sullivan, who had disappeared, caught Morris's eye. With her were the two widows, in appropriate black blouses. Louise Acton raised a brave smile as Morris kissed her on the lips. Phyllis Newton offered a reluctant hand.

"Oh, Morris," Louise said, running her hand through her short, dark hair, "I'm glad to see people happy."

"You deserve to be happy yourself," said Morris.

The glad noise was punctuated by a sharp, ugly voice behind Morris. He turned to see Eddie Hayward cursing a bartender for giving him the wrong drink. The apology from the old bartender, inundated with orders, didn't wipe the anger off Eddie's face.

Morris would have liked to dump the drink on his head. No fate could ever satisfy Eddie. He had played with all the guts you could ask for, finishing tenth, and except for the catastrophe on No. 13, would have had a run at defending his title.

"Kiss me, Morris," said Sullivan.

"In front of all these people?"

She kissed him instead. They might have been newlyweds in the happy chaos of a reception.

"Where did you find the widows?" Morris whispered.

"I went and dragged them out of their rooms,"

said Sullivan. "They need to be where life is happening."

"Yes," said Morris.

He turned at a loud, happy voice behind him, shouting to the crowd: "Let's drink to the great city of Seattle, home of The Masters champion!" The man shouting was not entirely sober. They drank to that. "Let's drink to the title going back West . . . where it belongs!" shouted the same man, provoking a sudden recollection in Julia Sullivan: the West . . . where this terrible story or murder seemed to lead.

"Morris, I think I'll go to the room now and change before dinner," said Sullivan. "Our widows didn't want to stay long." She moved to gather them up like a mother collecting her children.

"Sure," he said. "I'll make the rounds of the Old Guard, and come and change myself." It would give him time to talk with the detective about his theory, if he could find him.

Morris dropped by the pressroom and stood, watching old friends labor over ancient nouns and verbs. The room was strangely silent in this era of the word processor. In the old days, portable Royal typewriters would be beating out the prose like the rhythm section of a cheap band. It made him sad to miss the sound of it. The detective was nowhere in sight.

"Was it greatness we saw?" asked Walter Edwards, his gray hair leaning over his forehead, as if it, too, were struggling with his story.

"A great effort," said Morris.

"What is our champion, thirty-four? Well," said

Mr. *New York Times*, "Hogan found his greatness late."

Neither of them ventured to say that Mr. Couples would ever rival Mr. Hogan. But then, who would?

"Anything new with the murders?" asked Walter, looking over his shoulder at the hotshot crime reporter from the *Times*, back on his feet after his stomach illness, trying to explain over the telephone to the news desk the absence of anything happening on the murder front. He didn't seem to be finding a receptive ear.

"No," said Morris, truthfully. "I don't know anything new." What he had come to suspect was another matter, which preyed on his thoughts. Where the hell was Detective Henry Fannin when you needed help? With luck, he thought, his idea would amount to nothing but an attack of nerves.

Morris found his way again into the clubhouse, which had become considerably less crowded by the departure of the champion. There were only a few stragglers in the bar, all of them quiet with fatigue. No detective among them.

Morris stepped out onto the lighted terrace. The sun had escaped the day, leaving night surprised among the dark shapes of the trees. A terrific commotion came from over toward the cottages. Morris poled himself forward with his cane, his whole mind irrationally fearful for Julia Sullivan.

CHAPTER ELEVEN

Flashlight beams cut long patterns in the dark. Morris collided with a Pinkerton man rushing toward the clubhouse and held him up to keep him from falling.

"What's happened?" asked Morris.

"Fellow killed . . . under a car . . ."

Morris recognized the Pinkerton man, Barton, James Barton, who had stood guard over Melvin Newton's dead body. Barton's large head sat right down into his shoulders. He was excited and could hardly catch his breath.

"Who was killed?" asked Morris.

Barton shook his large head, nearly losing his cap. "Got to call an ambulance."

"For a dead man?"

Barton left the question in the air as he struggled on toward the clubhouse.

Morris followed the general commotion, which was coming from behind Newton Cottage.

"Just what we need, another body," he said to himself. He felt no guilt to be relieved it was a "man" who was killed and not a woman. God knows who? Morris recognized the curly red hair caught in a flashlight beam. "What happened?" he said to Detective Henry Fannin.

"Morris. You won't believe it. Eddie Hayward is lying dead under that automobile." He pointed toward a large, apple-red Buick.

"Jesus," said Morris, "that's *my* rental car. How did he get under there? Can't you get it off of him?"

"It was locked. We just smashed in a window," said the detective. "We'll roll it off. But not just yet. I want to get photographs. Eddie's plenty dead. We checked immediately."

Morris remembered Eddie's flash of anger at the old bartender less than an hour ago. Well, Eddie would have no more arguments with fate. "Who was driving the car?" Morris asked, suddenly fearful it might have been Sullivan, pulling the rental keys out of his pocket and handing them to Fannin.

"I don't know." The detective shone his own flashlight into the ghastly face under the left front tire; all the softness had contorted into pain and horror. "My guess—from the looks of him—both of his legs are broken. . . . He was hit more than once . . . maybe knocked down and then run over. It's not a pretty sight."

"No chance it was an accident," said Morris. "No innocent driver leaves a three-thousand-pound automobile locked and parked on top of a man."

"No," said the detective. "I've got Pinkerton men at both entrances of Newton Cottage . . . and just sent one, James Barton, to the clubhouse to call an ambulance—and to see that nobody leaves or enters."

"I ran into him," said Morris. He pointed to what had been Eddie Hayward. "How long has he been under there?"

"Not long. He's still oozing blood. The Pinkerton man, Barton, found him. He heard a noise—a shout—maybe fifteen minutes ago . . . about 7:30, give or take five minutes, he said. He didn't hear anything else, but drifted over this way. Saw the car at this odd angle. Shone his light under it. Blew a whistle he carries. I was in the parking lot at the clubhouse and came running."

"Well, the only people who wanted to kill Eddie are those who knew him," said Morris.

"All too true. Once again, we're not looking for a stranger."

"Listen, I have a wacky theory," said Morris, "but I need your help. . . ."

"It'll have to wait, Morris," said the detective. "I've got to deal with a body, not a theory."

"I understand. Have you seen the familiar body of Julia Sullivan?" Morris rarely used her first name, unless it was a crisis or some special moment.

"She's in the cottage. I saw her through the front

window when I shone my light inside. Does she also have a key to the rental car?"

"Yes," said Morris. "But it would be easy enough for someone to hot-wire it; it's a typical General Motors car."

"Maybe," said the detective. "It would also be easy to lift the key out of her purse. I've seen it lying in the kitchen myself."

"True," said Morris. "But the person would have to be in the kitchen. It seems to me you have your regular cast of suspects . . . and a murder as deliberate as the other two." Morris ached to tell the detective what he had come to believe.

Heels thudded down the driveway, and the tall, thin police photographer came running. He took his shots, looking over his hooked nose, as casually as if he were photographing a wedding. Detective Fannin made the cold-blooded decision to leave Eddie under the car until the medical examiner got there. Nothing was going to bring him back alive now. Dr. Karen Moseley got out of a sports car in a red jumpsuit that made her look about twelve years old. She gave Morris a kiss on the cheek. He thought, *nothing like a string of murders to make old friends out of new acquaintances.*

The detective gave Dr. Moseley the keys to the rental car. "Check him out under there first. See what it tells you. Then have one of the men back it off him."

She went straight to work, merely nodding her head.

"Let's go inside," said Detective Fannin. "And hear the cry of the innocent."

Sullivan welded her arms around Morris's neck as if to save him from demons in the night.

"What happened out there?" she asked in his ear. "They won't even let us on the porch."

"It's Eddie Hayward," said Morris. "He's dead. Under *my* rental car."

"I swear! I haven't driven it!" Her face might have been that of a small girl who had lost her lunch money.

"I know. This was no accident. The Buick is locked and parked on top of his head."

The room seemed to gasp. Morris looked away from Sullivan to see all of them in the cottage, standing in the living room, near enough to hear him. They all spoke at the same time, a collision of nouns and verbs and panic.

Detective Fannin, with his arms folded, waited for them to run out of words. "I want to speak with you—one at a time," he said. "We'll talk in the kitchen. Mr. Compton, let me start with you. I suggest the rest of you wait in your rooms. It goes without saying, no one is to leave the cottage until you've spoken with me."

Michael Compton stood, reluctantly, in a shirt with no tie and a pair of trousers with no belt. The whistle sounding in the parking lot and the subsequent noise and lights must have startled him out of his dressing room. Morris had never before seen him without his composure intact.

"Am I to come with you, also, Detective Fannin?" asked Aeriel Compton, already dressed for dinner in a dark blouse and silver pendant that flattered her thin, aristocratic presence.

"I'll send Mr. Compton for you after we've finished," said the detective. He nodded for Morris to follow them into the kitchen, saying to him quietly, "You might catch something I miss."

Morris nodded and followed after them.

The detective got straight to the point. "Where were you, Mr. Compton, between seven o'clock and seven-thirty?"

Compton held his arms away from his body, as if his state of undress spoke for itself. "I was just out of the shower and getting dressed. The phone rang once, and I answered it. Then I heard a whistle and shouting. The windows were up in my bedroom. It's too cool for air-conditioning." He stopped, as if he were talking too freely.

"Who telephoned?" asked Morris. The detective had not said he was to ask questions. But it came naturally.

"I don't know," said Michael, touching his hand to his mussed silver hair. "It was a wrong number."

"What time was that?" asked Fannin.

"I'm not sure. My watch"—he looked at his bare wrist—"is still on the dresser. Maybe it was seven-fifteen, a little later."

"A man's voice or a woman's?"

He thought. "A woman's. Definitely. I have no idea who."

"Who did she ask for?" asked Morris.

"Listen. It was a wrong bloody number. Nothing

else," said Compton. "She asked"—he thought about it—"for somebody named Walter. I had to think. There isn't a Walter in the cottage. I told her that."

"There's a Walter Edwards," said Morris.

"It was not his wife's voice," said Compton. "It was a *Southern* voice, not a New York voice. What the hell difference does it make?" He was put out by the interest in the phone call.

"Did your wife hear the phone ring?" the detective asked, ignoring his petulance.

"I have no idea. She was dressing, I suppose, or reading in her own room."

"Doesn't the phone ring in both bedrooms?"

"Yes. For God's sake, yes. You'll have to ask her if she heard it."

"Wasn't she curious who called?" asked Morris. He thought Compton might actually strike him, and that would have been a sight. The last of the New York elite, taking a civilized poke at a huge, past-tense sportswriter. Morris couldn't help grinning.

Michael saw no humor in it. "We haven't seen each other in the last . . . oh, hour. Since we came over from the clubhouse to dress for dinner. Aeriel was already in the living room when I came down to see what the fuss was about. . . . Another death." He avoided the word *murder*. "I can't wait to leave for New York. I've got a final committee meeting tomorrow," he said, as if reminding himself of his obligations to the tournament.

"Before the whistle," said Morris, "did you hear a shout? Or the lunging engine of a car? Or what might have been a car striking a man? Through your open window?"

Compton closed his eyes to heighten his concentration. "I might have heard a shout. I was watching ESPN, seeing what they had to say about the tournament. If I heard a shout, and I think maybe I did, I didn't pay any attention. And I wasn't aware of a car engine or of a collision. I'm sorry."

"Does it shock you that someone killed Eddie Hayward?" asked the detective.

"No. I mean, yes, of course it shocks me. I mean Eddie was an obnoxious man; it's easy to see how he could have enemies. I frankly admit I despised him."

"But not enough to run a three-thousand-pound automobile over him," said the detective.

"No." Michael ran his fingers through his hair, as if to sustain his composure.

"Did you go outside at all after seven o'clock?"

"I told you, I was dressing."

Detective Fannin left the question hanging in the air.

"No," said Compton. "I haven't left the cottage in nearly an hour. But you'll have to take my word for it."

"Did you take Eddie to the TV interview room after his final round today?" asked Morris.

"Yes." Compton touched his open collar as if the missing necktie left him vulnerable. "You know the defending champion must put the green coat on the new champion. Eddie was in a wretched mood. He was openly cursing the 13th hole and a

ruling he got there, some question about where his
ball entered the hazard; it cost him another two
strokes, on the way to a *nine*. I was afraid of what
he might say on television."

"Did he speak to you of the failed casino deal
since yesterday?" asked Morris.

Compton avoided his eyes. "No. I didn't speak
to him before this afternoon. He was furious about
the one hole, costing him a chance to defend his
title."

"That's all you talked about on the way to the
interview room?"

"We stopped at the bar for Eddie to get a drink.
A double Scotch."

"You had no sense that Eddie was nervous about
anything?" asked Fannin.

"As I said, he was furious. He thought we should
'plow up the goddamned 13th hole and start over.'
That kind of thing. I can't say I felt a drop of sympathy for him," admitted Compton.

"Did Eddie ever speak to you about the other two
murders?" asked Morris.

Compton shook his head as he thought, then
looked up: "Yes. After Gerald was found . . . dead . . .
I saw Eddie in the bar. Much later that night. He said,
if I can remember, 'Golf's a dangerous sport. All this
fake goodwill. Anybody in the game will fucking kill
you, even those who don't play. . . . ' He said something very like that. I asked him what he meant. He
said, 'Careful, or you'll find out.' "

"What did you think he meant by that?" asked
the detective.

"I wasn't sure. I'm still not. It seems likely he meant we were in danger. Certainly, we now know that to have been true . . . at least for Eddie." Compton looked down at his long, well-manicured hands, as if they held the answer.

"Do you imagine yourself to be in danger?" asked Morris.

Compton shook his head. "I don't know. I don't know what to think. After three murders."

"Thank you, Mr. Compton," said Detective Fannin. "I'm going to have to ask you and your wife not to leave Augusta without checking with me."

"I've got to get back to New York by Wednesday," said Compton.

"Maybe by Wednesday we won't need you. But I can't promise it. Please ask your wife to come down. If you remember anything else Eddie might have said, please let me know, immediately."

Compton turned, more fragile in his shirtsleeves, and went out the kitchen door.

"What do you think Eddie meant?" asked Fannin.

Morris said, "Sounds like he didn't trust somebody in the game of golf."

"A player, do you think?"

"If Compton was quoting him accurately, Eddie didn't necessarily fear a player. What did Eddie say? 'Anybody in the game will . . . kill you, even those who don't play. . . .' "

"I can understand Melvin Newton being caught

unaware," said the detective. "He was the first victim. Why weren't the other two more careful?"

"Who expects to be killed on a golf course, in fading daylight, with thousands of people making their way through the trees? And hundreds working on the grounds?" said Morris.

"Yeah, you're right . . . and who looks to be run down by an automobile in a private parking lot?" said Fannin.

"Gerald was maybe excited about meeting a young woman," said Morris, "and Eddie couldn't get the 13th hole out of his mind."

"Where do we go from here?" The detective might have been asking himself the question.

"Let me tell you what I think," said Morris, anxious to have the opportunity. "It won't take but a minute." It took three minutes.

"Oh, shit, Morris!" said Detective Fannin.

"I've already used the expression."

The detective turned over Morris's idea in his mind. "You could be right about everything, and it still does not tell us who killed the three of them."

"I hope that's true," said Morris, but he did not believe it.

"Let's talk to them all," said Detective Fannin, "then we'll check it out."

Morris nodded. It was awkward, suspending his own judgment. But the detective was right: even if what he imagined actually happened, what did it prove?

There was a tap on the kitchen door. Aeriel

Compton stepped inside the kitchen, as formally as a guest for high tea.

"Mrs. Compton, I have to ask you what were you doing between seven and seven-thirty P.M.," the detective said, as gently as the question could be posed.

"Reading," she said, "until the terrible whistle blew outside my open window. Then I came down to see what was happening."

"Before you heard the whistle . . . did you hear a shout from outside?" asked Fannin.

She shook her head, no.

"Aeriel, did you hear the telephone ring?" asked Morris.

She looked at him oddly, but didn't hesitate with her answer, "No."

"Doesn't the phone ring in both bedrooms?" asked the detective.

She nodded. "Yes."

"What were you reading?" asked Morris.

"Gibbons," she said.

"Which volume?"

"The second."

"The years of the Christian persecution. Unhappy times in the Roman Empire," said Morris. "Possibly you were so deep into that world, you didn't hear the phone?"

She thought about that. "It's possible. It's happened before. I'm used to my maid answering the phone. Do you know that it rang?"

Detective Fannin ignored the question, asking, "Had you spoken with Eddie Hayward in the last twenty-four hours? Or did you have the opportunity to hear him speak with Michael, or anyone else?"

Aeriel Compton touched her lips with a slim finger. "No. Michael did speak to me *of* him. He said he couldn't bear to think of Eddie Hayward repeating as Masters champion. I agreed with him. He didn't measure up to Bob Jones's idea of a champion—a wonderful player with a sense of sportsmanship. He was not an appealing man."

"To beautifully understate the truth," said Morris.

"I'm going to have to ask you if Michael was in his own room between seven and seven-thirty P.M.," said the detective. "In a court of law, you wouldn't have to answer that question."

Aeriel lifted her chin and looked directly at him. "I could not see through a closed door. But I knew Michael was showering and dressing and very likely watching the sports channel on television . . . to see what was being said about the tournament. If Michael says he was in his room, then I believe it . . . absolutely."

"Thank you, Mrs. Compton," said the detective.

Morris waited until the door closed. "I can understand her not hearing the phone ring. I've been in the office writing, in the old days, and not heard four lines ringing at once."

"Do you think she would lie to protect Michael?" asked Fannin.

"Of course. The question might be, Would she kill to protect him?"

Morris, I don't believe that woman killed anybody."

"Probably not. But don't doubt she is tempered steel."

Morris was surprised to see Sid Norton stick his shock of entirely white hair past the kitchen door, smiling under it with his drinking man's ruddy face.

"I didn't know you were in the cottage," said Morris.

"I was here in the kitchen, fixing myself a quick Scotch," said Norton, "when I heard the whistle blow. I went outside. But the detective, here, ran me back inside. It puts me in an awkward position, Morris . . . but I was here to meet Eddie."

"About what?" asked the detective.

"About a gun. I . . . He grabbed me at the clubhouse and said, 'Come over to the cottage. And bring the spare thirty-eight. I've got something to tell you.' I have no idea what he meant to tell me. That was about an hour ago . . . about seven o'clock. I got away sooner than I thought I could. I beat him here. And I brought the thirty-eight." Sid pulled the handgun out of his jacket. "I was waiting here in the kitchen when I heard the whistle."

"Did you hear a shout before that?" Morris asked, taking the gun, which had not been fired recently, and handing it to the detective.

Sid turned his head, as if it could help him recall a shout. "I don't know. The window's open. I heard voices. Maybe somebody shouted." He squinted his eyes. "Maybe I did hear a shout. But I'm not sure. If I did, it didn't mean anything to me."

"Did it shock you that Eddie was killed?" asked Detective Fannin.

"I can't believe it yet," said Norton. "Guys like Eddie . . . you don't think of 'em as victims."

"What do you mean?" asked Fannin.

"Eddie was the kind of guy who would get a man whipsawed in a bad bet . . . and take all his money and the car he was drivin', if he didn't look out. A dangerous man, Eddie. And a very nasty drunk."

"Was he drunk?" asked Morris.

"Oh, yeah. And he was dog-cussing the 13th hole." Sid laughed. "I got to say, that hole caused the most popular nine of the tournament. I don't know a player who could stand Eddie Hayward. I know I couldn't."

"Why did he want this thirty-eight caliber handgun?" asked Morris.

"He was afraid, just like the rest of us. I put a new shaft in his driver before today's round. A bit stiffer. Eddie has a quick swing. I think it helped him. We weren't buddies. Never have been." Sid light a cigarette. "But when I was working on his club, he hung around. We got to talking about the killings. If there would be any more. Neither of us knew a damn thing. But I said I kept a thirty-eight in the pro shop and a spare one in my car. He wanted to know if he could buy the spare thirty-eight. I said he could borrow it. Then I forgot about it."

"Did Eddie mention anything specific he was afraid of?" asked Morris.

"We were just talking," Sid said, looking for a place to dump the ash off his cigarette. Finally, he dumped it in the sink.

"So, what was Eddie Hayward frightened enough about to need a handgun?" asked the detective.

"What he said doesn't mean shit," said Sid. "You know Eddie and his big mouth."

Morris and the detective waited.

"He said he was afraid of Tom Spears," said Sid. "Now, that is ridiculous. Tom is one of the finest men ever to play in this tournament, much less win it twice. I think Eddie made some remark about Jerusha Benefield, and Spears grabbed him by the collar and threatened to whip his ass. Now, that I believe."

"What did Eddie say about Spears?" asked Morris.

"Nothin'. Except, he 'didn't trust him.' That he was 'finished and dangerous.' I told Eddie he was full of shit. That Tom wouldn't hurt anybody. Still, he wanted to borrow the gun. He said I better keep my own gun handy. That there were others 'as dangerous as Tom Spears.' It's amazing Eddie could play as well as he did in the tournament, no better than he was swinging, and I think he was really scared. Of somebody. And I don't think it was Tom Spears."

"Why not Spears?" asked Morris.

"He was just angry with Spears," said Norton.

"But he was scared of somebody. So am I. I just don't know who to be scared of."

Detective Fannin said, "You two tell me: Why would Newton and Acton consider hiring Eddie as their club pro if they built their casino and golf course? He would not have been a popular choice."

"Eddie isn't a popular choice as a dead man. He must have brought something we don't know to the equation," said Morris. "Maybe he had some pull with the gambling commission. Maybe he had some awkward information on both men."

"I could believe that," said Fannin.

Morris leaned with one big hand against the refrigerator. "Did anybody ever kill three less appealing people?"

"No," said the detective. "But when they strap you in the electric chair, they don't ask if you killed a sweet guy. Sid, did you see anybody here in the cottage . . . in the last hour?"

Sid nodded his head, yes. "I saw our chairman, Michael Compton, comin' in the front door in his shirtsleeves. . . . Had somethin' up under his arm . . . shoes, I think."

"When was that?"

"Must've been a bit after seven. Maybe ten after. I didn't look at my watch," said Sid.

"Did he see you?" asked Morris.

"I don't know. I don't think so. I just looked out from the kitchen. He seemed to be in a hurry. I didn't speak."

Morris looked at Fannin and bit his lip.

"Thank you," said the detective. "You'll be around the next few days?"

"I hope to be around a couple of more years," Sid said, smiling. "Of course, the club shuts down after the tournament. But I have plenty of work to get done before I leave for the summer."

"Thank you for your help," said the detective. "Morris, will you get Tom Spears?"

Spears's tan seemed to have grown one beat deeper in the Georgia sun. This time he was not fingering a golf tee.

"I was asleep," said Spears before they could ask him the first question. "I was on my feet all day. I walked the last nine holes with Couples. I was so drained, I felt like I'd played. I had a drink in the club. Came over here to my room and lay down and fell dead asleep."

"What woke you?" asked Morris.

"I'm not sure. A sound, maybe. It's too cool for air-conditioning. My window was up. It looks over the parking lot out back. At first, I thought I was dreaming. Then I heard voices and feet running. I stuck my head out the window. Couldn't see much. I put my shoes on and came downstairs. They wouldn't let us outside."

"Did you see Eddie after his round today?" asked Morris.

"Yeah. He caught me in the bar. Started in bitching about the 'lousy 13th hole,' which is a very great golf hole. And I told him so. I saw the shot he tried to make to the green. It was a ridiculous gamble for a man near the lead. Of course, it hit a tree and kicked in the woods. I told him it was his own fault, not the hole's."

"What did he say?" asked Morris.

"You wouldn't want to hear. Eddie said I reminded him of 'another asshole, always taking up for the golf course . . .' "

"Did he say who?"

"No." Spears shook his handsome head. "I had already tuned him out, anyway."

"What else did he say?" asked the detective.

Spears thought. "He was looking for Sid Norton. He didn't say why."

"Did you have an argument recently with Eddie?" asked Morris.

"No. I only told him I would whip his ass if he made another suggestive remark about Jerusha." Spears smiled.

"That's not an argument?"

"No. It was a promise. I could have done it, too, Morris. Funny, I can't swing a club with my hands. But they make good, solid fists."

"I believe it. What did Eddie say about Jerusha?"

"Just gutter stuff. About her moving to Paris. And what he was going to do to her in Paris. He was making an ass of himself in the locker room."

"Nice guy, Eddie," said Morris. "He would have been a good man, 'if there had been somebody there to kill him every fifteen minutes.' With apologies to Flannery O'Connor."

"Did you know Eddie was borrowing a handgun?" asked the detective.

"To protect him from me?" Spears laughed.

"Maybe. But to protect him from somebody. Did he mention to you he was afraid?"

"He couldn't swallow his own spit when I was talking to him," said Spears. "That was this morning, before he went out to the practice range to hit some balls. I just stopped in the locker room to wish good luck to some old friends, none of whom was Eddie Hayward. And Eddie started in about Jerusha."

"You didn't go outside from seven P.M. until half past," asked the detective, "and you didn't see anybody who did?"

"I was sleeping until sometime after seven," said Spears. "Something woke me up. Around seven-fifteen. And I came downstairs. That was it. I didn't have a chance to go outside or to see anybody who had been outside."

"Remind me not to piss you off," kidded Morris, his own big hand on Tom's back.

"I don't think you would need a handgun to protect yourself, Morris."

"Don't be too sure," said the detective. "Thank you, Tom. Please don't make plans to leave town without talking to me."

"No," said Spears, as he left the kitchen.

"Let's talk to the Benefields," said the detective.

"Why not. Do we take them one at a time?" asked Morris.

"Yes. Let's start with Mrs. Benefield."

Morris fetched her. "It's always a treat, walking down the stairs with a beautiful woman."

Jerusha laughed. "Morris, you can always make me laugh, even at the worst of times."

"That's the best time to laugh," said Morris. "You didn't kill the bastard, did you?" Morris was surprised that he could block out his own thoughts and talk as if they were going down to dinner.

"No." The fun went out of her gem-green eyes.

"No, what?" asked the detective, who stood in the kitchen door.

"No, I didn't kill him," said Jerusha.

"Did you know one of your friends threatened to whip Eddie for making a sexist remark about you?"

"No. Who?" asked Jerusha. "What did Eddie Hayward have to say about me? I hardly knew the man. And I couldn't abide him."

"He was just making an ass of himself," said Morris. "He was good at that. And at golf. He wasn't worth a damn at life."

"Who threatened him?" asked Jerusha. "Tell me, Morris."

"Tom Spears."

"Oh. He didn't actually hit him?"

"He didn't have to. Eddie shut up. But he was getting himself a handgun."

"To protect himself from Tom Spears? That's absurd," said Jerusha. "Tom's a perfect gentleman."

"But not a guy to go to 'fist city' with," said Morris. "We don't know who Eddie was truly afraid of. But he made it plain he was afraid of somebody in the 'game of golf,' not necessarily a player."

"But not a woman?" said Jerusha.

"He didn't make that clear. Why do you ask?" said Morris.

"You're talking to me . . . a woman."

"That's for sure," said Morris.

"What were you and Edgar doing from seven P.M. until now?" asked Detective Fannin.

She took a deep breath. "We made love," she said, embarrassed. "I know the maid will tell you we normally sleep in separate bedrooms, but we were together at that time." Now she was even more embarrassed, but determined to be frank.

Maybe to protect Edgar, thought Morris.

She might have read his mind. "Edgar has been so upset at my going to Paris. I'm still going," she insisted, as though they were attempting to dissuade her. "I fell asleep. It must have been just about seven o'clock. Edgar was sleeping too. I woke up with a terrific whistling in my ear. It was coming through the window. I was alone in the bed. I think I cried out. I know I did. Edgar came in from the sitting room and asked me, 'What's the matter?' I wasn't sure. There was a lot of activity outside. I put on a housecoat. And we came downstairs."

"Did Mr. Benefield hear the whistle?" asked the detective.

"I don't know. He must've. Or he heard me cry out. Or he heard both," said Jerusha.

"Had he been in your rooms all the time?" asked Detective Fannin.

"Yes. Or I'm sure he was. We went to sleep together. He woke up first. He was getting dressed for dinner, and letting me sleep until the last minute."

"Had Eddie spoken with either of you since Gerald Acton was killed?" asked the detective.

Jerusha thought about it. "I don't think so. I despised Eddie Hayward. And Edgar didn't care for him at all. We've known him for years, from the time when Edgar was still playing tournament golf. He had an unfortunate personality."

"Well said. At least our murderer is killing all the right people."

"That's quite terrible, Morris." Jerusha could not suppress a tiny smile.

"Are you afraid . . . for yourself or for Edgar?" asked the detective.

Jerusha drew her housecoat more tightly around her. "Yes. I'm afraid for us both. But even after three murders, it doesn't seem real. We eat breakfast and lunch and dinner and watch golf on a beautiful course and somebody dies. It's surrealistic."

"If that means, who can tell what the hell is happening? . . . you're right," said Detective Fannin. "Thank you for your help," he added. "Let me ask you not to fly off to Paris without letting me know first. And would you send Mr. Benefield down, please?"

"What do you think, Morris?" asked the detective.

"I think Edgar is crazy to let her go to Paris alone. But why did Edgar pick that specific time to make love to her?"

"It would be tough to convince a jury that anytime was a bad time," said the detective, allowing himself half a smile.

"The truth is, he could have woken up anytime. And been outside in a minute," said Morris.

"It's possible," said the detective.

There was a tap on the kitchen door. Edgar Benefield came inside with the sure step of an athlete. Like Spears, his tan had gone a beat darker in the Georgia sun, and the gray at his temples was more pronounced.

"Care for a cup of coffee?" asked Morris. The pot had announced it was ready to be served.

"Indeed," said Edgar.

The detective poured three cups. All of them took it straight.

"To 'better times than these,' " quoted Morris, lifting his own cup.

The other two drank to that.

"Your wife told us you two were sleeping together at seven o'clock," said Detective Fannin.

Morris had to smile at the euphemism.

"Yes," said Benefield, with no embarrassment.

"When did you wake?" asked Morris.

"I didn't look at my watch." He looked down at his empty wrist. "It's still on the bedside table. But it must have been a little after seven o'clock. I went in and turned on the local TV news. They had gotten as far as the weather."

Which would make it nearer seven-ten, thought Morris, *a very clever alternative to being down in the parking lot, killing Eddie Hayward*. "What is the forecast for tomorrow?" asked Morris. "Not that any of us are going to be flying out of here."

Benefield hesitated. "More of the same, I think. I wasn't really listening. I was waiting for the sports, to see what they would say about the finish of the tournament."

"They'll be saying plenty on the ten-o'clock news," said Morris. He looked out the kitchen window. The detective's men were keeping a small army of reporters and cameramen away from Newton Cottage. Morris could imagine CBS crews unpacking their TV equipment. Killing two anonymous Augusta National members was one thing, but killing the defending champion of the Masters tournament, who had finished among the top ten players in this year's field, was something else.

"What did you hear from behind the cottage?" asked Detective Fannin.

"Several shrieks of a whistle," said Benefield, his cup rattling on his saucer. "Then my wife cried out. I think the whistle must have woken her. I ran into the bedroom to be sure she was all right. I could see a flashlight outside and heard feet running and heard cries. I didn't know what was happening."

"What did you do?" asked the detective.

"We went downstairs. We went out on the porch, but the Pinkerton man wouldn't let us in the driveway."

"What did you think had happened?" asked Morris.

Benefield shook his head like an aging aristocrat, deliberating the history of his family. "I had no idea.

But I was afraid it was—" He didn't finish the sentence.

"Another murder?" said Morris.

He nodded yes.

"Who did you imagine had been killed?" asked Morris.

Benefield sat his cup and saucer on the counter. "I had no idea."

"You didn't imagine it could be Eddie Hayward?"

"No. I didn't imagine it could be any specific person."

"You competed against Eddie. In fact, you came within one stroke, as I remember, of beating him for the National Amateur. I also remember, Eddie was just as nasty then as he was as The Masters champion. How do you remember him?" asked Morris.

"The same as you," said Benefield. "He was not an honorable man." He might have been speaking of one of the early, lesser Romans.

"Then you weren't shocked to hear he was murdered?"

Benefield put his hands in his pockets to consider it. "No. I suppose I wasn't. He didn't belong among the champions; even the Augusta National members would agree with that."

"Do you think a member killed him?" asked Morris.

Benefield shook his head. "I can't say. But I agree with what you and the police have said: Why would a stranger kill any of them?"

"Why? That's the question," said Morris.

"Had you spoken to Eddie today?" asked the detective.

"No," Edgar said with finality. "I avoided him whenever I could."

"You won't have to avoid him anymore," said Morris.

"Did you leave your rooms anytime this evening, after you woke up from your nap?" asked Detective Fannin. *Nap* was a nervous euphemism for his time in bed with his wife.

"No," said Benefield, with the same finality.

"Well," said Morris, "I believe this 'unlovely champion,' as somebody identified him, parked my automobile on top of himself."

Benefield could only smile at that unlikely possibility.

CHAPTER TWELVE

Morris and Detective Fannin went up the stairs to find Julia Sullivan, who was sitting with the two widows in Louise Acton's suite.

Louise and Phyllis Newton sat on opposite sides of Sullivan on the long couch, as if to divide the gruesome events of the week by two.

More likely, thought Morris, they despised one another. All of his sympathy was with Louise, who stood to kiss him on the cheek. Sullivan kissed him on the other cheek and patted his arm like a small boy who had done his homework without being fussed at. Phyllis Newton continued to sit with her "tragedy" wrapped around her as securely as her late husband's estate.

"What can you tell us, Morris?" asked Louise.

"Not much you don't know. Eddie Hayward is dead. Run over by my rental car."

"Someone took my keys out of my purse," said Sullivan, holding up the black purse as dark evidence.

"When did you last see them?" asked the detective.

"I haven't seen the keys since we rented the car. Morris drove us over here. Anyone could have taken them. I've left the purse all over the cottage, and the clubhouse, too, for that matter."

"Where were all of you around seven o'clock?" the detective asked, including the three women in the question. He couldn't imagine any of them as likely suspects.

"I was in my room," said Phyllis Newton, as if her presence was of paramount importance. "You may call my lawyer in New York. We spoke on the phone three separate times before he could understand what I wanted to know."

Morris thought, *And what she wanted to know was how much was she now worth.*

"Julia and I were together," said Louise Acton. "As soon as Julia was dressed for dinner, she knocked on my door. We were just talking, remembering the good times, and looking to the good times to come." She smiled at Julia.

"We heard the whistle and the commotion in the parking lot," said Sullivan. "We ran down the stairs, Louise in her bare feet. It was a huge confusion. We spilled out on the porch, but the Pinkerton man told us to stay inside. That's it, Morris, from the home front." She looked to Morris as though he were the presiding detective in the matter. Unspoken in her eyes was the question: "What do you know?"

You'd be surprised, thought Morris. He did not miss the edge in her voice of what else she might have to tell him.

"Morris and I have to make a phone call," said the detective.

"We'll be in our rooms," said Morris to Sullivan. "I'll come get you in a few minutes."

Her curiosity threatened her patience. "I'll swap ideas with you," she said.

"Do you want me to call?" asked Detective Fannin. The look in his eyes said, "I'd rather have a barbed-wire enema."

"He's your buddy," said Morris.

"But it's your idea."

"Get him on the phone, and I'll talk to him," said Morris. In truth, he had met the man twice. Even interviewed him once when he was researching his book on the Ryder Cup and wanted to check out an anecdote that had to do with the Walker Cup, which was named after the man's grandfather. Turned out the anecdote was true and made it into Morris's book.

This time the detective's call was intercepted by an aide. It took more than a little convincing to have him put the president of the United States on the phone to a young detective in Augusta, Georgia.

"Please . . . just tell him I'm calling," said Detective Fannin, in his most formal voice. "Tell him we've had another of the golf murders at Augusta

National. Someone has killed the defending champion of The Masters. The president is helping us." With the last sentence Fannin was stretching the truth from Augusta, Georgia, to Washington, D.C., and he rolled his eyes at Morris as if he expected to be arrested for subverting the White House.

The aide put Fannin on hold, and during the long wait the detective propped up his legs in false bravado and rested his telephone elbow on an end table. Suddenly he sat up as if he had been called to attention: "Thank you, Mr. President, for speaking with me . . ."

"Yes, sir," said the detective, "we've had another murder. Someone has killed defending Masters champion Eddie Hayward. . . ."

"Yes, sir . . . No, sir," said Fannin.

Morris could only imagine what the president had asked him.

"Yes, sir . . . it's possible you might help us . . . on a vital detail. If I might turn the phone over to former Associated Press writer, John Morris . . . Yes, sir . . . that John Morris, the golf writer . . . I'll put him right on, sir. . . ." Detective Fannin handed the receiver over to Morris with the relief of a man passing a five-hundred-pound weight.

"Morris." The president said his last name as if they were old friends.

"Yes, Mr. President. Thank you for speaking with us."

"Terrible news about the golfer, Hayward. What happened to him?" The president sounded truly disturbed.

"Someone ran him down with an automobile."

"It couldn't have been an accident?" asked the president.

"No, sir. Whoever did it left the automobile on top of him." Morris squinted both eyes at giving the unfortunate selective detail to the sitting president.

"I see." The president did not hesitate. "How can I help you?"

"Sir, you remember . . . the first victim here—Melvin Newton—had recently entered your private telephone number in his pocket calender—"

"Yes, but I did not know the man!" The president's voice was suddenly as hard as an executive veto.

"Yes, sir," said Morris, "but may I ask you if you have had any recent dealings with the publisher and president of Benefield House . . . Edgar Benefield?"

There was quite a pause on the White House's end of the line.

Then the president said, "Morris, is this conversation on the record?"

Morris bit his lip. "Mr. President, I'm retired from the Associated Press. And I'm not speaking here as a journalist, but as a friend of Detective Fannin's. I don't know that our conversation would ever need to be made public. But then . . . even private conversations—however innocent—have a way of becoming public when the subject is murder."

There was another pause. "I understand," said the president, a certain resignation in his voice. "Yes, I have had recent conversations with Mr. Benefield. In fact, I am negotiating with Benefield

House to publish my memoirs when my presidency is over. I've long admired the publishing house, and I went to school with Edgar's older brother. My father knew his father. In fact, our grandfathers knew each other. I do plan to stand for reelection, Morris. You can see that any book negotiations—which came about rather accidentally when Edgar and I ran into each other at a state function . . . you can see how the negotiations, at this time, could be awkward for me. We don't plan to publish the book until I am out of public life. Nor do I intend to take any advance money before that time."

"Yes, I understand, Mr. President," said Morris. "Detective Fannin will have to speak for himself, but very likely your negotiations with Benefield House could remain confidential information."

Fannin was nodding his head with heavy enthusiasm.

"Why do you ask if I know Edgar Benefield?" the president asked, all curiosity.

Morris told him.

Another long pause. "I see," said the president. "It's all possible . . . but a bit of a reach, don't you think?"

"Yes, sir, it is that," said Morris.

"And entirely out of character," said the president.

"Yes, sir. Entirely. But then, murder so often seems to be," said Morris.

"Please let me know what you find out," said the president. "I'll leave word to patch you through to me immediately." He did not find it necessary to insist again on confidentiality.

"Yes, sir, Mr. President. And we do thank you."

"Morris?"

"Yes, sir."

"I did enjoy your book on the history of the Ryder Cup. I know my grandfather would have gotten a kick out of the story you included about him and how the Walker Cup came about. I enjoyed it myself."

"Thank you, sir."

"Good luck to you." And the line was dead.

Morris put down the receiver in his hand, but not the weight of regret. He gave a quick summary for the detective of what the president had said.

"Oh, shit," said Fannin.

"That and worse," said Morris, sick at heart.

"You believe that's what happened?" said the detective. "You don't agree with the president that it's 'a bit of a reach'?"

"I believe it happened. Even though it's madness," said Morris. "Do you want me to come with you, to confront him?"

"Yes," said Detective Fannin. "Do you think he's still dangerous? Or has he finished what he came here to do?"

"I can't answer that," said Morris. "But any man who kills three other men is dangerous . . . even if he's asleep. I want to check on Sullivan first. And let her know what to expect."

"While you do that, I'm going to call over to the

clubhouse. I think we need a backup . . . just in case. Stop back here, Morris, after you talk with Sullivan."

He nodded.

Morris rapped on the door to Louise Acton's suite. She answered it herself. The room behind her seemed to be empty.

"Where's Phyllis and Sullivan?" asked Morris.

"Phyllis went to her room to lie down," said Louise, opening the door wider for him to come inside. "Sullivan wanted to see Jerusha about something."

"In-her-rooms?" Morris ran the words together in his concern, pointing with his cane down the hallway.

"Yes," said Louise. "Is something the matter?"

Morris shook his head and poled his way down the hall.

He rapped on the door to the Benefields' rooms. No one answered. He hit the door again with the head of his walking stick. Nothing. He tried the handle. It turned, and the door opened to an empty room. He walked through the sitting room into both of the bedrooms. The beds were made. The clothes were hanging in the closets. Jerusha's large everyday purse was lying on top of a vanity table. Morris looked inside the purse: her credit cards and driver's license were there, with a modest stack of twenty-dollar bills. But around him the room was empty. The other bedroom, the bathrooms. Nobody. It was as if Edgar and Jerusha Benefield had left town with no forwarding address. Probably they were all downstairs, having coffee, thought Morris. But he stretched his bottom lip tautly over his teeth and bit it with concern. He looked again in the sitting room. Nothing on the coffee table, just copies of *Architectural Digest* and *Southern Accents* magazines, seemingly untouched. Nothing on the sofa or the cushions of the chairs. Nothing at all to indicate Julia Sullivan had ever been in the room. Maybe the Benefields were at the clubhouse, having drinks. Maybe Julia was with them. He caught himself thinking of her first name, as he rarely did, and yet, there was no call for crisis . . . he told himself.

Morris left the suite, not bothering to close the door behind him, forgetting the existence of Detective Fannin in his own rooms. He swung his stiff left leg down the stairs. The big living room was empty. But he heard a noise in the kitchen.

Morris shoved the kitchen door open, startling Aeriel Compton, who dropped an empty coffee cup, which shattered on the hardwood floor.

"Oh, goodness!" She held her hands to her thin face, as if she had destroyed a family heirloom.

"I'm sorry . . ." Morris bent as though to catch the shattered pieces in his free hand. "I'm looking for Sullivan. It's important. Have you seen her?"

"Yes," Aeriel said, smoothing the sides of her skirt, her composure again intact.

"Where?" Morris startled Aeriel Compton again, taking one of her slim hands in his own huge one.

"Oh . . ." She actually blushed at her confusion, something Morris had never seen her do. He offered no apology. He was all intensity, and she could feel it in her hand. "Yes . . ." said Aeriel, after a deep breath. "Julia just left . . . through the back door . . . with Jerusha and Edgar. . . ."

"Oh!" Aeriel bent toward the pain in her captured hand.

"I'm sorry," said Morris, releasing it. "It's terribly important: Did they say where they were going?" His intensity frightened her, as much as if he was still squeezing her hand.

"I don't know . . . yes . . . for a walk," she said, suddenly remembering, as if that fact could expel all the tension in the room. "Edgar said they were going for a short walk."

"Did Julia say anything?" Morris asked, keeping his voice steady with an act of will, his large hand choking his walking cane.

Aeriel thought, then shook her head. "No. No, she didn't. Nor did Jerusha."

"Was Edgar carrying anything?" asked Morris.

Aeriel looked at him strangely. Then shook her head. "Only a flashlight . . . and a sweater over his arm."

"Shit!" said Morris.

Aeriel stepped away from him, as if she feared for her life. "What's the matter, Morris?" She trembled like a small bird on a wire.

"They left through the back door!" said Morris, more as an accusation than a question.

Aeriel folded her thin arms in front of her. "Yes. But Edgar didn't say in which direction they were going . . . just 'a short walk' was all he said."

"How long have they been gone?" Morris asked, his eyes one savage line of hatred.

"Not more than . . . a few minutes. Just now, in fact . . ."

"Listen . . ." He took Aeriel Compton by the shoulders, feeling her narrow bones through the thin blouse. "Detective Fannin is upstairs in my suite. . . . Go there immediately and tell him what you just told me. Tell him I'm outside, looking for them. He'll know what to do." Morris almost lifted her off the floor. "Do it now. Lives may depend on it."

Morris ignored her garbled question and scrambled through the door onto the back porch. A thin light was burning in the porch ceiling, a hopeless intrusion on the endless dark.

He went down the steps without touching the banister. Something on the last step caught his eye, a faint yellow reflection. He almost lost his balance stopping to pick it up. A card—he held it to the thin ceiling light—a library card from the *Denver* public library . . . belonging to *Julia Sullivan*. She had managed to drop it. Somehow *she knew*. She was not walking in the dark of her own free will. Morris could have bent his cane double with his bare hands, and it once was a two-iron in the happy bag of Monty Sullivan.

Julia Sullivan stumbled deliberately and Benefield caught her arm in an iron grip.

"No," he said. "You can't stop here. You can go back when we get to the pond. We need to be alone. It's our journey, not yours." There was a frightening absence of all passion in his voice. He flicked on the flashlight to see the path ahead and quickly flicked it off again, making the night even darker than before.

"I won't leave Jerusha," said Sullivan, catching her old friend by the arm. She could feel the terror in her slim frame.

"No, Julia," said Jerusha, her voice diminished in her throat, like a small child's after a nasty accident. "It's our affair. . . . When we get to the pond, you go back to Morris. Help him understand . . ." She couldn't finish the sentence.

If only Morris understood, thought Sullivan, dragging her feet, finding reasons again to stumble in the dark, this time all the way to her knees. Edgar couldn't see to find her hand, but grapped her jacket sleeve in the dark and pushed the barrel of the gun against her back.

"Up with you," he said, with no more compassion than a farmer herding a sheep to the slaughter.

Sullivan, stalling for time, began again to speak to him. "Edgar, no matter what has happened, Morris and I are your friends. And Jerusha loves you. We will see that you get help—"

Help was the wrong word. He pushed her, more roughly than before. "It's too late for all that," he said, his voice still flat and merciless, as if it had already decided to leave his earthly body. "I can't live in America alone," he said. "I've lost everything. I can't go back."

"Then kiss Jerusha good-bye and let her go with me," said Sullivan, stopping where she stood.

"No. I won't go alone," said Benefield, pushing

her forward, toward the slope that she knew ran down to Eisenhower Pond.

"It's our trip, Julia," said Jerusha, her voice not quite so lost inside her. "Edgar doesn't have to . . . go alone. And you go back to John Morris."

"I won't leave you," said Sullivan, making up her mind what she would do. She couldn't fight Edgar Benefield. For all his once gentlemanly ways, he was an athlete and a powerful one. But she wouldn't leave Jerusha. And she wouldn't bow her head, waiting for a bullet. She could feel the evenly mowed grass under the thin soles of her shoes. She could see what she imagined to be the level blackness of the pond, suddenly stretching out before them.

Morris forced himself to wait, panting in the dark, aching to rush off in all directions. Where would he go? Through the woods down toward the 10th green? There was no path. . . . It would be tough going unless they broke out into the 10th fairway, and Edgar wouldn't do that, leaving the comfort of the trees for the open spaces . . . and the lights of the clubhouse shining behind the 10th tee. . . . And Rae's Creek swung around to the left of the fairway . . . at the bottom of an awkward ravine . . . easy to fall into in the dark . . . Edgar was not an awkward man, in anything he did. No, he would head for Eisenhower Pond. He knew the path easily enough, even in the dark. And he had a flashlight. And no fear of stumbling on any living soul. And under the sweater, what did he have? Morris did not give himself a chance to doubt his logic. . . . He started in a swinging, stiff-legged gallop, careless of running headlong into one of the great pines ... poling himself across the uneven ground with his cane, covering the distance with awkward, remarkable speed.

"Did you hate Melvin Newton that much?" asked Sullivan, easing herself behind Jerusha Benefield in the dark, with one arm around her waist as if to comfort her.

"He stole my family's company," said Benefield, as though to himself, his voice still oddly flat and merciless. "You tell them that." He might have been speaking of a lost civilization, left far behind him. "I could have saved Benefield House with a deal for a casino. All of the cash flow I would have ever needed. It was my idea. They stole it from me. They meant to cut me out. . . ."

"Even though your mother's family could have gotten a license?" said Sullivan. "Did Eddie lie to you also?" Just keep talking, she thought, anything to get his mind off what he meant to do.

"Eddie cheated all his life. He cheated me out of the U.S. Amateur. . . . We were all even on the last hole and his ball moved in the rough. . . . His own caddy told me . . . years later. . . . He also lied about Nevada. . . ." He laughed the deadest laugh Julia Sullivan had ever heard. . . . It echoed off the top of the black, unseen water in the pond. . . . "But I killed the deal—and the three of them—and now it's time to leave. . . ." He flicked on the flashlight, sending a beam directly into Jerusha's terrified face, drawing a gasp as if she had been struck with a fist.

He was raising his gun hand under his sweater ... when Sullivan lifted her foot and set it against his side and gave him a vast shove, with all her strength. He lost his balance, his arms wheeling as if he could catch onto the dark ... the flashlight tumbling theatrically in the air until it sank, still burning, like a beacon from the bottom of the pond, and then he was down himself with a terrific splash into the shallow water. Not waiting to hear him struggle, Julia lifted Jerusha Benefield in the air, pulling her, dragging her back from the pond, toward the tall, heavy shadows of the trees. A shot exploded toward them, louder than a bomb on top of the water, the flash terrifying in the night, as if it were seeking them out personally to be destroyed. Jerusha screamed until Sullivan slapped her face hard enough to burn her own hand. Both of them fell, but Sullivan dragged and pulled Jerusha to her feet and set her running, staggering. . . . Sullivan was glad to smack into a tree and stumble behind it. Now they were off the path, crashing through the brush, glad to feel it tearing at their legs. . . . Other shots exploded from the pond, but the flashes were too far behind them to be seen.

Morris was amazed to see the flashlight illuminate Jerusha Benefield, and did not stop when he saw the light spinning in the air. The shot that came afterward seemed to explode through him. He lowered his head and ran toward the gun flare as if to catch it in his teeth . . . and now he was running, lumbering on level grass, and when the subsequent shots detonated over the water he threw his cane and spread his huge arms and dove into the dark and the water and the dim figure standing over a strange light under him, until he smashed him into wet, shattering pieces, the two of them drowned in the lighted water, Morris clutching something, a man's thick shoulders, until he found his neck and head and drove them into the mud, legs kicking under him that might have been minnows, hands clawing at his own, nothing, not even ripples, until he lifted his own head and drew a breath and held with all his great strength until the struggle was the same as the water . . . all stillness.

Morris came out of the pond, careless of the water and the mud, limping without his cane, lowing in the night like a seabeast come to land. He shouted her name . . . in separate shouts: "Sullivan! Julia! It's Morris!" He could not bear the silence and the memory of the shots. He cried the names again . . . like the last survivor of a great massacre.

He heard a noise . . . from the dark . . . from deep in the shadows of the trees. Then he could hear . . . it was his own name being called. And the voice, even in a shout, could only belong to Julia Sullivan.

"Come give me a hand!" he shouted back, tears mixing with the pond water on his face. "I've lost my damn cane."

* * *

When Detective Fannin reached them on the path, Morris had Sullivan under one wet wing and Jerusha under the other. It was impossible to know who was holding up whom.

"Good Lord!" said the detective, playing his light over Morris's sodden, mud-covered head and clothes. "We heard shots. What happened?"

"Your boy's down in the pond," said Morris. "He won't be getting out by himself."

"Is anybody else hurt?" asked the detective, playing the light over Sullivan and Jerusha Benefield.

"We hurt all right," said Morris, "for an old friend who died some days ago; his body just joined him. Now get the damn light out of our eyes and get us to a Scotch and water."

It was a tie as to which felt the best, the shower or the dry jacket or the Scotch. Sullivan and Jerusha huddled under sweaters as if they, too, had been submerged in pond water. Sullivan shivered to think what might have happened to the two of them.

"You saved my life," said Jerusha, for the fifth time.

"So, as the Chinese say, I'm responsible for you as long as you live," said Sullivan. "I'll be checking up on you; expect houseguests in Paris."

Jerusha smiled with her green eyes for the first time in a long night.

A rap on the door and Detective Fannin stuck his head inside. "We found him. The damn flashlight was still burning."

"Have a drink," said Morris, pushing the Scotch toward him.

"Yes," said the detective, pouring a stiff one in a glass without ice. "Here's to life," he said.

They all drank to that.

The detective sat a small tape recorder on the coffee table. "For the record . . . what the hell happened?"

"You first, Morris," said Sullivan, squeezing up against him, not letting him farther away than the thickness of his jacket.

"We were following Fred Couples up the 18th hole, you and I," said Morris to Sullivan. "I was thinking of all the famous names who've won The Masters that he was about to join . . . when from nowhere, it hit me: the president's name . . . in Melvin Newton's calender. All at once I understood . . . the president didn't call Newton. That's why he didn't recognize his name. The president must have been talking with Edgar Benefield . . . and probably about publishing his memoirs." Morris took a long pull on his own Scotch. "Immortality comes to the minds of presidents about the end of their first term . . . especially when there is no guarantee they will be reelected. Henry"—Morris nodded toward the detective—"called the president . . . and I was right. He had been negotiating with Edgar for his memoirs . . . when Edgar had to sell the company to Melvin Newton. Edgar hated selling it. And soon enough, he hated Newton. I believe Edgar used the president's name—and the deal for his memoirs—to get Melvin outside alone . . . and he took him to a pond named for another president . . . Eisenhower. And he killed him in a second, and the real Edgar Benefield died with him."

"Oh, Morris," said Jerusha, "I killed him when I decided to move to Paris." She bit her lip but had no tears left to cry.

"No, babe. His life had been coming apart for a long time. It was nobody's fault, maybe not even his own." Morris was not sure he believed that; a current of weakness had run through Edgar Benefield as long as he had known him, had kept him from being the golf champion his talent had predicted, but he had been a lovely man. "We'll remember the Edgar we all used to know," Morris said, and meant it.

Sullivan put both arms around Jerusha to squeeze away the pain.

"How did you get onto him, Sullivan?" asked Morris. "I knew you had something to tell me after Eddie was killed. But there was so much confusion, and Henry was about to call the president . . ."

"Yes," said Sullivan. "I was going to remind you of something Edgar said the first day we were here . . . that he was 'an Eastern American person' . . . that he couldn't live anywhere else . . . that he 'had a hard enough time visiting Mother when she moved back West.' I remembered, Morris, that his mother came from *Nevada*. That his grandfather had been governor of Nevada."

Sullivan said, "I thought Edgar might have been involved in helping Melvin and Gerald get a gambling license there. Of course, I couldn't know that the whole thing was his idea . . . to try and save his publishing company."

Jerusha Benefield, in a small voice, said, "If I hadn't been so unhappy . . . I might have known what Edgar was involved in. . . . I did know he flew out to see his mother, and he talked on the phone with her attorney several times, but I wasn't paying any attention . . . I never listened in on his conversations."

"I made a terrible mistake," said Sullivan, shivering in spite of the sweater around her shoulders. "I asked Edgar about it . . . with Jerusha sitting in the room. I asked him if his mother's family, coming from Nevada, had had anything to do with Melvin's attempt to get a gambling license. Edgar seemed so normal . . . I wasn't afraid of him. . . . Whatever he might have done, I never dreamed he would harm Jerusha . . . or myself. But he lost it . . . right in their sitting room." Now Jerusha was hugging Sullivan. "He must have already known that he would kill himself . . . and Jerusha too." Sullivan felt it was the time to say the awful truth aloud. Jerusha was able to weep again, but did not close her eyes at the memory. "He already had his gun in his jacket pocket," said Sullivan. "He threw a sweater over it and picked up a flashlight and said we were to come with him. He was so . . . detached, so . . . dispassionate. I knew if I screamed, he would shoot us right there. I had no doubt about it. I was just playing for time. I was hoping you would be in the hall, or on the stairs, Morris, but I was terrified, also, at what he might do if you were. We only saw Aeriel Compton in the kitchen. She paid us no mind. It was like a bad movie. We were on the porch. And then we were in the dark. And you know what happened . . . you sounded like a one-legged Rooster Cogburn coming down that hill, Morris." She laughed in spite of herself. Even Jerusha smiled.

"Yeah," said Morris, unable not to chuckle at the thought of himself in a quasi-gallop in the dark. "I'm always coming to the rescue of some dizzy brunette from Colorado . . . with her tail feathers on fire."

"Now, there's a thought," said Sullivan.

"I can't help you. I'm dying of pneumonia," said Morris. "Tell me," he said, seriously, "how the hell did you get him into the pond?"

"I kicked him in," said Sullivan. "He switched the flashlight on Jerusha and left me in the dark."

"We all know how dangerous you are in the dark," said Morris. "Remind me never to carry a flashlight."

"Do you still think Edgar meant to kill Newton and Acton at the same time?" asked Detective Fannin.

"Yes. There's no way to prove it, but I believe it. You might talk to Louise, see what she remembers," said Morris.

"I already have. She says she has no idea if Edgar asked Gerald to meet him anywhere that Sunday night. She's flying straight to New York. Says if we want to talk to her, we can talk to her there."

"It took a desperate man to kill Acton on the golf

course," said Morris. "Edgar must have seen him with the woman engineer, and called him, and said she wanted to meet him down by the 10th green. And when he came, Edgar stepped out of the Port-o-let and killed him, careless of who might have been there to see it. Lucky for him, nobody was."

"Not the action of a sane man," said the detective. "I wonder when he stole the car keys from Sullivan's purse?"

"Could have been anytime this week," said Sullivan. "I haven't tried to use them."

"He must have seen Eddie drinking in the bar, and waited for him behind the cottage with the engine running," said Morris, "and Eddie never knew what hit him. It's true what Edgar said, Sullivan—Eddie's ball did move in the rough that last hole at the U.S. Amateur. We all suspected it. Edgar's own caddy complained about it. But we could never write it. There was no evidence . . . no camera on the ball."

"I guess Eddie . . . at the last," said Sullivan, "would rather have had the one-stroke penalty."

"I can't believe you said that," said Morris.

"I had a terrible mentor," said Sullivan, her old wicked smile back in place.

"What about the Augusta National golf tees?" Detective Fannin asked. "Why did Edgar leave them with the three victims?"

"He must have had a reason," said Sullivan. "Some signature . . . that meant something to him we may never understand."

"Much of the best of his life was golf," said Morris, "and maybe he wanted something of it in his death. He wasn't killing the three of them . . . he was killing himself."

"In the left pocket of his jacket," said Detective Fannin, opening the palm of his right hand, "he had these two tees."

Their dark-green reality dominated the room.

EPILOGUE

Morris puzzled over the money and finally opened his hand for the old news vendor to pick out the correct change. A damp breeze was coming off the Seine. The streets were not crowded with tourists. There was just enough traffic to give energy to Paris, the most beautiful city in the world. He was even moved to try out his halting French:

Toute France . . . est un grand vent souffle . . . haut votre pantelon.

Sullivan buried her head in the sleeve of his great winter coat. They stepped onto the Pont Marie, with its beautiful, unequal arches, crossing to the Île St. Louis. A working canal boat, with a white goat improbably on the deck, passed under the bridge. The pale green water in the river was as clear as Morris had ever seen it. He hugged Sullivan to him. They might have been two remarkable characters in *A Moveable Feast*.

Sullivan's head was bobbing up and down in the sleeve of his coat.

Morris stopped in the middle of the bridge. "What are you doing?"

She tried to get her breath and couldn't. She was giggling against his coat. She tried again.... "Do you know what you said to that Frenchman?" She lost it again in the sleeve of his coat.

Morris could not take his eyes from the *grisaille*, the falling, everywhere, grayness of Paris, and rising through it, the great corridor of classical buildings along the river Seine. The wind in his face might have been blowing from two thousand years ago. He only hoped he had caught a hint in his words of the greatness of the moment.

Sullivan tried to say ... tried again.... "You said ... you said, 'All France ... is a great wind ... blowing up your trousers....'" Sullivan was afraid she might laugh herself off the bridge into the pale green water.

"Never mind," said Morris, "he knew what I meant."

"Is that why he's giving you that gesture with his hand and fist?" Sullivan said with a laugh, looking back over her shoulder.

"It's probably a very warm French tradition," said Morris.

"I bet it is," said Sullivan, almost strangling to keep from laughing.

They stepped off the bridge. They might have

been standing peacefully at sea on the small river island, one of the most coveted addresses in all Paris. The seventeenth- and eighteenth-century houses rose up, leaving the narrow, toylike streets in permanent shadows.

"Is this where you are buying my Christmas present?" prodded Sullivan. "Plenty of shops here, Morris," she encouraged him.

"We're close," said Morris, mysteriously.

They followed the small, shop-lined Rue Budé to the Quai d'Orléans, which commanded a powerful view of the Seine and of the great, medieval Notre Dame rising over the Île de la Cité, which lay across an iron footbridge, the only truly ugly bridge in Paris.

"It's a sin," said Sullivan; "they can look out their window and see this scene anytime they want to . . . free of charge."

"I don't think," said Morris, "this address is free of charge."

"Well, rent doesn't count," said Sullivan.

"It doesn't if you fly your own jet plane to Paris."

"I couldn't drive my car here from Colorado," said Sullivan, with her usual logic.

"Do we just ring the doorbell?" asked Morris, puzzling over the street address.

Sullivan shook her head. "You'll get us arrested yet. They live two doors down."

"Of course," said Morris, stumbling forward in another language, for all the world like Inspector Clouseau.

There was no doorbell, but an old-fashioned, brass door knocker instead.

Jerusha Benefield swung the door open, as if she had been waiting all day for them to knock. Morris knew the language for a hug around the neck.

Sullivan and Jerusha greeted each other in a blizzard of French. Morris could only guess why Jerusha was laughing at him until she was crying.

"Come on upstairs and have a drink," said Jerusha.

"With true Scotch and lots of ice?" said Morris.

"All the ice your glass can hold," said Jerusha, hugging him again.

"Watch that!" said Sullivan.

The view out of the living room was, indeed, sinful. And hanging over the mantel was a painting of that very view at night that would break your heart into tiny pieces, and remind you, thought Morris, of Matisse's long-ago work in fog-shrouded London, but in the original hand of Jerusha Benefield.

Morris raised his glass. "To the good times. And to the painter who made that painting."

"Wait! I'll drink to all of that." Coming through the door, as darkly handsome as twenty years ago, was Tom Spears.

Now it was Sullivan's time for a hug around the neck. Morris was careful to barely shake Spears's arthritic hand.

Tom filled his glass and raised it: "To the good times to come, and to the painter of that painting!" They all drank to that.

Morris touched the frame of the scene of Paris.

"I think you've found your life," he said. Jerusha did not deny it.

"You two look wonderful," said Sullivan. "I hate you both . . . for living in this city."

"Come on to Paris," said Jerusha. "There's a dreamy house for sale . . . three doors down."

"We'll take two," said Morris.

They all drank to that.

"When did you get in?" asked Tom.

"Two nights ago," said Morris. "It took my pilot an extra night to get over her jet lag. It took me an extra night to shut both of my eyes."

"You flew your own plane?" said Jerusha, to Sullivan.

"You just get up in the air and fly," said Sullivan. "I loved speaking French to the flight controllers. I don't know if they were having as much fun. I think they wanted me to land in a larger country."

Then Sullivan said, "That's enough bullshit. Let's get down to the hot gossip. How long have you two been living together?"

"Sullivan!" said Jerusha, with fake embarrassment.

"I came to visit . . . about two months ago . . . and I forgot to leave," said Spears. "I love it here. They can't draft me into a pro shop . . . this island is too small for a golf course. And this house has the most beautiful owner in Paris . . . and certainly the best painter."

"Watch the bullshit," said Jerusha. "I can't wait for you to see some of Tom's work, Sullivan." Jerusha caught Morris's eye.

"I'd love to see it."

"You will," said Spears.

"Who needs another drink?" asked Jerusha. Everybody needed another drink. She filled all their glasses.

"Well," said Jerusha, "let's talk about it. Tom and I decided we would be like Morris and Sullivan, and have no forbidden subjects."

"Dr. Karen Moseley told me," said Morris, "that Edgar had a lot of blockage in the arteries to his brain. She said there was no way to determine if it influenced his behavior."

"She called me, personally," said Jerusha. "She was very professional, but very sympathetic."

"Had you seen a difference in him?" asked Sullivan.

"Thinking back on it . . . yes," said Jerusha. "He'd grown so distant. So beyond reach. He had headaches and dizziness from time to time, but he'd been subject to headaches all his life. I thought his withdrawal was just age . . . and all the financial trouble with the publishing house. And maybe time and trouble were a large part of it. I know I'll never get all of the guilt out of my bones." She had a sheen of tears in her eyes.

"Without you, he would have self-destructed years ago," said Sullivan. "Morris is right . . . he was a lovely man."

"Funny," said Morris, "Edgar is the only one of the four that any of us will miss."

"Louise Acton is coming over next spring," said

Jerusha. "She's coming as a bride. She and her friend are going to get married after all."

"Listen to the silence in this room," said Sullivan, looking from Tom Spears to John Morris.

"Where did you say you kept Tom's work?" said Morris.

"Coward," said Sullivan, laughing into her glass.

"We have a his and her studio on the top floor," said Jerusha. "Follow me up the stairs. You don't need to belong to a health club in Paris. You just climb up and down the bloody stairs."

Two flights up, Jerusha opened the door into a long, high room with a skylight running the length of it. The end wall was one large window, and they were looking down on an unmatched view of Paris in December. The four of them looked on in silence, as if waiting for the city to speak to them.

"I know when the lights come on, it must break your heart," said Sullivan.

"Yes," said Jerusha. "And speaking of breaking your heart . . . look on that wall. . . ." She pointed toward a set of eight mounted and framed pen-and-ink drawings.

Sullivan headed way across the room, while Morris hung back with the other two. She stopped in front of the first drawing . . . and tilted her head in appreciation of the young woman with her long hair hanging to one side, laughing at the damn world. Morris was again amazed at her laughter on the canvas in pen-and-ink cross-hatchings. By the time she was seeing herself, looking over Monty's head, her chin resting in his hairline, singing some

Irish drinking song, Sullivan was crying. She stood in front of each of the eight drawings, tears streaming down her face, seeing herself sitting on the terrace at Augusta National like the mistress of Baron Alphonse Berckmans, and standing in a great crowd around a golf green, and sitting alone in the bar with a quality of sadness, and imitating some hilarious, improbable golf swing to the glee of a half circle of writers, a young Morris among them, and hugging Morris's own neck in the last scene, sitting on the hood of his old antique Packard.

"Well, that spoils Christmas, your present comes a couple of weeks early," said Morris.

When she could speak, Sullivan, making no attempt to dry the tears on her face, said to Tom Spears . . . "You did these?"

"I'm guilty," he said, loving her tears.

"When?"

"When they happened."

"When Monty was alive . . . when we were all young?"

"Yes."

"I never knew . . . I never saw you paint anything," said Sullivan.

"It was a secret vice," said Spears.

"It won't be secret long," said Jerusha. "He's having an exhibition . . . here in Paris . . . next spring."

"Thanks to you."

"Thanks to your work. It's a sin for a painter to be more beautiful than his paintings . . . don't you think, Sullivan?" said Jerusha, taking Spears's ruined hand in her own.

"Were we ever that young?" asked Sullivan, turning again to the drawings.

"Oh, there's plenty of young still in us," said Morris.

Sullivan ran into his arms like the closing scene in an old Hollywood movie when Gary Grant was still a young man. Morris laughed, thinking it would be wise not to make the comparison.

"What are you laughing at?" asked Sullivan.

"Time," said Morris.